DEAD SKY

WESTON OCHSE

SOLARIS

First published 2019 by Solaris
an imprint of Rebellion Publishing Ltd,
Riverside House, Osney Mead,
Oxford, OX2 0ES, UK
www.solarisbooks.com

ISBN: 978 1 78108 668 1

10 9 8 7 6 5 4 3 2 1

A CIP catalogue record for this book is available
from the British Library.

Designed & typeset by Rebellion Publishing

Printed in the US

DEAD SKY

Other titles by this author

The Task Force Ombra Series
Grunt Life
Grunt Traitor
Grunt Hero

Seal Team 666 Series
Seal Team 666
Age of Blood
Reign of Evil
Border Dog

The Afterblight Chronicles
Blood Ocean

Tomes of the Dead
Empire of Salt

Multiplex Fandango
Halfway House
FUBAR

For everyone who has ever served in Afghanistan, knows the taste of dust in their mouths, hates driving down the pot-holed roads, stares warily at passers-by, and looks lovingly at T-Walls.

Thanks especially to Screamer, Rocko, and Private Pile. This book is for you.

"Concepts, like individuals, have their histories and are just as incapable of withstanding the ravages of time as are individuals. But in and through all this they retain a kind of homesickness for the scenes of their childhood."

—Søren Kierkegaard

Chapter One

Our Lady of Atlas in Exile

THE WORST THING about having other people inside your head was that not only were you forced to come to terms with everything you'd done and seen yourself, but you're presented with an entirely new universe of someone else's PTSD. Flashes of women he'd never seen, alluring, kissing, cuddling, then dying, the emotion of it choking off his air. Flashes of a young boy standing on a train platform as the train pulls away, the point of view getting farther and farther away until the child is nothing but a dot on the gray English horizon, never to be seen again, the regret an impossible weight. Flashes of a woman's fingers scratching the skin of an orange. Flashes of hundreds of men dead and dying on battlefields, spears, arrows, and jagged bones jutting from their bodies as their eyes sought salvation from a cold blue unforgiving sky. All of this and more slammed over and over into Boy Scout's shattered mind until all he could do was drool, his mind reeling from the invasion and terraformation of the intruder.

Boy Scout sat in the corner of the Hermit's Cabin, face half lost in shadow. His chest heaved. What could be seen of his face was pale and covered in sweat. His hair dove in every direction. His eyes stared blankly at a place thousands of miles away that he'd never been to. His breathing eventually slowed, and for the first time in an hour he moved, a hand coming up to wipe the drool from his mouth, and then after wiping it on his pants, scraping the sweat from his brow.

He'd been back in Afghanistan.

Just not *his* Afghanistan.

Not any Afghanistan he even remotely knew.

But that was his new reality. When he was tired or lacked control, they surfaced like bodies in backwoods swamps that wouldn't stay down. Putrid, rotting things whose stench was of dead and bloated bodies, oranges, and dry desert air. So far he'd counted four of them—entities or whatever they were—all inside of him, all unfortunate souvenirs from the monster that had chased him while he'd been in The White.

The memory that had just had him in its greasy grasp was of a warrior. More importantly, he'd been a survivor. Still, the memories had been like his own, and he'd relived them as if he'd been the one in battle, the very idea of him so comingled he was becoming more and more uncertain of what was his own and what was from the others. He, him, I, was, is... all of it merging into a single being who was irrevocably not himself.

Like now, the memory of the battle still beating in his chest like his heart was a spear smacking the edge of a shield at the instant two armies collided. Just moments ago, he'd been laying beneath bodies, the stench of death and offal enough to make him want to retch, the crushing press and weight of his brothers almost too much to bear. He didn't dare move. That he was still alive among so much death was his secret and to move or make a sound would reveal his presence, even as British troops staggered drunkenly and exhausted between piles of the dead. His eyes were open and his entire horizon was the dead face of Ahmad, his friend and brother in arms, eyes open and glazed, teeth visible through bloody cheeks from the savage cut to his face made by one of Her Majesty's cavalry swords. And it was through Ahmad's glazed, dead eyes that he was able to see the reflection of what was occurring outside his pile of bodies.

The occasional cry was cut off, then followed by laughter and rough language.

Gunshots were few, probably conserving ammunition when the blade of a bayonet or sword would suffice.

Everything else was silent, so much so that his own breathing seemed impossibly loud. He tried to regulate it as best he could. That he was buried beneath the flesh of his own people had been a godsend. Had they not mistaken him for dead, he'd be at the end of a sword himself. But as it was, he'd passed out when the British soldier had struck him in the head with the butt of a rifle. Even now the side of it felt broken open like a pomegranate that had over-ripened on the tree.

Suddenly he smelled smoke and burning fat. He knew what it was before he saw the orange and red reflection in Ahmad's eyes. The soldiers were setting each pile of bodies on fire to rid themselves of the need to bury them. He felt the rise in him at the incredible sacrilege, but then realized he was in one of the piles. And it wasn't long before it was his turn.

He saw the burning torch come and light Ahmad on fire. He felt the heat of his friend, even as it raged hotter and hotter until pieces of Ahmad dripped on him. He fought the urge to scream, then realized he was losing his ability to breathe. He wanted nothing more than to push his way out of the pile, to be free of the bodies of those he'd so recently fought beside. His hands and arms began to shake. His legs quivered. He felt himself release his own feces into his pants as he tried against every impulse not to move. Finally, he couldn't take it any longer and gasping for air, pushed Ahmad off of him and clawed his way through his burning brothers to solid ground. He rolled to quench the flames that had begun to lick at his skin, then when he came to a stop, he opened his eyes, expecting the swift brutal ending from a sword.

But all he saw was black sky, the glorious stars that had been there since he'd first stared up in awe as a child obliterated by the smoke from his burning brothers. He turned his head and watched as the soldiers in red coats moved away from him, lighting pyre after pyre of the dead, each burning pyre a bonfire of memories never to be shared over more friendly fires during more friendly times when his country wasn't being invaded by the selfish. And then he saw it, his stars, not in the sky but recreated on the *terra damnata* of this smoking, hard-scrabbled slag, the burning never able to be reflected in the billowing dead sky that had so recently been the perfect heavens he'd once walked proudly beneath.

*   *   *

A SHADOW DARKENED the rest of Boy Scout's face as the door opened. He lifted the great weight of his head and peered from the darkness towards the doorway. He was pinned to the back wall by the stark ray of bright like a butterfly pinned to felt. The black silhouette of a monk stepped into the light.

"The abbot wishes to speak with you," came a trembling voice from someone who could not have imagined an inkling of the horrors Boy Scout had seen.

He opened and shut his mouth several times, but his lips were impossibly chapped, peeling and bleeding in places.

The monk stepped forward and held out a water bottle.

Boy Scout took it and glanced at the label, something he'd bought himself thousands of times at a store.

As if in apology the monk said, "It has been blessed."

Boy Scout unscrewed the cap and drank without touching the plastic. The water was cold and invigorating. He drank it down, feeling more alive and more himself with each gulp. Out of the corner of his eye he watched the young monk, noting the shifting of his feet, the fists balled at his side and his slight lean away from the man in the corner as if what he had was contagious.

But then, Boy Scout was possessed of a sort. Not William Peter Blatty possessed, or at least he didn't believe so, but he was possessed nonetheless, and the brothers and sisters of Our Lady of Atlas in Exile knew it, which was why he'd been given the Hermit's Cabin. The recent death of their hermit had made it unoccupied and they had yet to select another.

Boy Scout let the hand grasping the empty bottle fall to his lap. "Time," he managed to say. "What time is it?"

"Sext has just concluded. The abbot wishes to speak with you." The monk wore the simple brown robe of a Trappist. Sandals on his feet. Hair cut evenly around. Fresh faced and still free of lines that would one day etch all of his worries. "One of your friends has come. She... she has news."

Boy Scout brightened. *Lore. Preacher's Daughter.* He'd barely seen her since his return to the States. Then again, he'd barely seen anyone. He had his own personal drama to deal with, something he'd kept from the prying eyes of the military doctors, camouflaging his multiple possessions with his too-real PTSD.

He struggled to stand.

The monk shuffled from one foot to the other, still not willing to come closer.

Boy Scout found the edge of his chair and used it

to push himself to a standing position. He hadn't exercised in months and his body felt like it. The only other time he'd felt as weak was back in the fugue when he'd been overweight and a junkie. But that hadn't been real, just a projection in their minds as he and his team had lain mentally incapacitated in an ancient cistern complex in the ass end of Afghanistan. He fought back a lump as the memories of the deaths of Criminal and Narco and Bully assaulted him, almost as fresh today as they had been when they happened, memories of them never far from his thoughts—when he had his own thoughts.

He let the young monk lead him out the door of the cabin and down the well-manicured dirt path. Ponderosa and sugar pines hugged the sides of the walkway like sentries, shrouding the walker forever in dappled gloom. The pine scent was strongest when the Santa Ana winds blew. After a few moments, the pines gave way to a wide-open space of freshly cut grass, the smell of it and loam heavy on the air. A wide, multi-armed one-story white stucco building sat in the middle of the lawn. Once the home of a Golden Age Hollywood director, the structure had recently been turned into a monastery, after the original Atlas monastery in Algeria closed down due to the wanton murder of monks by a savage and uncontrolled terrorist cell. The roof was made from mud red tile and shadowed by royal palms and California black oak, the latter already turning bright orange, the color of the flames he'd so recently seen reflected in Ahmad's eyes. At the corners and off to the left were areas of solitude. Beside each were planted Pacific dogwoods, their willowy branches delicate compared to the stout thickness of the sprawling oaks.

This had been Boy Scout's home since he'd returned from Landstuhl Medical Center, where he and his surviving team had recovered. Nestled in the heights of the San Bernardino Mountains, the abbey was a place of contemplation that many had used to discover who it was they wanted to be, and most often whether or not they were close enough to God. God had nearly nothing to do with Boy Scout's presence however, except for it being the bright flame that had been the inspiration for the abbey and the calling of those who named it a permanent home.

He got more than a few stares as he emerged into the clearing.

The other monks knew of him and many had seen him, but Boy Scout kept to himself, trying to master the things inside of him that kept trying to surface. And there were the day visitors, those up from Los Angeles or other points south, coming as a Christian tourist to experience, if only for a moment, how the Trappists lived in their solitary lives so near one of the most pulsating centers of modern civilization and the universal heart of worldwide cinema.

Boy Scout knew he looked like a wild man, with his six weeks of unshaven beard, hermit hair and disheveled, sweat-stained clothes, but he didn't care. What he did care about were the people. Not that he was worried someone might do him harm, because no one would ever think to look for him here, but his anxiety from his last deployment and everything that had transpired had set him on such a fine edge that more people than he could keep track of made him feel overanxious. So he hurried, head down, eyes scanning, to the side door marked *Private*. It wasn't until he was inside that he breathed a sigh of relief.

The young monk escorted him into the Trappists' private dining room—red tile floors, white walls, rough tables made from great slabs of hewn redwood. Most of the tables were filled with silent, hunched monks, using chunks of bread and a spoon to eat whatever was in the bowls. Five nuns sat at a single table, doing the same.

About half of those present glanced at Boy Scout as he entered, but the moment they saw him, they turned back to their meals.

He clocked each of them but kept his head

lowered, the pressure of being around people almost too much.

They stopped at a table occupied only by a single monk, older and bespectacled, his face heavily scarred. He smiled when he saw Boy Scout.

"Monsieur Starling," he said in a French accent. "Would you please join me?"

Boy Scout had met Abbot Dominic de Cherge the first day he'd come to the monastery and seen him several times hence, but they'd never really spoken. Boy Scout's best friend, McQueen, had arranged Boy Scout's stay through an old acquaintance from the French Foreign Legion. The original Atlas Abbey— *Abbaye Notre Dame de Atlas*—was located in Tibhirine, Algeria, and was the site where seven monks were kidnapped and murdered during the Algerian Civil War. The abbey was all but shut down after the incident. Many of the surviving monks went to the monastery annex in Fez, Morocco, but a large contingent, sponsored by the Archdiocese of Los Angeles, traveled to the San Bernardino Mountains and reformed the Abbey in Exile. The abbot was the brother of one of the monks who had been killed, and after tracking down the Algerian terrorists who'd done the terrible deed, gave himself to the church. So as Boy Scout sat, he was aware that de Cherge was not only the head of the abbey, but also a former brother-in-arms.

"Thank you for joining me, Monsieur Starling." The abbot waved his hand and two monks arrived, one with pitchers of beer and water and the other with a bowl of stew and some bread. "Please, eat and let me tell you of some news."

Boy Scout stared at the man before him. Once handsome, burn scars now puckered the entire left side of the man's face. But what Boy Scout noticed was the calmness emanating from the man. Here was someone who had led before and knew the benefits of remaining calm.

He nodded, lowered his head, and tested a spoonful of the stew. Fish of some sort in a thick broth with potatoes and onions. He tore off a piece of bread and began to eat in earnest. He was hungrier than he thought he'd be, but then he'd been living on raw fruit and vegetables with only the occasional pot of broth for weeks.

"I know some of what happened to you in Afghanistan," de Cherge began, his accent making the words dance but still intelligible. "We have been watching for any Mevlevi Sufi and have been increasingly aware through our association with the Archdiocese that the Mevlevi are searching for something, probably you."

A voice whispered in Boy Scout's mind, *please don't kill me daddy,* then was gone. He'd become so used to the interruptions that he didn't even pause. He poured himself a beer and closed his eyes. "I have something they want," he said.

De Cherge nodded. "So it seems. The center of the activity surrounds the Turkish Consulate in LA. We've been tracking the Mevlevi, but there's really no way they would even know where you are."

Boy Scout glanced up at the same time a woman's voice said, *I remember when you used to care about things other than yourself.* A feeling of self-doubt and loathing blossomed and died inside of him. Boy Scout pushed it aside and asked, "Have you any experience with…" He didn't know how to finish the sentence.

"If you mean do we have experience with possession, then yes. I have witnessed it, as have several others, although the official line from the church contravenes the obvious." De Cherge grinned, his lips twisting only on the unburned side. "You are not possessed. I've been close enough to feel the evil that comes from such things. What you are, however, is unknown. You say there are many inside of you?"

"I can never be sure. It seems as if there are four distinct sets of memories that must come from the consciousness of former travelers. One appears to be from the eighteen hundreds, probably around 1842 during the first Battle of Kabul. I call him Ahmad's

Friend and he was a warrior. Another seems to be more recent—henpecked, no self-confidence; I have visions of a modern Arab city, but not Afghanistan. Maybe North Africa. I'm not sure at all who or what he is. He's been mostly silent. Then there is a boy with memories of a mother and oranges. I still haven't figured him out."

"And the fourth?"

"He's been hiding. I get a few things now and again. I think he's English, but there's something about him that's different. It's like he's two people. One fairly recent and another who's far older than the others. Maybe one or two hundred or even a thousand years."

"So old," de Cherge said.

"I get intense smells. I'll wake and think the room is filled with the scent of jasmine and oranges, but of course these are nothing but the memories of scents."

"Do you worry that they might take you over?" de Cherge asked. "That would be my greatest fear."

"Mine as well. At first that was my worry, but now I think they talk to each other. I think they spend more time trying to discern who they themselves are than who I am."

"What if they eventually come together as a united front?"

Boy Scout paused, then put his spoon down and pushed the bowl away. "That's a hell of a thing to say." De Cherge had just voiced what he'd been thinking but had been afraid to say out loud. He didn't want to give the entities any ideas. As it stood, he didn't know how much of his mind they had access to or if they could know real time what he was thinking. All he could do was frown as he crossed his arms and leveled his gaze at the abbot.

After a moment de Cherge's eyes widened slightly. "Yes. Of course. I understand." Then he shook his head. "This is all new. I'm trying to understand... to help."

"You have helped," Boy Scout said. "You gave me a place to recuperate. A place to deal with my—particular—issues. What other news do you have?"

"I'm informed that you will be leaving us. Madam May will be arriving shortly to escort you to your next endeavor."

Madam May? Oh, Preacher's Daughter. Lore. Then he remembered how he must look. He brought a hand up to his face and then his hair. It had seemed proper to live as a wild man as the wildness raged inside of him, but now that he seemed to have more control, he felt as if his outward appearance should present the same. Plus, if they were going to be traveling, he couldn't be seen as if they'd just pulled him off the street.

"Is there a place I can—do you have…"

"Certainly. We can get you cleaned up. When you're done eating, just let me know."

Boy Scout leaned forward and asked, "Why is it really that you're helping me?"

De Cherge leaned forward as well, his face serious. "The Mevlevi are known to us—what they've been doing—sending hostage travelers into Purgatory, what they call The White—in order to troll for certain entities. Their presence has been heavy in North Africa for the last fifty years. Both in the Legion and in the church, there have been notices to be careful while traveling. Twice I led units against them in Algeria and twice they escaped me. Maybe if they hadn't escaped me you wouldn't be here now."

Boy Scout thought of the ancient cistern and the ten-foot-tall *daeva* the Mevlevi had been using as a power source. Then he remembered the field of buried bodies, thousands of them and no room to bury more. "No, I think they've been doing this far longer than the Legion has even existed. Still, I appreciate your efforts."

The abbot shook his head quickly. "*Ce n'est rien*. It is no problem." He stood. "Now if you are ready, we shall make an improved version of you for the world to see, *non*?"

Boy Scout started to stand and watched as his left arm swept everything from the table and onto the floor, while his right hand grabbed the abbot, clenching the fabric of his robe at his throat. Boy Scout jerked the man halfway across the table, then leaned in and with furious spittle said, "I'm going to rip out your throat and shit down your neck."

Only Boy Scout wasn't doing this.

Only he was.

But it wasn't him.

Not really.

Chapter Two

Abbey Commissary

DE CHERGE TRIED to pull away, but the being inside of Boy Scout wouldn't let him. Red hot anger filled him as if he'd just ingested the whole of the lava from a volcano. He felt his biceps bulge as he ripped the abbot across the table and onto the floor. Behind him he heard shouts and a scream. Inside he wanted to scream for help, as out of control of himself as he was in the many channels of his dreams. Outside he did scream, guttural French epithets at the top of his lungs, barking mad, elephant roaring, as an anger held back for decades finally found a breach in the wall, exploding forth.

The words flowing over his snarling lips held the curving lilt of a beautiful language, but even without knowing what he was saying, the cut and slash of it drew psychic wounds upon de Cherge's stunned face.

But his words weren't his only violence.

Boy Scout sat on the abbot's chest.

His right hand began to rise and fall.

First a flat hand, it slammed repeatedly into de Cherge's scarred face.

Then it turned into a fist, striking the man's ear, his eye, his throat.

But de Cherge wasn't merely a punching dummy. He'd been a captain in the French Foreign Legion and knew how to take care of himself.

Recovering from the shock of the attack, he brought his left knee up hard, catching Boy Scout in the kidney, folding him.

Boy Scout reeled with the pain, but the thing that had control of him had no concern about any damage being done to the body, evidenced by him not even hesitating as he continued to rain blow after blow onto the Frenchman.

Boy Scout balanced himself with his left hand on the ground beside de Cherge's face and it was this arm that de Cherge wrapped his own arm around. He trapped the arm, pulled, then brought around his right knee, propelling Boy Scout off of him.

Boy Scout felt himself rolling and knew the move. De Cherge kept the momentum of the roll until he was on top and Boy Scout was on the bottom.

He grabbed his assailant's wrists and held them, shouting, "Stop it. No more." He was already breathing heavily and the strain on his face as he tried to contain Boy Scout's violence was showing from beneath the blackening bruises. "I said *stop*."

Boy Scout watched as his body sagged, then slacked. It was like Pain TV. He was part of it but in body only. All he could do was watch as whoever had taken him over used his own jujitsu.

De Cherge loosened his grip and relaxed, probably thinking that Boy Scout was obeying his command, but instead, Boy Scout bucked his hips and then grabbed de Cherge's hand, pulling it into him, then spinning beneath the Frenchman until he had the arm in an arm bar, his legs over de Cherge's chest, the arm pulled straight, straining at the elbow to not break in two as Boy Scout pulled hard and continuously on the wrist.

OHMYGOD! he wanted to scream, prisoner to his own actions.

Then a *crack* as the arm broke, followed by de Cherge's scream.

A hand grabbed at Boy Scout and began to pull him away, but he wouldn't let go of the arm. The movement made de Cherge scream again and again, hyperventilating his pain into a world gone mad. The bone ripped through the skin, blood gushing.

Hands grabbed at him from all sides. Some pulled his hair. Another had him under the neck, heaving back. Still others clawed at his wrists, prying de Cherge free of his grip. He felt the pain and pull of it, but his body didn't respond; instead, once his hands were free of de Cherge, they sought other opportunities. Whoever had their hand under his chin soon discovered what it felt like to have their hand locked, twisted, then broken at the wrist— the scaphoid process shattering like plaster from a wall.

The owner of the hand screamed and fell away.

Boy Scout surged to his feet, twisting around and gripping the arm of the hand that was in his hair. He caught the arm between his own left arm and body, then spun to his right, his weight and momentum ripping it out of the socket.

The owner of the arm screamed as well.

In fact everyone was screaming…

…FOR HIM TO STOP.

But whoever or whatever had him in its grip wasn't ready.

The monks and nuns who had been previously gently eating were now standing, wide-eyed. Some had their fists balled, ready, or at least they thought, to fight. Others had their hands to the sides of their heads, as if the image of him was so unbelievable—which it was. Not a single person remained sitting. De Cherge and a pair of unnamed monks lay on the floor, each cradling the grievous injury Boy Scout had visited upon them.

He threw back his head and laughed.

But on the inside, he was ready to cry. He could only stand by, passive, as his body was turned into a violence delivery machine, his hands the lethal weapons they'd always been but without the governing mechanism that was his conscience. It was like being behind the wheel of a car careening through a crowd without being able to stop it, turn the wheel, or even bail out, which he would if he could. The claustrophobic emptiness of The White had never seemed so inviting.

Two monks ran at him.

Boy Scout grabbed one by the hair and used the man's own momentum to hurl him past, where he tumbled to the floor and against a wall.

The other caught Boy Scout in the shoulder with a kick, but he was too slow in the retrieval.

Snatching the leg, Boy Scout brought his own leg up and then down at an angle on the inside of the monk's planted leg, dislocating the knee in a sickening crunch. Not happy just to do some damage, Boy Scout brought his fist up and slammed it into the side of the knee of the leg he was holding. Then he let go, dropping the monk like a sack of trash.

Another monk came at him, swinging his fists like he knew how to use them.

Boy Scout stood his ground, his hands open and at his sides.

The monk struck him in the face with a right, then a left, then a right again.

Boy Scout's head moved incrementally, but he made no notice of pain that blossomed with each blow.

The monk struck him again, flush in the center of his face.

Boy Scout felt a blinding hurt, then the warmth of blood as it cascaded from what was surely a broken nose, but he still made no move.

"Stop it! Stop fighting us," the monk yelled.

Boy Scout didn't miss the irony of the man's statement as his body stood there doing nothing.

"*Toz filk was filli gabuuk, ya kalbd,*" Boy Scout said.

He recognized the Arabic, but didn't understand the words.

The monk's eyes narrowed, then he hauled back and delivered a punch that knocked Boy Scout down.

But he stood back up as if the blow hadn't even registered, a pathetic, wild-haired version of the Terminator.

Boy Scout began to fight from the inside, but it

was like fighting while floating in midair. He had nothing to grab, nothing to hold. The frustration of it was incredible. He'd been in his body for thirty-nine years and never once considered where his consciousness resided. But as sure as he knew he'd been mindjacked, he knew that wherever his consciousness was, the others were there as well. If he was in the cistern with the *daeva*, he'd have been able to enter The White at will and—

A thought occurred to him even as he was punched again.

He didn't need the *daeva* to enter The White. The travelers inside of him hadn't had the luxury of a *daeva* to help them transport. They'd entered it at different times and in different places. How had they gotten inside, then found him as he visited The White, then made it out? Was it something like this? Did they seek to leave their body and then get stuck in the nothing place, a sort of purgatory where the only thing you could control was your own visage? He felt violated; he didn't want to lose his body to some other entity. They'd had their bodies. They'd had their chance. Through fate or consequence, they'd decided to leave theirs behind and he'd be damned if he'd let this being have his body.

And why had he stopped fighting?

Why was he just standing there taking a beating when he could easily—

Because the entity or whatever the fuck it was busy doing something else, which could only mean...

Boy Scout concentrated. He had no real idea what he was going to do. He'd never astral projected before, and he hadn't ever really believed in it, but since he had at least three visitors inside of him, he could conveniently say that his situation had definitely changed. Not that he was actually going to astral project, but it was the only metaphor that he could think of for what he was trying to do.

He knew he didn't want to return to The White, so instead he imagined the universe as the exact opposite. *Black*. A complete void of white without even a star to mar the Abyssinian universe he was attempting to create. Darker than dark. Blacker than black. A universe where nothing existed except himself, his place, and the core of his existence.

He blocked out sight and sound.

He blocked out the pummeling he was taking.

He blocked out the anxiety he felt and the fear he had that he'd never be free of this new, terrible existence.

The same concentration he'd once used to sight in on a target at nine hundred meters with a Barret .50 he applied to this moment, sighting in on nothing but the possibility that there was a place he could inhabit.

The same concentration he'd used when he was in a Close Quarters Battle stack, responsible for a single sector as they entered a room where he knew hostiles were and could only aim at a certain area, convinced that his teammates would have his back because they had the same training, he applied to this moment.

The same concentration he gave when scanning the side of the road for IED signs, he applied to this moment.

And he was there.

Or nowhere.

A universe of nothing but blackness.

The opposite of The White.

The *Black*.

And like in The White he couldn't see himself, at least not until he decided to will himself into a temporal existence. And even then, without a light source or a way to see, he'd never be able to see his own being. He just had to feel his way. He'd had the same problem moving in The White. Without legs and feet, how could he step? But he'd solved the riddle by merely willing himself forward, somehow moving without a sense of movement.

His sixth sense kicked in.

The feeling of being stared at.

The feeling of not being alone.

The feeling of a shape beside him in the dark.

He reached out with his mind and felt it... something pressing... something that had no give. He tried to push against it and felt it move. It grew larger and heavier. He pushed harder and it was as if a balloon popped. The smell of jasmine. A street scene from an Algerian market, basket weavers selling their wares beside a flower merchant. A sky going from gray blue to dark blue. The call to prayer in the voice of an old man, vibrato in its earnestness.

This, too, dissolved until there was less than nothing.

Then came lightness.

Piercing.

Blinding.

He blinked back tears as the light seared into him.

Then he realized that his eyes were open and he was no longer in The Black.

Preacher's Daughter stood before him, confusion and anger on her face.

She brought her hand around and slapped him hard.

He felt it and it hurt.

She brought her hand around again and this time he grabbed it.

"Stop. It's me," he said.

"About damn time." She looked around at the downed men and the scattered tables. "You certainly made a mess, didn't you?"

Boy Scout sighed and realized that the simple motion of it made his face hurt. In fact, his face hurt just from doing nothing. But that didn't matter. He was back. His body was his own. And for one incongruous moment, he was happy. So he smiled and in doing so, capped a chapter on his life that had been pure insanity.

Then he turned and felt the lights go out inside of him.

Chapter Three

Abbey Infirmary

THE SMALL, FOUR-BED infirmary was a busy place thanks to Boy Scout. When he woke up eighteen hours later, two of the monks he'd assaulted were in beds across from him. One was asleep, the clear plastic tube of an IV attached to his left arm, his right arm in a cast from hand to shoulder. The other was awake and regarded him with a smoldering anger. Both of his legs were in casts and slings that hung from the ceiling. The empty bed beside him had been pushed against the wall to allow de Cherge to be there. He sat in an arm chair, his right arm in a wrist-to-shoulder cast, cradled in his left hand.

Boy Scout felt like he was one big mottled bruise. His face was a cooked sausage and his chest and stomach ached from deep within. His lips were two dry twigs that gave way to the vast Sahara of his throat.

De Cherge handed him a glass of water.

Boy Scout took it and drank it slowly, his gaze steady on the one-time French Foreign Legionnaire turned Trappist abbot. When the glass was empty, de Cherge took it from Boy Scout and set it on the bedside table.

The act of adjusting to a sitting position made Boy Scout groan and grab for his stomach, but he pushed through and managed to do it without passing out.

"We took you for x-rays at Twin Peaks and they came back negative. No broken ribs and no internal injuries," de Cherge said.

Boy Scout glanced once more at the other beds and polled his conscience. He'd done that. He'd put them here. He was pissed that his body had been used to deliver such violence—such damage. His anger was almost enough to overcome the shame he felt for doing what he did even if he wasn't in control when it happened.

"How are they?" he asked, staring at the monk who stared back as if he wanted a rematch.

"Brother Frievald had a bad reaction to the anesthesia they used when they went to repair his shattered wrist. He's going to be fine, but they are keeping him under until his heart rate and vitals return to normal. Brother Khost has about a fifty percent chance of walking again. You dislocated both of his knees. One was only a subduction, but the other was a complete dislocation including tearing the patella tendon."

."And you?"

"Complex fracture of the radius. I'll be fine. I've had worse."

Boy Scout nodded and lowered his head. "Of course, you have. You do realize that it wasn't me, yes?"

"As I understand it, after discussing your condition with Madam May, one of the entities inside of you was able to take over. But it was pretty plain to me when we were fighting that it wasn't you."

"How's that?"

"For one, I don't believe you can speak French, or if you did, you wouldn't have a Berber accent."

"I pegged the entity as North African. I was thinking Morocco."

"Could be. That or Algeria. The Berbers frequented both areas."

"What's the other reason? You said *one* so there must be a *two*."

"The way it refused to fight at the end and allowed Brother Sebastian to pummel you. I could tell you were fighting it on the inside. Trying to make it stop."

Boy Scout thought for a moment, then shook his head. "I only wish that were true. I think it was busy trying to find a permanent location. By the time I figured out how to find it inside me, it disappeared. It somehow knows more about this than I do, and I don't doubt that it will try again."

De Cherge's eyes narrowed. "This is not something I wish to happen again. The brothers are worse for wear. As it stands, you will be leaving in a few days. Do I need to find a way to keep others safe from you?"

By *keep others safe* Boy Scout had no question it meant either locking him up or chaining him down. "I hope that won't be necessary. Something else bothers me," he said, changing the subject. "The entity knew jujitsu, and not just *any* jujitsu. I myself am a blue belt in the Gracie Brazilian jujitsu. I might be able to buy that the entity had come across Japanese Small Circle jujitsu, but I can't believe for one moment that it knew Brazilian jujitsu."

"I was thinking the same thing, although I can't tell the difference between the two."

"There are variances. I've watched enough to know."

"My question, big boy, is why you don't know how to speak French?" came a female voice.

Boy Scout turned to the door.

Preacher's Daughter closed it behind her. She glanced at the wounded brothers, then shined the light of her wicked grin on Boy Scout. Just shy of six feet, she had the lithe build of an athlete. She wore black jeans with a tucked in T-shirt and a black denim jacket. Altra runners hugged her feet. Her high cheekbones hinted at American Indian ancestry. Her blonde hair was pulled into a pony tail. An army of tiny diamond studs hugged each ear.

"Why would I know French?" he asked.

"Clearly the Algerian used your skills at jujitsu to fight the abbot, which means that it had access—has access," she clarified, "to your skills and knowledge."

"And?"

"Jesus, Boy Scout. Is that what you've been doing for six months? Feeling sorry for yourself?"

He glanced at her, then away.

"Have you been skulking about in the dark all weepy-eyed because some other entities entered your body without as much as a by-your-leave? Because if that's it, you need to relook your attitude. Clearly whatever is inside you—this Algerian—has been biding his time so that he could finally be in the driver's seat, during which he learned jujitsu from you."

She poked him in the chest. *Look at me*.

Grudgingly, he turned and looked at her, shame weighing his movements.

"This Algerian also probably learned most—if not all—of your TTPs"—tactics, techniques, and procedures—"in addition to reliving your three-day fuckfest outside of Clark Air Force Base in the Philippines in 1986. That you haven't even tried to do the same to them is shameful."

And he knew she was right.

"You have four enemy combatants who have hijacked you and instead of hijacking back, you're hiding in a corner. Are you Boy Scout or Girl Scout? Do you get fucking merit badges or are you a cookie seller?"

"I think you're being unfair to Girl Scouts."

"Fuck Girl Scouts. I was a Girl Scout and I spent more time in front of grocery stores trying not to get groped while my mother tried and usually succeeded to one-up the other mothers while us kids stood at the doors one step away from selling our bodies for a few extra calories."

"I think you might have issues," Boy Scout mumbled, wishing she'd leave and let him slip back into his pity corner.

"Issues?" She stepped forward. "You want to see issues? I'll show you some fucking issues." She glanced at de Cherge. "And you! You should have been advising him better."

De Cherge raised an eyebrow. "Advising? *Moi?*"

She snapped her mouth shut and curled a lip. She seemed about to say something else but turned on her heel, opened the door, then slammed it on her way out.

The room was silent for a long minute.

Boy Scout was the first to speak. "She's right, you know? I should have been trying to figure things out better." He shook his head. What had he been doing all this time? "The problem is I don't know where to start."

"But you said you were able to find the entity."

"I sort of stumbled into it. I wasn't sure at all— I'm still not sure what I am doing."

"I think I might have an idea," de Cherge said.

Boy Scout sat up a little straighter and almost avoided wincing.

"We have a nun who recently came here from Turkey. She was possessed by a demon and exorcised. She might have some insight into what you're going through."

"A nun possessed by a demon?"

"She's better… mostly." De Cherge gave him a faraway look. "You'll have to see for yourself. She knows about your problem and has shown some interest, but… you have to understand the sort of damage a possession can do."

An image of Boy Scout standing in the middle of the commissary being hit and unable to do anything about it strobed through his mind. "I'm just beginning to."

"Then it is settled."

"De Cherge?"

"Yes."

"Can you arrange to have chains put around my waist and me bound to them?"

De Cherge seemed to be about to argue the point, then looked down and nodded once. "I can arrange that."

"I think it's for the best."

"I, as well."

Chapter Four

Atlas Meditation Grotto Number 4

THE NUN WAS Sister Renee de Lydia, originally Jessica Fontaine. Born in Los Angeles, the daughter of a Catholic missionary, she'd been active in school and a cheerleader for her high school football team until her father had moved the family to help restore the Sumela Monastery in northern Turkey. She'd initially fought the move away from her friends and everything she'd known, but soon came to love the eighteen-hundred-year-old cliff-hugging Eastern Orthodox Monastery. She'd had the run of the place and rapidly found her solace in the beauty of the Black Mountain and its hawk's view of the surrounding countryside.

Soon after she turned eighteen, they began the excavation of the monastery's St. Barbara Chapel to bring back the icon that had been buried by the Greeks who'd fled persecution in the 1920s. One of the holiest artifacts of Christianity, the *Panagia Gorgoepekoos*, was an icon of the Virgin Mary alleged to have been painted by the Apostle Luke. She was one of the first to see the uncovered icon and that moment changed the path of her life.

Not only did she decide to give her life to Christ at the moment she spied the impossibly beautiful Virgin Mary, but something was let loose that had been guarded by the icon. Something that would not only result in the deaths of her mother, father, brother, and seventeen other workers in the monastery, but would also come into her and inhabit her for seven hundred and sixty-three horrific days.

Boy Scout observed the small figure of the young woman in her black and white habit. When she turned to him as he approached, he saw the haunted eyes amidst a comely but shadowed face, and he knew that something terrible had happened to her. He'd seen that same look on an old woman in Croatia who'd watched as every man and boy in her town was shot and shoved into a ditch by a squad of Serbs. He'd seen the same look on a young boy whose sister had just been evaporated by a roadside bomb in Iraq. He'd also seen that look on a picture of an old Jewish man returned to Auschwitz, the memories of the Holocaust both personal and global.

De Cherge had made it so that they wouldn't be disturbed, selecting one of the several secluded meditation grottos on the property for the meeting.

Boy Scout approached slowly. His hands were cuffed, the chains running from them through a belt at his waist, then down to cuffs around his ankles. One of the officers at the Twin Peaks police department had loaned them to the abbot without question, probably because he'd seen his fair share of craziness.

He watched her watch him as he approached.

She sat on a backless stone bench, knees together, hands in her lap.

He positioned himself on an identical bench across from her, mimicking her position not only because it was less threatening, but because it was all his chains would allow.

Bougainvillea with giant red flowers surrounded them, creating a solid, leafy wall of shrubbery. The grass beneath their feet was thick like it could only be in California. From somewhere off to his right a bird whistled occasionally, its bright notes the only sound other than an occasional bristle of wind through the leaves.

He let a minute pass before he introduced himself. "Hello, I'm Bryan Starling. I was hoping you might be able to help me."

She cocked her head much like a bird and regarded him. She chewed at her lip for a moment, then asked in a voice older and more worn than she should have had, "What does it feel like? Does it feel like you're full up and there's so much pressure your skin will explode? Does it feel like fingernails are scratching the inside of your brain, occasionally tapping, like they're either eternally bored or sending you hidden messages in Morse code? Does it seem as if someone is whispering to you right on the edge of your hearing, telling you something you really need to hear, but can't quite manage? Does it feel anything like this? Does it feel anything close to this?"

As she spoke, he imagined everything she said and was horrified by the questions. When she finally finished, he slowly shook his head and said, "No. It feels nothing like that."

"Then you have no idea how bad it can be. Do you know who they are—the things inside you?"

"One is an Afghan. I call him Ahmad's Friend because of a thought we once shared. Another is a North African—a Berber according to de Cherge. The third is a boy who has remained silent. The fourth keeps hidden. But there seems to be something else, something I can't yet discern." He swallowed. "But I feel it… watching me."

"I'd be most worried about that one. After all, what's it doing while the others are busy?"

Again, she offered a dreadful ponder, one he didn't even want to think about.

"How do they present?" she asked.

"When I dream, I sometimes dream of things that must be their memories. Occasionally, I'll find myself in a fugue—no, not a fugue. I don't know what to call it. One moment I know what's going on, then there's lost time followed by a moment where I once again know what's going on but think I might have gone somewhere. Yet I never really moved." He laughed self-consciously. "Does that even make sense?"

"It does. How did they get in you? Do you know?"

He laughed again, this time in pain and remembrance. He told her about the mission they'd had in Afghanistan with the three giant burning objects in the sky... so much like UFOs, but something far older and of an original Earth quality. He told her how they'd all thought they were going crazy, dreaming of the same burning sky, a girl, and a goat which turned out to be some crazy psychopomp representing something all too real. He explained how they'd awoken in an ancient cistern, mind-linked to an even older Zoroastrian being known as *daeva*, put there by the Mevlevi dervishes, an order of Sufi mystics who were using strangers as lures to troll The White for their missing leader and even more ancient beings. He told her of the Falling Man, and the Napalm Girl, and then the Burning Monk who spoke to him, then of the spider creatures that had climbed down his throat, then the escape, then the explosion that almost killed them all, and finally the whispering that began in earnest then disappeared, worrying him even more because he knew there were things inside him that should never have been there.

She sat still through it all, staring at him through eyes that seemed to be unblinking. Once it was done, she stood and turned her back as she paced to the corner of the grotto, hands behind her back. He could see her inhale deeply several times, as if she were trying to control a rush of emotion. When she settled, she began to speak, her back still to him, but her low voice clear.

"People generally aren't raped, so they don't understand how one can feel so violated. I think you have a taste of it—the violation. I can hear it in your voice. I went to Santa Monica High School for a year and was raped by a football player named Will Rigalski. I was fifteen then and thought it would be the worst thing to ever happen to me. I felt unsafe and my father found out and decided to try and make me safe again by taking me halfway across the world. Then when I was eighteen and in that old monastery halfway across the world, I *did* feel safe. I felt safe before we dug up the Virgin Mary. I felt safe before we unleashed it. What the Greeks hadn't mentioned when they'd fled the monastery in 1926 was that when they buried the icon, they'd buried with her a hollowed-out bible that held the spirit of a major demon, one who, when it saw the residue of pain in my eyes, was eager to resurrect that pain and enter me, unbeknownst to almost everyone."

"Did it have a name?"

She whirled about so fast and her anger was so sudden that he flinched.

"This is my story. Do not speak until I have finished."

He gulped and nodded. The transformation from calm to someone who seemed keen on tearing his arm off had been fantastically swift.

She turned back around, but not before he saw the tears that rimmed her eyes.

"I'm sorry for that," she said. "The exorcist said that I'd have some PTSD from the possession. Funny about PTSD. I thought you had to go to war or something. Whoever thought a girl would have it because an ancient evil invaded her mind?"

She shuddered and continued. "Its name was Kimaris. The Lemegeton labels it—" she glanced at him as he stared blank-eyed back. "Sorry, the Lemegeton is also known as The Lesser Key of Solomon. It's a spell book of sorts from the mid-seventeenth century. The Lemegeton indicated Kimaris as the sixty-sixth demon in the *Ars Gotea*—the first book of the Lemegeton, drawn from arcane books from far earlier. The Lemegeton describes the demon as a majestic warrior riding a black horse. It has the ability of locating lost treasures and holds the rank of marquis in Satan's court. It supposedly has thirty legions at its beck and call. But that's all marketing some seventeenth century group of men in dresses created to make up for the fact that they have—" She inhaled and shook her head. "I mean, that's how Kimaris is described, but it's anything but that. I found the demon to be a sniveling little bother, then when it had me locked out of my own body, it proved itself as cowardly as it was devious. There was nothing majestic about it at all, except perhaps the ignorance it displayed in thinking I wouldn't fight to have my body returned to me, toe to soul and all."

Sister Renee turned to look at him, once again with the face of someone who'd been well-haunted. "Then I was the one trying to explode out of my skin, scratching at the inside of my own brain, tapping messages to a self who'd been hijacked by a sixty-sixth rate fallen angel. Ever want to do something but been unable to do it? Ever tried to take a step or lift a finger and not be able to?" She nodded. "Yes. I can see from your face that you know."

She moved to him so quickly he thought she was going to hit him, but instead she shoved her face toward his until they were separated only by inches. "How did it feel to be helpless?"

"It felt—it felt..." He lowered his eyes. "I have no words for it."

She backed away and began to pace again. "Then you know. You know what it's like."

He watched her walk back and forth, wondering how it had been for her to be locked out. Had she been screaming from the inside like he'd been? "De Cherge said you might be able to help me figure out how to get rid of these things."

"My exorcist called them travelers. He was aware of their existence and checked me for their possible presences. But it didn't take a genius to figure out I was possessed. He concentrated his efforts on ridding the world of demons one little fucked-up girl at a time." She shook her head again. "Sorry."

"These travelers... how did he check for them? Make sure it wasn't a demon?"

"Automatic writing. He gave me a blank notebook and a pen and had me fill it up. He told me not to think about what I was writing, just to write as fast as I could, using whatever words came to mind. He didn't even want me to form complete sentences, just get whatever was in my mind on paper."

"And did you do this?"

"I did. The hardest part was in the beginning because I thought I was so stupid for not being able to write complete sentences. But once I got over that, it went quick. Fifty-five minutes and I was done."

"How did he check it?"

"He looked for patterns. For missing words and phrases. For words and phrases that said something. He searched for foreign words written in languages I didn't know."

"What did he find?"

"He said there was nothing extraordinary except in the space of fifty pages I'd used the word God three hundred and forty-seven times."

"That seems excessive."

This made a grin flash across her face, lighting it like a bolt of lightning might illuminate storm clouds. She came and sat across from him again. "It was. So, he had me do it again. And again, I used God three hundred and forty-seven times."

"Hardly seems like a coincidence."

"That's what he said. So, we tried it a third time and you know what happened?"

Boy Scout shook his head.

She grinned madly. "I didn't use it once."

He didn't see the correlation.

"Father Emmett explained it to me. If I had travelers, there would be entire sections or passages in their language or in my language describing things and concepts for which I am not aware. But possession by an actual demon is different. The demon knows we're trying to find it. It knows to hide. It knows we're trying to find signs of its evil."

"So, the three hundred and forty-seven times was its attempt to color your writing with Godliness."

"Yes. And without thinking it repeated the same thing it did before, until it realized what we were doing and then swung all the way back so that the letters G-O-D did not appear in sequence at all, either front to back or back to front."

"How could someone possibly keep track of such a thing?"

"Exactly. That's how it works. As a conscious entity, my mind has other requirements. To stand. To speak. To do physical things. An entity has no need so can concentrate like I cannot. Automatic writing or psychography is not an exact science. In fact, Father Emmett said it takes a certain amount of art to read the results. The bottom line was that I was possessed and there were no travelers inside me."

"What would he have done had there been any inside of you?"

"Astral projection," she said matter-of-factly.

The very thing he'd been considering doing if he only knew how. But coming out of the mouth of a Catholic nun, given to her by a Catholic priest, seemed a little bit new age for the stogy Catholic church. So he said as much.

"Demons have been possessing humans for far longer than the Catholic Church has been around. Fallen angels have been trying to get corporeal form long before Christ was a zygote. Exorcising a victim often requires techniques borrowed from cultures and religions from across the breadth of time. Astral projection is what helped me keep my soul away from Kimaris during the worst of the infestation. It needed my soul to merge with and I denied it that, so to get me back he took it out on me."

Seeing the question in his eyes, Sister Renee added, "He cut me—one tick mark for each day he was inside of me."

She wore long sleeves and her dress was down to her ankles so he couldn't see where she'd been cut. Then he remembered what de Cherge had said about the length of her possession and was staggered by the number. Seven hundred and sixty-three days. The tick marks had to be all over her. Everywhere.

She nodded to him as his eyes widened in silent horror.

"Where is Father Emmett?" he asked softly. "Maybe I can get him to help me."

Her face hardened. "You won't find him anytime soon. Kimaris took him and they both disappeared."

"Took him as in… Oh my God. Aren't you worried he'll be back?"

"Not in the least. What's a young woman compared to an expert on Christian demonology? Kimaris upgraded. There's no reason for him to come back. My guess is he wants to find a way to get to Rome."

Boy Scout thought about the idea of a possessed pope and shuddered. Then a thought came to him that might be even worse. "There's another possibility. What if he's looking for others like him? You said he's number sixty-six? What about the other sixty-five? What if he managed to get them all together? That truly would be Hell on Earth."

Chapter Five

Atlas Meditation Grotto, Later

THEY MET SEVERAL more times over the next few days—each time in the grotto, his hands and ankles cuffed and chained together. Sister Renee began to teach him how she learned to leave her body. They both felt that the astral projection taught to her by Father Emmett was his best hope at discovering who his travelers were and possibly being able to communicate with them. The idea that he could actually converse with the entities on a level playing field held a certain excitement to him. Certainly far better than him screaming to get out from behind the glass walls of his mind.

"You have to take a leap of faith," she finally said on the first day. "You just have to trust me that this is a thing."

"It's not that I don't trust you," he said. "It's just that I can't see myself doing it."

She leveled her gaze and said each word slowly. "Leap of faith."

He laughed and sat back.

"What's so funny?"

"Just that you were so serious. You remind me of one of my college professors the way you just said it, with your head down and your eyes so piercing."

She crossed her arms. "Now you're just making fun of me."

He sat forward. "I'm not. Really, I'm not." He licked his lips and regarded her for a moment. "Do you know where that term came from—*leap of faith*?"

She shook her head.

"Søren Kierkegaard. He was a Danish philosopher. He posed that faith wasn't something based on evidence, but rather something that lived in one's self-doubts. I know it sounds like he's arguing against himself, but listen. What is the evidence of love or belief in God? There's detritus like a shoe box full of love notes or the Bible, but are they really evidence? Do they really prove anything? Kierkegaard theorized that in order for someone to truly believe in something they couldn't touch, see, or feel that they needed to doubt it and then recognize that they had doubts."

"So, you're saying that if I doubt then it proves I believe?" she asked, her eyes squinting around the problem.

"Basically. Think of having to leap over your doubts to get to where you can believe."

"What about blind faith?" she asked.

"I think that's for idiots and lemmings. To not approach life intellectually is to allow someone else to dictate your future."

She nodded. "That's deep. You learned all of this?"

"I lived all of it."

"In the church we deal with our doubts all the time. I'm far from perfect and I often have doubts, but there are small things that make me keep going."

"Same here," he said. "I've doubted several times that I'd survive a particular battle, but I always do."

She grinned at his response. "Based on your doubts, then, you should believe in the astral plane and astral projection."

He thought about this for a moment. "I'm willing to believe, yes," he flashed a grin, "but my faith is wavering."

"Remember, if you doubt, you truly believe." She flashed him a grin. "At least according to old Søren."

He laughed a combination of nervousness and hilarity. "You got me there."

"Then let me see if I can't make your faith stronger," she said. "I can confirm that you have travelers. I have seen them. They are like bright shadows of you in the darkness."

And so, the lessons began.

"Each of the seven chakras represents a step to locking away your body and then leaving it. You must lock each chakra or something could come and inhabit you."

"Do you mean had I known this to begin with this might never have happened?"

"From what you tell me, it wasn't in the best interests of the dervishes to explain ways to defeat their plans."

Her voice had grown softer and her eyes seemed brighter since he'd first met her. He wondered if the almost constant and close contact between them might be an antidote for some of her misery. He hoped it was, because her presence certainly made him feel better... *safer*. That she'd gone through something possibly worse made him listen more closely—like he had in Ranger school when his instructors began telling war stories, him in awe of them until he had his own memories, realizing then that they'd shared theirs to try and get the memories out of themselves.

"Each of the chakras has a name," she said. "There's no reason to memorize the original names for them because the words have no magic. Just know them for what they are called in English and where they are located on the body. From bottom to top they are the root, sacral, solar plexus, heart, throat, third eye, and crown. Each chakra is a place of power. A focal point. While each chakra has other characteristics, for the purposes of projection, you just need to be able to visualize where each one is."

She'd gone on to explain that the chakras ran in a straight line from the base of the spine to the top of the head, indicating where each one existed.

"Now imagine that all the power inside of you is located in each of the seven chakras. Beginning with the root chakra, you shift the power from each one into the one above it until all of your power is in your crown. From there, it's only a matter of effort to push your power, which is your soul or your consciousness, out of your body and into the astral plane. This is what they call astral projection."

He'd laughed at her then, and almost lost her as a mentor. He'd been forced to explain. "You have to understand that until recently, I didn't believe in anything I couldn't see, hear, touch, lick, or fight. All of this is so new to me, it's still taking some getting used to."

Then she'd pinned him with a level gaze and asked, "And you think I'd always planned on being possessed?"

From that point on he kept his wonderment and self-deprecation inside.

"The idea of astral projection exists in most cultures. Even certain Amazonian tribes believe that they are able to fight each other in a sort of soul fight on the astral plane. But it's not easy. Many who attempt it try and fail. The secret is being able to concentrate so completely that you are able to tune everything else out."

"How long did it take you to be able to do it?" he asked.

"I was more motivated than most. I was locked out of my mind. Already under the heel of Kamaris. Father Emmett spoke to it and I listened. The message had always been for me. Projecting myself was the only way Father Emmett could really talk to me."

"How long?"

She sighed. "Weeks."

He imagined her trapped, her body being ravaged by the thing inside of her, while she desperately tried to get away and failed... over and over and over.

"Eighty-nine days to be exact."

"And on the eighty-ninth day?"

"I climbed out of my chakras, locked them behind me, and left my body."

He frowned. "When you say lock you mean…"

"It's helpful to imagine each chakra as a lock. You design it. It can be simple or complex. It's up to you."

"What do yours look like?" he asked.

"Mine?" she asked. "Initially they were something you might find at a hardware store. Something I might put on a school locker. But now they are complex with many moving parts. Each one looks like a lotus."

"Were you ever afraid you'd be lost—that you wouldn't be able to come back?" he asked.

"I was hoping for that. I didn't want my body anymore. I just wanted to be done with it. But you are tethered to yourself. You can't lose yourself unless you really try."

"So, it worked."

"Father Emmett was waiting for me. He waited for me as he'd done for each of the eighty-nine days."

"What did he say?"

"That's when he told me his plan to set me free."

Boy Scout opened his mouth to speak, but felt a great weight pull at him, as if an immense anchor was attached to his psyche. Slowly at first it pulled him away. Down and down and down he went, until he was no longer in the grotto but instead at the entrance to an underwater cave. The press of the ocean against his skin was incredible. A great beast awaited him inside the cave. He couldn't see into the stygian blackness inside the opening, but he knew something immense was in there, something not human. It moved and he felt the displacement of water pushing against him, but still he didn't see anything. It was then he realized that he was underwater, and he sought to breathe. When he opened his mouth, water surged down his throat and into his lungs. He gasped. His body became a question mark. Then it straightened into an exclamation. Back and forth from question to surprise as his hands clawed at his throat. Then the beast moved forward, just a shadow, but enough for Boy Scout to see the outlines of a face, humanlike, and eyes that glowed with malevolence.

Something grabbed him.

He slapped it away.

It grabbed him again and he felt pain on his face.

Then he was back.

In the grotto.

Not in the water.

Sister Renee squatted next to him, as did Preacher's Daughter.

"What… what… I couldn't breathe," he stammered.

"Where were you?" the sister asked.

"Under—something immense waited for me—*wanted* me."

"Enough of this," Preacher's Daughter said.

Where had she come from? Boy Scout noticed she was wearing strange glasses—like something John Lennon might wear at a carnival.

She handed a pair to him. "Put these on. We need to go."

He accepted the glasses and put them on. Lights blinked on the frames surrounding the lenses in different combinations. The lights constantly drew his gaze. He found it immediately hard to concentrate on one single thing.

"What the hell are these?" he asked, sitting up.

She also wore body armor over a T-shirt. Her legs were covered in jeans that ran into her Merrell shoes. "Our protection against the dervishes. Our protection against their dance."

"The dervishes? Here? How?" he asked, but she just kept nodding.

"No time." Lore stood and held out her hand.

He took it and let her help him to his feet.

"We've got to go. McQueen is waiting."

She quickly unshackled him. Everything was happening so fast. Boy Scout didn't want to go—he wasn't ready. The grotto was safety. The monastery was safety. He wasn't ready to go back into the world. He wasn't ready to fight the dervishes again.

Preacher's Daughter grabbed his hand and pulled him so hard he had to follow.

He noted two last things.

The worry on Sister Renee's face as he departed.

And that his clothes were entirely soaked through.

Chapter Six

The West Lawn

GUNFIRE ATE AT the silence of the monastery in small, nasty bites.

Boy Scout idly identified pistol and machine gun, the latter firing so fast they had to be Uzis. He'd thought the old weapon of choice for drug smugglers had gone out of style when Don Johnson was still rocking sockless loafers and sport coats with T-shirts on *Miami Vice*. The buzz of nine-millimeter rounds was accentuated by the louder sounds of a .40 caliber and several nines. But as violent as the rounds promised they'd be, they energized him.

Now at the edge of the grotto, he also heard the sound of a helicopter hovering.

He jerked his hand away from Preacher's

Daughter and grabbed her wrist in turn. "What's going on?" he asked.

"Are you back or am I talking to an eighteenth-century traveler?" she asked, one eyebrow raised.

"I'm back. Now what's going on?"

"The dervishes found you. They want the things inside of you."

"They can have them. Are you packing?"

She reached behind her back and pulled out a pistol. "Try not to hurt yourself."

He accepted the Walther PPQ, pleased at how the grip fit perfectly into his hand, checked the magazine, loaded a round, then pointed it at the ground.

"I don't think it's that easy, boss."

"Where's McQueen?"

"He has an exfil plan." She glanced at him. "You ready?"

He growled at her, then found himself running to keep up, his body aching with each step. She stayed within the tree line, allowing the tall pines to shield them as they circumvented the green lawn. As he ran behind her, he saw several monks with pistols firing back at a group of men who were firing using the aforementioned Uzis. The good thing about Uzis was you could put a shit ton of rounds down range. The problem was they rarely went where you aimed. Then it hit him.

"You had me guarded?"

"What? You don't think there's an order of Trappist monks who carry nines to prayer?" Preacher's Daughter laughed as she ran. "That was McQueen's idea. Freed us up to do some research—you know, trying to get those things out of you."

"Who paid for it?"

"We did a GoFundMe. It hit huge on Twitter. What do you think? Came out of your combat pay. De Cherge insisted anyway. He didn't want his people injured."

"I sure messed that up, didn't I?" Boy Scout said, struggling to breathe. He hadn't done any exercise in months and his body felt as much. "Where are we—"

They skidded to a stop at what had been his home for the past few months, the Hermit's Cottage.

McQueen stood waiting for them, wearing the same goofy glasses they were. On him the glasses made him look like the old pro-wrestler, Randy Savage. Not only did he have the super muscular build, but he also had the chiseled face with a bushy Fu Manchu mustache. He wore one of his old shirts from when he was a bouncer at a gay bar in West Hollywood, tucked into 5.11 tactical pants. The shirt was hot pink and said COME YANK AT HANKS in white letters.

Boy Scout felt his heart hollow a bit at the sight of his old friend. They'd been through so much together and knew secrets neither of them would tell another soul.

McQueen held out a kit bag.

Boy Scout took it and emptied it on the ground. Soon he was donning his body armor, with a chest rig holster for his Walther, a belt with a dump bag in back, and a suite of grenades, some smoke and some fragmentation.

"We got word they were coming minutes before they arrived," McQueen said.

"Any idea how they knew I was here?" Boy Scout asked.

"Emails from the monastery to the Archdiocese of Los Angeles detailing a fight and three seriously wounded monks," McQueen said. "I found these guys from 4Chan who are working for us now. They've been following the dervish hacks, mainly because they're all originating from a diplomatic IP. My 4Chan friends totally want to fuck with the dervishes."

Boy Scout held out a hand. "Enough. Later on, the details. What's the plan?"

"I figure they have all the roads blocked, so if we want to get out, we go up."

"The helicopter is their ride?" Boy Scout asked.

"Was their ride," McQueen corrected.

Boy Scout grabbed the glasses and tilted them up. "And these? You sure they work?"

"We're in the middle of field testing them," McQueen said with a smile.

"Then why are we—" Boy Scout stopped and stared. "You mean *we're* the ones field testing them? So we could just see one of the fuckers dancing and end up in a fugue somewhere? I've played that game before and I don't like how it ends."

The dervishes had tricked them before, making them believe that they needed to stay in a fugue in order to get back to their own reality, when in fact Boy Scout and his team had been used to try and attract just the sort of beings he was hosting. He remembered the field of dead bodies, hundreds, perhaps thousands of them—each body representing a human who had been tricked and forced to fugue until their bodies gave up. As healthy as McQueen was, he'd almost died in the fugue, his body feeding on itself as it tried to survive. And all of it from the dervishes, who had the studied ability to dance in such a way to cause the human mind to flip, sending the viewer into an immediate trance.

And to think everyone thought the dervishes danced to be nearer to their god.

"Ready?" McQueen asked.

Boy Scout nodded and glanced at Preacher's Daughter, who did the same.

"You want to lead?" McQueen asked.

"This is your show."

McQueen moved forward and checked his glasses. "Glasses on. Stay on my six." Then he was off at a slow jog toward the sound of gunfire.

Boy Scout hesitated only a moment, his muscle memory kicking in. He was soon close enough to McQueen to count the hairs on the back of the man's neck. Although Boy Scout didn't look, he could feel Preacher's Daughter doing the same behind him. He checked to make sure his glasses were flashing, then pulled his pistol from his chest rig.

They broke free of the brush and onto the wide expanse of grass. Two dervishes remained standing. One was dancing, the other laying down covering fire. The dancing dervish wore a long dress with a conical hat that allowed his movements to be accentuated, drawing the eye, making one look in wonder. Monks and nuns lay on the grass where they'd fallen, dead or wounded from one of the nine-millimeter bullets that had been sprayed across the grounds, or by trance, their minds and bodies no longer in synch.

Behind and to the left of the dancing dervish stood an old Blackhawk style helicopter, its blades whirling.

One of the monks who had been firing back was attempting to crawl away from the dervish with the Uzi, who was clearly stalking him.

McQueen opened fire, breaking into a sprint and aiming at the dancing dervish.

Boy Scout opened fire as well, his target the dervish with the Uzi.

Preacher's Daughter ran for the chopper.

Boy Scout's first two rounds missed, but he saw the next two hit as the man reeled back as if punched. But as he turned, the small-barreled submachine gun swung towards Boy Scout. Instead of diving out of the way, he gritted his teeth and kept firing, catching the man in the arm, hand and then the Uzi, the force of the rounds from his Walther slamming the dervish back and back and back.

Rounds whizzed by his face and ear, but Boy Scout never deviated as he ran towards his target. He'd spent six months exiled from the human race, living in and out of the dappled shadows of his mind because of men like this. If only he had every one of them at the end of his pistol and an unlimited supply of ammunition. But with one pistol and one target, he settled for firing all ten of the Walther rounds, the last one at point blank range into the dervish's look of surprise.

Then Boy Scout turned and sprinted toward the chopper.

Preacher's Daughter was almost there when it started rising off the ground.

He nearly shouted as she took two running steps

and leaped to grab a skid, both arms, and then a foot hooked over it before the ungainly-looking aircraft roared up, turned and twisted away, soon gone from sight.

Boy Scout's mouth fell open as he realized he might never see her again. She'd been like a daughter, a partner as good as any he'd ever had— better in fact.

McQueen skidded to a stop beside him.

"I counted three. One was already dead. I got mine and you got yours."

Boy Scout turned to the other man. "Are we sure? What about the guards?"

"Two dead. One ran. Another was wounded and trying to crawl to safety."

"One ran away?"

"That's what the wounded guard said."

"Sure don't make help like they used to," Boy Scout said.

De Cherge exited the monastery carrying an old pistol in his left hand. He glowered left and right as he stalked towards them. Several other monks followed behind him and began to go from one downed member of the monastery to the next, probably assessing if they were dead or tranced.

A moment later, de Cherge snarled a command in French, then switched to English. "Why did you bring them here?"

"You knew the danger," McQueen said. "We reached out. You offered. You even took money."

"Had I known—"

"Had you known what?" McQueen asked. "Don't go getting self-righteous on us now that what we were afraid of happening actually did. They found them through your emails about the fight." He pointed at the abbot's chest. "You were the one who caused them to come."

"I want you to go," de Cherge said, gesturing to the driveway and the road that wound towards the Rim of the World Highway.

"De Cherge—" Boy Scout began, but was cut off by a chopping of the pistol.

"Don't. Do not say you are sorry. That's all you have been since you came." He cursed in French. "You need to find another reality."

"I intend to."

Just then the chopper returned.

All of them spun towards it, watching it flare over the trees before landing where it had taken off only moments before.

Boy Scout had thought her gone. Maybe dead. "Do you think?" Boy Scout asked.

McQueen raised an eyebrow. "Had you any doubt?"

Boy Scout had had a dozen doubts, but he shouldn't have. Trust in the team... always.

"Come on," McQueen said, grabbing Boy Scout's wrist. "Let's get out of here." He glanced at de Cherge and gave the man a nod. "Let's change your reality. "

Boy Scout allowed himself to be tugged away and was soon jogging beside McQueen. When they reached the chopper, they climbed inside. Preacher's Daughter sat in the right-hand seat, her pistol to the head of the man in the left seat.

"Either of you know how to fly this thing?" she asked.

They both shook their heads.

"Then it looks like it's you and me for a little while more. Besties," she said, grinning dangerously. She poked the gun firmly into the side of the pilot's head. "Let's get out of here and don't even think of crashing this thing or I'll shoot your pecker off before you ever hit the ground." She adjusted the aim of her pistol accordingly, then gave the same dangerous grin to Boy Scout.

"Ready, boss?"

He nodded.

She turned back to the pilot. "Okay, Buzz Lightyear. To infinity and beyond."

The chopper wobbled, then lifted into the air. In seconds they were over the trees and past the highway, San Bernardino a thousand feet below.

Chapter Seven

Twentynine Palms

"Where are we going?" Boy Scout asked.

"Twentynine Palms. There's a man who's been looking for us and I think it's about time we make introductions."

"Who's been looking for us?"

Lore glanced at McQueen, who took over.

"Seems someone with half a brain actually went to the cistern and investigated. They found the bodies and some other strange things they couldn't explain. While the military officially believes our story that we were captured by Al Qaida and managed to escape, no one ever put everything together. Turns out now someone has—some Army lieutenant named Poe."

"Since when are we worried about a lieutenant?"

Boy Scout asked.

"Since he belongs to a unit no one has ever heard of and one I can't find any information on. I even tried to go through Government Supply Agency and do a backdoor search through acquisitions, but his unit doesn't use GSA."

"Everyone uses GSA," Boy Scout said.

"Exactly. Hence my concern."

"What do you think he is?" McQueen asked.

"My guess? Some sort of *X-Files* meets *SEAL Team 666* dude."

"Both great shows," McQueen said. "I streamed them in rehab, although Triple Six never really lived up to its hype."

"Says you," Preacher's Daughter said. "The SEALs have a dog, though. Mulder and Scully never had a dog."

McQueen rolled his eyes. "I bet you loved Lassie and cried when Old Yeller died."

"Know how they check if someone is a human and not an alien?" she asked, her smile getting ominous again. "They make them watch *Old Yeller*. Those who don't cry get shot in the fucking head."

Boy Scout shook his head. "Easy, Lore. We're all friends here."

She waggled a finger. "Don't mess with dogs. I bet McQueen's a cat person," she said, as if it were the gravest of insults.

Boy Scout sighed. "A couple things. One, there are no aliens. Two, everyone cries when Old Yeller dies. And three, there's nothing wrong with cat people. That's like getting mad at crazy people. They just don't understand. Now back to the problem at hand. Who is this Poe guy?"

Preacher's Daughter pointed out the windscreen. "We'll find out soon enough. He's down there waiting on us."

"With handcuffs or a handshake?" Boy Scout said.

"We'll know in a moment."

"Hey, boss?" McQueen asked as they began to descend.

"What?"

"How do you know there aren't any aliens? I mean, I'm only asking because we were most recently hooked up to some sort of ancient demon like we were lights and it was a battery."

And it was in this moment when Boy Scout felt he was truly back. Sure, he had a few mischievous travelers inside of him, and sure, he could be hijacked by one of them at any moment. But he was once again the Boy Scout he'd always been, previously destined to be a high school English teacher, a former US Army Ranger, now leader of a Tactical Support Team. Neither Narco, Bully, nor Criminal had survived Afghanistan. They'd need to rebuild the team. While they might never go back and provide diplomatic security for MANTECH, they still needed to be a cohesive unit. Their mission was still on, and would be until Boy Scout was free of his travelers and the dervishes were all killed or dissuaded from doing what they had been. That was going to be his life mission.

"Easy now," Preacher's Daughter said to the pilot. "Don't get any ideas."

"I'm just going to land," he said, his voice twangy with a Southern accent. "I can tell you now that I wasn't involved in any of this. This man hired me to recover his missing daughter... said she was abducted by a cult."

"And you fell for it?" she asked.

The pilot turned towards her for a brief moment. "Why not? Why would someone lie about that?"

"Who did they say they were... the men who hired you?"

"Didn't say anything and I didn't ask. Listen, I thought all of this was a rescue mission. I figured the man brought along backup."

"Didn't you see the weapons?"

"I'm telling you, he said they were going to rescue his daughter. I might like to fly under the radar and take a few shortcuts, but I'm not a criminal... mostly."

Preacher's Daughter gave Boy Scout a look. "What do you want to do, boss?"

"Check his credentials."

McQueen pulled his pistol free from his chest rig and held it chest-high, barrel pointed at a forty-five-degree angle to the ground. "Easy, chum."

"The name's Noaks," the pilot said. "Peter Noaks."

"Where are you from, Noaks?" Preacher's Daughter asked as she pulled the FAA license from the book in the front.

"Biloxi, Mississippi."

"Wallet?" she asked.

The pilot pulled his wallet free from a zippered compartment in the leg of his flight suit and handed it to her.

"What sort of name is *Noaks*?" Boy Scout asked.

The pilot shrugged. "Been a family name for at least a hundred years or so."

Preacher's Daughter read from his license. "Last name is Noaks, as he says. Peter K. Noaks. Lives in Long Beach. Helicopter is registered to Noaks Aviation at Long Beach Airport. How did they get hold of you?"

"A man showed up at the hanger last night with ten thousand dollars in cash. Asked me to help rescue his daughter."

"I get that, but how did he find you?"

"That I don't know. My name's known in certain circles. We're usually able to get people where they want to go if they know how to properly incentivize their request."

"Do you charge extra for illegal stuff."

"Easy on the *I* word, ma'am. Fact is, we intentionally don't ask a lot of questions. We like the ability to be agile at any time." He held up a hand as he listened to his headset. "I don't have clearance to land. No bueno on going to Twentynine Palms."

"How far out are we?" Boy Scout asked.

"Five mikes."

"Find a place and set it down."

Preacher's Daughter stared at Boy Scout a moment, gave the pilot back his wallet, and put the license back in the book.

Within minutes, they were standing on a patch of sand next to a highway. Across the street was a store named Space Cowboy Books that had a wooden alien out front holding a sign that said *WE'RE OPEN*. Next to that was a trailer park. A Walmart parking lot unraveled on the other side. The helicopter with the mostly-not-a-criminal pilot named Noaks was roaring westward, probably back to Long Beach and his eponymous aviation company.

"We going to use him later?" McQueen asked after looking around.

Boy Scout removed his glasses, made sure they

were turned off, and stowed them in his pocket. "If we need him."

"Do you think it was wise to let him go?" Preacher's Daughter asked.

Boy Scout nodded. "I doubt that the Mevlevi dervishes have their own air force. They'd need to find folks who work on the fringes for help. Guys like Noaks. If they can use him, then we can too. We're off the grid for a while anyway. Without Criminal's connections, we need to start making our own."

"What now?" McQueen asked.

Boy Scout gestured toward the bookstore. "Let's go inside and wait." He checked for traffic but there wasn't any. "Read any good books lately?"

The bookstore turned out to be tiny. The owner sat in a corner wearing a well-used cowboy hat. He had a narrow but pleasant face and seemed to be in his early thirties. When he saw their combat gear, he raised an eyebrow but didn't stray from his seat. Finally, he said, "Looking for a particular book?"

"Got anything on Zoroastrian demons and how to defeat them?" Preacher's Daughter asked.

"Not sure I have—" Then he held up a hand and stood. He scanned two cases, then reached in and grabbed a thin, dog-eared title. "Try this one. It's *The Cosmic Puppets* by PK Dick published by Ace in 1957."

Preacher's Daughter's smile fell. "Seriously?"

The owner nodded. "It's about a man who returns home only to discover that the town is missing things. Turns out there's a war between two Zoroastrian demigods and they've altered reality in their attempts to outdo the other."

Preacher's Daughter laughed hoarsely. "Sounds about right."

McQueen shook his head. "Please don't tell me I've been spending all my time noodling around 4Chan, Reddit and the rest of the Dark Web and the answers are in that book."

Preacher's Daughter glanced at him. "I doubt this is the cure, but there may be some clues it can provide. There's not exactly a host of empirical articles on what we're looking for. I know, because I've checked." Then she grinned. "Oh, and you might want to take off your glasses. You look like a disco version of a professional wrestler."

McQueen reached up and felt the glasses, then removed them, also making sure to turn them off. He grumbled, "Maybe I wanted to look like the disco version of a professional wrestler."

"How much for the book?" she asked the store owner.

The cowboy glanced at their armaments and shook his head. "It's free. No problem."

Preacher's Daughter thrust out a hip. "This isn't

a robbery. We'll pay for this."

He grinned weakly. "Okay. In that case, it'll be five bucks."

Preacher's Daughter reached for her hip pocket and then froze. "I don't have my wallet. I left it at the apartment. McQueen?"

"I did the same."

"Boss?"

"I don't even know where mine is."

McQueen snapped his fingers. "We have it."

All three turned to the bookseller.

"Can we borrow it?" Preacher's Daughter asked.

The owner looked from one to the other to the other. "You can really have it."

She shook her head firmly. "No. I want to pay for it. Problem is that I went sterile in preparation for a gunfight. Good news is the bad guys got shot to shit. Bad news is no wallets. I can come back later though with the five dollars."

His eyes narrowed as she told the story. "Seriously, I'm gifting you the book," he said.

She glared at him. "Don't make me shoot you."

He sighed, looked worried for a moment, then laughed. "Fine. You can borrow the book."

Then she smiled, turning to everyone. "See how things work out if you just have a conversation with people?"

A vehicle skidded to a stop outside.

"Looks like our ride is here."

A moment later, a tall thin army lieutenant with his blond hair cut high and tight strode into the store. He wore his starched ACUs like they were a second skin, but there were no unit or combat patches on it, nor was there a name tag. His uniform was sterile. Stone-faced, it didn't seem like the place many emotions lingered.

"You Starling, May, and McQueen?" he asked.

They stared at him instead of answering.

The shop owner pushed himself back into a corner, unsure if this was a meeting or something closer to the O.K. Corral.

Boy Scout said, "You must be Poe."

The man nodded. "I am."

"Good, we've been waiting for you."

"Exactly what I was going to say."

Chapter Eight

On a Dark Desert Highway

THEY ROARED DOWN the highway in a black Ford Expedition with blacked-out windows. By the feel of the suspension, the vehicle was also up-armored as well, which didn't make a lot of sense here in the good old US of A. Still, riding in the passenger seat with body armor and a chest rig reminded Boy Scout of all the times they'd ferried diplomats or senior military officials in and around Kabul, Afghanistan. The thousand times they'd been caught in the herds of Toyota Corollas around Masoud Circle or moved through the multiple layers of security in the Green Zone or funneled down Airport Road as they approached the main gate of Kabul International Airport all slammed into a memory sandwich that was impossible for him to digest.

Then the final time they were in an up-armored SUV, at last escaping the dervishes and the horrors of the cistern, heading for safety, only to hit an IED and come under direct fire from an ambush. They'd all been hit. He'd thought McQueen and Preacher's Daughter weren't going to make it, but they all did. The worst of it had been inside of him, whispers turning into threats, voices that weren't his own.

And now they were heading towards China Lake, according to the close-mouthed Poe. For what reason, Boy Scout couldn't be sure, but he'd be damned if he'd let a sorry US Army first lieutenant decide his fate. He had connections he hadn't even worked. Escorting and ultimately saving enough general officers had the benefit of future favors, ones he'd banked so that they could accrue interest.

They'd been traveling for two hours when Preacher's Daughter finally broke the silence.

She never did understand that all the power rested in the person being spoken to. McQueen knew it and had been pretending to sleep this whole time. Boy Scout certainly knew it, and had spent the hundred and twenty minutes trying to internally communicate with the travelers inside of him.

Whether she knew it or not, her patience had finally given out.

"I knew you were looking for us. You left your footprints all over the web."

Lieutenant Poe glanced in the rearview mirror, then back at the two-lane desert highway unrolling before him. "I meant it that way. You all know what you're doing. Your history tells me how dangerous you can be. Reports from the monastery indicate you haven't lost much of your dangerousness in the last six months. I guessed letting you know you were being looked for might be better than surprising you."

"It was you who dropped the information about preparing to come get us in Twentynine Palms?"

"I knew you'd need to get somewhere quick once the dervishes found your location. This was the closest military base where I could have any semblance of control."

"Not often an army lieutenant has control on a marine base," McQueen said.

"I have a letter that gets me pretty much what I want."

"Signed by your mother, I suppose," Preacher's Daughter put in.

"She wasn't available so I had to a get it from the chairman of the Joint Chiefs."

"Was it you who made them deny our helicopter landing?" Boy Scout asked.

"It was. Less red tape if I could get you outside the base."

"Even with the letter?" Boy Scout asked.

"Even with the letter. Never underestimate the ability of the military to be overly bureaucratic," Poe said.

Preacher's Daughter snorted. "Sounds like something Boy Scout would say."

"Some axioms are universal," Poe said.

"So what unit are you with?" McQueen asked.

"One you've never heard of."

"Try us. We've been around," Preacher's Daughter said.

"Special Unit 77."

"Never heard of it," McQueen said.

"You got me," Preacher's Daughter added.

Everyone was silent for a moment, then she asked, "What about you, boss? Every heard of this Heinz 57?"

Boy Scout noted that the Joshua trees they'd been passing had all but disappeared and now outside the window was all a wasteland of sand and low scrub. "I've heard of them. I know they did some work in San Francisco during the sixties and seventies. Not sure what they did after that."

Poe turned to him and a smile crested his face. "Now I'm impressed."

Boy Scout shrugged. "Don't be. I've just been around. Seen a few things."

"About that," Poe began. "I was hoping you

would let me help you. As I understand it you have several entities inside of you and probably want to get them out."

"You have a dust buster that can do the trick?" Preacher's Daughter grinned.

"Not exactly. But we do have archives of information you can have access to."

"Are you taking us to the super-secret Warehouse 13 where you have the Ark of the Covenant and a whole squad of exorcists?"

Poe all but turned around to stare at her, a perplexed look on his face. Then he looked at Boy Scout as if he wanted to ask, *Is she always like this?*

Seeing it, McQueen answered for all of them from the back seat. "She's like wine. You either get used to it or spit it out and switch to beer."

Preacher's Daughter put her hand on McQueen's arm. "Aww, that's nice. You compared me to wine. You... I think you're like a very hoppy IPA." She nodded. "Yup. That's it. You're the hipster beer that can strangle an unsuspecting drinker."

McQueen shook his head and offered a rare grin. "Trust me when I say I've never strangled any unsuspecting drinkers. They've all been expecting it." Then he looked at Poe. "I think the lady asked a question."

Preacher's Daughter fanned her face with her hand. "First wine and then he calls me a lady."

Poe cleared his throat. "There's no Warehouse 13 and there's no squad. The members of Seventy-Seven are dispersed in several remote locations in order to respond to certain events. We determined long ago that there wasn't any need for an office or a headquarters because most of us were never there."

Preacher's Daughter leaned forward and put a hand on Poe's shoulder. "You're telling me that there isn't a giant warehouse somewhere that contains magical and religious artifacts that the US government has determined are detrimental to the health and safety of American citizens?"

Poe glanced at her hand, clearly wanting it removed, but Preacher's Daughter kept it there.

"I'm not saying that," he said through a clenched jaw. "I'm saying that that's not where we are going."

Preacher's Daughter flung herself back into her seat. "Ha!" she cried. Then she held out a hand to McQueen. "Pay up. I told you I'd get him to tell me about his secret warehouse."

McQueen groaned. "Put it on my tab."

"Your tab's getting pretty long," she said.

Poe said, "Seriously? You made a bet?"

Boy Scout smiled for what felt like the first time in a long time. Being back among his team really was what he needed. He'd spent too much time alone—too much time in his own head. His team wasn't the same as it had been. They'd lost too many of their own. But they still had the three of them as the core and right now that's all that mattered.

"Why China Lake?" Boy Scout asked after a few moments.

"We have spaces there where we can base until we can discern the apex and terminus of the threat—both internally and externally."

"Glad you understand the nature of what's going on," Boy Scout said. "But I can't see where you alone are going to be able to assist."

Now it was Poe's turn to smile. "I'm not alone. I have access to networks you don't know exist. I have botnets to conduct searches. I have sock puppets to throw off those searching for you. I can also task click farms or a few super hackers to conduct DNS attacks."

"What good is that going to be against the dervishes?" Preacher's Daughter asked.

"Control information and you control the operation." Poe grinned, an eerie cousin to Preacher's Daughter's evil grin. "I'm basically going to weaponize the internet and make it our friend."

Chapter Nine

China Lake Naval Weapons Center

CHINA LAKE WASN'T really on a lake. Like much of the Western Mojave Desert, it was comprised of dry lake bed after dry lake bed. If one were to look on a map and see all the *lakes*, one might think it was a place to bring sunscreen and a bathing suit. But the Mojave Desert as a whole was one big beach that had the temerity to disallow the very idea of water. Boy Scout had read that on one occasion during World War II, several Germans in a prisoner of war camp, who had been provided maps of the area, fancied an escape. They built a canoe in secret and were able to escape—primarily because, being in the middle of nowhere, the guard force was intentionally thin. Discovering that the lakes and rivers on the map had long dried up, the

Germans eagerly returned to the camp, limping back and almost dead from dehydration.

Such was the Mojave Desert and all of its lakes.

Which was why the US government chose it as a place to conduct weapons testing. China Lake represented eighty-five percent of the navy's CONUS land holding and was the main place to test all of their aircraft and armaments. Although a town had built up around the main gate, the testing was conducted on ranges far from the homes, where an off-target or stray missile would only create another crater in an otherwise barren landscape.

Armitage Airfield was the main focus of the center. Top-secret plane designs took off and landed at regular intervals. Glimpses of them showed they looked more like artist conceptual spaceships at times than something in any military's inventory before being hustled into one of the hundred hangers surrounding the runways. It was in one of these development hangers that Special Unit 77 was given space, a suite of three offices and four bunk rooms carved out of a corner. The number 77 on the outside door was the only indication that this was dedicated to the unit, and with no indication what the numbers meant, they might as well have been invisible on a compound with a hundred such doors hiding secret designs and clandestine units.

All four of the bunk rooms had two beds on the floor and an equal number of end tables, lamps, desks and chairs. Each member of the team had their own room assigned.

As cozy as the situation was, Boy Scout felt a little claustrophobic. He wasn't sure if he was a guest or a prisoner. Before they went any further, he had a question he needed Poe to answer.

All four of them stood in the common area, which contained two couches, four chairs, a card table, a refrigerator and a television.

Boy Scout was dog-tired and he knew it showed. Still, he had to ask. "How is it you figured out our situation? I never did get the story about how you found out about us—how you were able to dismiss our cover story."

Poe grinned. "The one about where you were captured by Taliban members? Yeah, that was pretty easy to spoof."

"How come it was so easy for you but not for the other military investigators?" Boy Scout asked.

"They had no reason to believe that there was a supernatural locus. All of their investigation was based on finding evidence of Taliban occupancy. They found some buried supplies, probably used by the dervishes, which the investigators attributed to the insurgents."

Boy Scout processed this, knowing it made sense.

Still, he needed to be careful. "How did we even track on your radar?"

"The location was already known to us as being a supernatural focal point. The Black Dragoons had a mission planned that was eventually cancelled. Seventy-Seven had access to their mission plans and I posited, based on what we knew, what was going on at the location that your version of events was probably false—for all the reasons you needed them to be."

"Black Dragoons?" McQueen asked.

"Our British counterpart. They had a missing Royal Marine whom they believed the dervishes had abducted. Turned out they tried, and killed him in the process. The Dragoons found his body, but didn't get a go to take down the compound."

"Why the hell not?" Preacher's Daughter asked.

Poe shook his head. "There's a lot of oversight we deal with that would drive you all nuts. Let's just say that the highest levels of most modern governments are aware of various supernatural locales and entities, but are careful about how and when to engage them. Not only is there a fear we might lose, but also that the event might be broadcast on every news channel and social media page. No one wants that kind of attention."

McQueen snapped his fingers. "So those nutjobs on 4Chan were right."

Preacher's Daughter snapped her fingers back at him. "That's the real reason you're dispersed. Back in the sixties and seventies we didn't have cell phones. Heck, I've been told there were only three TV channels. Back then your missions and various events would have been less likely to make it into the mainstream media. But now—soldiers even take GoCams with them into combat."

Poe chewed the inside of his lip and gave a reluctant nod. "That's one of the reasons, yes. It's frustrating. As much as we know, there's so much we're not allowed to do."

"Did you go to the cisterns, then?" Boy Scout asked.

"I did."

"What did you find?"

"DNA from an entity that has no comparable reference, with seventy-two chromosomes."

Preacher's Daughter jerked her head back. "Wait. Humans only have twenty-three chromosomes."

"Right," Poe said. "Which means here was something there that wasn't human."

"The *daeva*," McQueen said, whistling. "So, it's real. Part of me was hoping it was all another fugue."

"Hush your mouth," Preacher's Daughter said.

"And then?" Boy Scout asked.

Poe turned to him and looked him squarely in

the face. "And then I began to track the dervishes. That's how I found you. I'd been able to track the other two, but you were well hidden." He added, "I want you to know that I'm here to help. You guys can go it on your own, but I encourage you to let me assist." He held out his hands, palms up. "That's it. I promise."

Boy Scout stared at him for a long moment, then grudgingly nodded. "That makes sense." He left the last part unsaid, hoping his stare might convey the meaning, *Just do me a favor and try not to fuck us.*

On that note they parted.

McQueen went to the Base Exchange to pick up some clothes for them as well as supplies.

Preacher's Daughter worked with Poe, who began showing her how to access the information they had, much of it on digital picture files of old papers that had been tagged with numerous words to help indicate the content and make searching faster.

That left Boy Scout to recover a bit in his new room. He'd taken a shower and managed to dry off. With no clothes to wear, he sat on a folded towel in the middle of his room, light turned off. Without any windows, the place was about as pitch black as it could be. He could feel the wetness of his hair, water still dripping from his beard. Although he'd toweled, his skin still felt as if it held a sheen of water. He could feel the muscles of his legs, unused to exercise, aching from recent exertion. His back ached from where he'd broken it on a jump into Panama during his first year in the military, when America decided to no longer be besties with Manuel Noriega. He also felt the wear in his knees, each one rebuilt at different times in an attempt to make him the man he'd never be again. The bruising of his face and torso were at a pain level of three now, which was basically how he'd gone through life the past few years.

He slowed his breathing as best he could, using his chakras as concentration points, just as Sister Renee had shown him. Part of him felt the astral projection was pure nonsense, but another part of him, the part that had been placed in the fugue and fed gruel for six months, believed that astral projection absolutely existed. So he ignored the smaller voice of doubt and focused on the idea of the possible, which rested at the base of his spine— the root chakra. The idea was to think of it like a switch. Turned on, it gave him access to his lower body. Turned off, his lower body ceased to exist.

Flick.

Gone was the pain in his knees and his right ankle that bothered him when it rained. He couldn't feel his lower body at all, as if he were floating just above the floor.

He inhaled and exhaled, then turned off his sacral chakra just inside of his stomach.

Flick.

He inhaled and exhaled, and turned off his solar plexis chakra.

But no flick.

He couldn't help but imagine the ragged edges of his chest where it had been ripped from his lower body. His breathing increased. He tried to ignore the image that had come horrifically unbidden to his mind, instead thinking of the darkness and a place where he couldn't see himself.

Flick.

His heart was next. The idea of removing something so intrinsic to his life seemed incredibly foolish. What if he couldn't come back? What if by flicking the switch he stopped his heart? He felt his breath hitch and then his eyes open.

Flick.

Flick.

Flick.

All of his chakras turned back on and he slumped, then fell back into the chair. He brought his arm to his forehead and choked back a sob. He'd failed. Again, he'd failed. Why was it so hard? Why couldn't he do what so many others had done? And then it came to him. Because he'd spent so much of his life concerned about the quality of his body;

erasing it from reality just wasn't in him. He tried to convince himself that it wasn't being erased, that this was just a process, but it was so hard. So hard not to use his body at all and be forced to use his mind. His body had rarely failed him and when it tried, he'd always pushed through.

Then Boy Scout realized he'd also gotten to the point where he'd act first and think later—or at least it seemed that way. He was thinking of instinctual movement. Wasn't his mind involved in instinct? Wasn't his mind already trained and informing his body first? If that was the case, why couldn't he just trust in Sister Renee's process and give his mind complete control over his body?

He remembered when he'd been in The White and how it was only his mind that controlled everything—his mind *was* his body, inventing it in real time while his real body had been in the putrid water of the cistern.

He lay there for a time, then fell into a deep sleep. His dreams were filled with things he'd done in foreign lands. Shooting, fucking, kissing, running, so many things that they all flashed into each other.

Then he slid into a time where he wasn't himself. He was a small man whose thoughts were simple and clear and whose ideas were so fascinating that Boy Scout didn't fight the direction they took; instead, he embraced them and in doing so, became entirely the other person.

Most people believe the sense of sight to be the most important to their daily lives. To not be able to see was so limiting, especially in the remote villages of the Hindu Kush. But for him, sight was an afterthought. It was merely a mechanism that enabled him to get from one place to another or to do things more efficiently. Smell was his most perfect sense, which he realized set him apart from almost everyone else. Who cared really about the sense of smell? Much of the time the smells were offensive, thanks to the Americans. All smell really did was enhance taste, without which more food would be palatable. He could lose his sight and his hearing, but still remain happy as long as he retained his sense of smell.

His earliest memory was smelling oranges from the fingertips of his mother's hands. He didn't know they were oranges then. He thought that was what his mother's hands smelled like. Then, when he turned six, he saw his first orange and thought how odd it was that the piece of fruit smelled like his mother. He kept the orange until it rotted, then cried when the smell went away. It was all he had of his mother—the smell of oranges. She'd been taken by the Americans, they said, but he'd later learned that it also might have been the Malik—the headman—from the village next to theirs. His eyes coveted his mother like they were hands, traveling where even eyes shouldn't dare go, his aunt had once told him.

They liked to blame the Americans for everything. That way those who were really guilty could walk the streets without fear of retaliation. They even blamed the Americans if there wasn't enough rain, or too much snow: *Their airplanes chased it from the sky*. But it wasn't the Americans he was after this day. It was the Malik, who he'd been following for six hours.

The Malik wore a white *ket* and a dark brown *partug*, tucked into his boots. What hair he had was a straggly gray. The side of his face had been burned during a firefight with the Americans, so his beard and mustache grew only on one side. He'd come to Kabul to buy better fighting birds from the Ka Faroshi Bird Market, but had stopped at several tea houses to meet with old contacts and once at an electronics store to buy gifts to bring back to his village.

He hung back from the Malik, hoping to blend into the crowds of people. He drove a scooter, so was easily able to follow the Malik's Corolla anywhere. The problem was when to deliver his message, for it was many years of planning that would culminate.

Now, as the Malik weaved through the bird

market, talking in low tones to old bird sellers, he couldn't help but inventory the smells. And the smells of Kabul were so much more present than those of his simple village, where as a youth he'd developed an inventory of the different smells of rocks and dirt. How granite smelled different than quartz and how basalt had a fragrance he looked forward to inhaling. But not here. In Kabul the smells were ever-present, overlapping until he almost gagged with confusion, his mind unable to parse the effervescence. He'd been forced to reach into his pocket many times, to scrape at the orange hidden within, then bring his fingers to his nose to clear his head. And every time he did, he was reminded of his mother and his reason for being here.

The smell of a watermelon was particularly joyous. Not only did it bring to mind summers and celebrations, but it covered up the offensiveness of the plastic explosive he was wearing in his vest. If watermelon was the smell of life, then the noxious chemicals in the small blocks all wired together were the smell of death—which was fitting.

He paused and watched as the man chewed on a watermelon piece.

No, now would not be the time to deliver his message. He could not do that to one who had just taken a bite of watermelon.

He continued, taking in the different aromas of each bird and their feed.

The Malik paused and purchased a chukar partridge. These reddish-gray birds were prized for fighting and looked as if they were bandits with black bands across their eyes. This one smelled of talcum and tobacco, left over from the man who'd handled it. Grizzled with the kind of wrinkles that hid memories in their seams, his face was also colored by the smoke constantly coming from his cigarettes. He could see the pack of them half hanging from a pocket of his ket—Marlboros— once again Americans being American.

Then the Malik turned, the wicker cage held high above his head. He passed him, heading back towards his car.

He waited a moment, then turned and followed, passing the nice man with the watermelon breath. The crowds began to thin as the two of them headed toward the end of the street. The smells of the city began to intrude again and once more he scraped the orange and brought his fingers to his nose. Mother. Bliss. A message to be delivered.

He decided that the time was finally right.

Everything was in the right place, his memories, the ochre smell of pollution, the sensibility of there being some sort of unfortunate collateral damage. He'd scratched the orange so many times, there was only a tiny patch of peel left, the rest of the fruit covered by the gauzy white of the pith, so similar to the cotton blankets they placed over the faces of the dead.

He took one last scratch, leaving the orange dead and heavy in his pocket. He brought his fingers to his nose and inhaled intensely. It must have been loud, because the Malik turned around.

"Why are you following me?"

He didn't know how to respond. He just smiled and continued sniffing.

"I demand to know why you are following me," the Malik said, furious because of the other's lack of response.

He reached into his pocket and pulled out the orange, now devoid of that which made it smell so wonderful, an ache of an odor that was less than a memory, redolent along the gauzy funeral wrap. He held it out to the Malik, who accepted it without thinking.

"You killed this. The orange would have lived had you not come to Kabul."

The Malik's eyes narrowed and the right side of his face crinkled, the left burned side remaining unmoving. "What is this? I don't understand."

"You took the smell of oranges from me. Now I will take the smell of everything from you."

Before the Malik could do anything, he reached into his other pocket and found the actuator, given to him by the same person who gave him the vest he wore beneath. Everyone has enemies. It was not just the Americans who were targeted. Sometimes, some of their own needed to go. So said the enemies of the Malik. The boy closed his eyes, one hand on the actuator, one hand with orange-scented fingers near his nose. He inhaled gently this time and could almost hear the voice of a mother he couldn't remember. Had he been more attentive to sound than he was of smell, he might have been able to remember what she sounded like. Had he been more attentive to sight, he might have remembered what she looked like. But his attention was on smell and he remembered those fingertips as she held him, as she fed him, and as she traced circles of love on his cheeks. He remembered the orange and the sensation of the smell filled him with joy.

He depressed the actuator and delivered the message, pieces of him and his memories of his mother's fingers expanding violently into a universe where the Malik and his fighting bird couldn't possibly exist. A place where a simple boy with a piece of fruit and a memory could change the life of terrible man with a burned face and a penchant for stealing other people's mothers.

And the universe turned volcanic with sizzling white static.

Chapter Ten

China Lake, Later

BOY SCOUT WOULD have fallen out of bed had he not been already on the floor, so disturbing and disorienting was the dream. How he'd gotten into the mind of a suicide bomber he'd never know, except he had. He realized what had happened as he thought those words and sat back, stunned. Apparently, one of his accidental travelers had been a suicide bomber. Did the bomber even know where he was? Did he think he was in Heaven or in some strange purgatory instead in the mind of a middle-aged former US Army ranger? Somehow Boy Scout had been able to connect with the consciousness of the traveler. His mind couldn't have possibly invented a plot surrounding the orange and the missing mother.

But why didn't he know the bomber's name? Would he know his own name if he wasn't referred to? He supposed not. It's not like he was always thinking in the third person.

A knock came at the door.

He sat up in the darkness. "What is it?"

"Got some stuff for you," came McQueen's voice.

"Bring it."

The big man opened the door and the light from the hall enshrined him in the darkness.

"Why are you sitting naked on the floor in the dark?"

Boy Scout smiled. "Do you really want to know?"

McQueen rolled his eyes and put two bags on one of the beds. On his way out of the room he said over his shoulder, "It wouldn't hurt you to get a tan. Just saying." Then he closed the door.

Fifteen minutes later, Boy Scout was dressed in generic contractor apparel—tan cargo pants, black polo, combat boots. What really made him happiest was the new underwear and deodorant.

He bumped into Preacher's Daughter out in the hall.

"Coming to get you. I need to show you what we've got."

"You've got something?"

Her eyes sparkled. "You have no idea the assets Poe has at his disposal. We've pretty much tracked down the dervish network."

"Is that what we're calling it? The dervish network?"

They entered the main suite of offices—two private offices with the doors closed and a main work area with several computer stations and a central conference table. McQueen was currently sitting at the table with a Starbucks coffee cup in one hand and a croissant in the other.

"Trying out to be the next Starbucks hipster spokesperson?" Boy Scout asked.

McQueen eyed him over the top of his cup, steam curling around his face, froth on the edges of his Fu Manchu mustache.

"Let me guess," Boy Scout said. "Pumpkin spice?"

"You know it," McQueen said. He reached into a coffee caddy and handed a coffee to Boy Scout.

"Please don't say it's pumpkin spice," said Boy Scout, reaching slowly for the cup.

"You're safe. Your boring café Americano won't turn you into a hipster, which I know is your greatest fear."

Boy Scout took the cup and inhaled the aroma, relishing in the deep blackness of the brew. As he sat heavily on one of the chairs around the table, he said, "I'd never make it as a hipster. I can barely dress myself and I count on the disapproving looks of others to tell me if I'm matched correctly."

"There's always remedial training," McQueen said.

Boy Scout was about to reply when Preacher's Daughter broke in. "Boys. Will you please stop?"

They turned their attention to her and Boy Scout noted for the first time that Poe was standing behind her as she sat at a computer workstation.

Poe stood ramrod straight, his head cocked to the side as he watched them—more a scientist observing animals in their natural environment than a lieutenant in the US Army.

Boy Scout took a sip of his coffee, leaned over and grabbed a croissant, then gestured toward Preacher's Daughter and Poe. "You may begin."

Poe mouthed the words as if he couldn't believe them, then turned slowly to Preacher's Daughter. "If you please," he said to her.

"While we were trying to find out about the things inside of you, Poe has been tracking the dervish network. With the help of CYBERCOM, he was able to lock down seven static IPs, which then allowed him to tap into CCTV systems, both private and public, to obtain visual identifications for future biometric searches."

She stood and went over to a whiteboard, then

spun it to face them. Pictures of twelve faces were taped to the board with names written below each one in red marker. The faces were arranged in a circle with a big question mark in the middle.

"We've identified that these twelve individuals have been actively searching for you." She grabbed the red marker and put an X over three of the faces. "These three were killed at the monastery, which leaves nine."

"How can we be sure there aren't more out there?" McQueen asked.

"We can't," Poe said. "But now that we have these nine, CYBERCOM helped with a biometric algorithm that's been sent out to all the ALPRs in SoCal. With automated license plate readers recently cued to also conduct facial recognition, we'll not only be able to track where these nine are, but who their friends are. It helps that all of the dervishes are Turkish. Using predictive technology, the ALPRs will notify us if any new predicted threats are near any of these nine. Meaning if the program thinks the person might be of Turkish descent, then it will catalogue and follow that person as well."

"What about—" McQueen began.

"In the event one or more of the nine are partnering with someone not of Turkish descent, then the ALPRS will catalogue that individual and inform us."

"Where are they now?" Boy Scout asked, finishing his croissant.

"Three are in Beverly Grove. Their consulate is off Wilshire Boulevard."

"That's high cotton," McQueen said.

"How do you know there aren't more than this? There have to be more people of Turkish descent in LA than these guys," Boy Scout said.

"We don't," Preacher's Daughter said. "If they don't have a link to one of the known targets or the Turkish Consulate we ignore them."

"So, there could be more," Boy Scout said.

"Or less," she said. "But we are pretty sure about the ones we've identified. Four more are near the monastery, probably trying to conduct an investigation, find out where we went."

"Not if de Cherge has anything to do with it," McQueen said.

Preacher's Daughter nodded. "The dervishes know there's a general police BOLO out on them, so they're being careful."

"Wait," Boy Scout said. "Why did we inform the police?"

Poe grinned. "We didn't, but our hacker friends set up a fake website a week ago and dangled information that there was a BOLO on you three, which lured the dervishes to our site. The dervishes think that they've hacked LAPD Command

Central, but they're only on a mirrored front page. All the subordinate links are ours."

Preacher's Daughter nodded. "It's genius, really. We can dangle information in front of them and also see the sort of information they're trying to get. Knowing what the enemy doesn't know is almost as important as knowing what they know."

"So the police really aren't looking for them. The dervishes just think they are," Boy Scout said.

"Correct." Poe nodded. "And the remaining two are at Long Beach Airport."

Boy Scout and McQueen looked at each other.

"You know what that means, right, boss?" McQueen asked.

Boy Scout's mouth tightened. "Anyway we can release a real BOLO on those two?"

"It might be too late," McQueen added.

Boy Scout said. "What about it?"

"You're worried about the pilot," Poe said, eyeing Boy Scout.

"I am."

"Don't worry. We've already been in contact with him. When we saw where they were heading, we sent information to Mr. Noaks and recommended he find another place to roost."

"Who did you say you were?" Boy Scout said.

"A friendly three letter agency who is friends with Boy Scout."

"A three-letter agency could be anyone. But with your name attached, it was more easily believed," Preacher's Daughter said.

"Do we know where he went?" McQueen asked.

"Vegas. Mr. Peter K. Noaks is in Vegas," Poe said, then paused as his telephone beeped. He answered it and everyone watched as his eyes widened. "I'll be right there." Then to the room he said, "We have a visitor."

"What? How?" Preacher's Daughter asked.

"I'm not sure, but she asked to see Boy Scout, Preacher's Daughter, and McQueen," Poe replied. "Any idea who it could be?"

Everyone shook their heads then watched as Poe left the room, an expression of contemplation and worry playing out across his usual stoicism.

Chapter Eleven

China Lake Command Center

WHEN HE LEFT, Boy Scout filled the others in on his dream with as much detail as he could.

"I think you're right," Preacher's Daughter said. "He's definitely an accidental traveler. He probably doesn't know how to communicate to you."

"Have you wondered if you can create a construct—a reality for him that he understands?" McQueen asked. "Sort of like a video game in your mind for him to live in?"

Boy Scout stared at the big man for a moment. "I understand the concept, but I am not sure of the process."

"Have you tried to re-enter The White?" McQueen asked.

A memory plowed through reality and took over.

Boy Scout was nowhere and everywhere. He couldn't think. He couldn't see anything except a kaleidoscope of spinning shades of white, dizzying, sickening. His essence had broken into so many parts that he couldn't even form a sentence. Unintelligible jabbering filled his mind. Were these his own thoughts? Or was it from something else? The spinning was beginning to slow. His mind was coming back together. He could see pieces of himself forming as if he'd been a porcelain doll and his parts were flying back together of their own volition.

A hand.

A forearm

A booted foot.

The mating call of a monkey came from behind him.

He spun and in his dizziness, fell to the ground. Only there was no ground. He was now upside down in front of the nightmare creature running towards him. In the split second he took to take it in, he saw a giant spider with more than a hundred legs coming toward him. Instead of central eyes, it had a face that was constantly changing into everyone he'd ever known.

Again came that sound, emanating from the lips of his mother's best friend, Rebecca. Then from the mouth of his drill sergeant, Sergeant First Class

Reddoor. Then from the mouth of a girl he'd dated three years ago, Connie. The same sound, but different faces.

The monstrous entity was closing in.

More pieces of him were coming together but he wouldn't be whole by the time it arrived.

Boy Scout willed himself to flee, then found himself moving backwards at impossible speed.

Again the universe shrieked like the scream of the King of all Kings and he was once more blown apart.

The dizzying kaleidoscope returned, and after a time of sickness, piece by piece he came together once more.

The mating call of a monkey came once again but this time much softer. Then another and another. There seemed to be dozens of monkeys. Then he saw them. The spider creature had blown to bits as well, but instead of reforming into a whole, it was now hundreds of smaller spiders, all rushing toward him. He'd barely started to reform when three of them crawled up his essence. He batted at them, but he only had a single hand. He struck one and it flew off, shattering into even smaller spider monsters that came back at him. One got onto his back and he tried to reach for it. That was the moment when one skittered onto his face and climbed down his throat.

He gagged, trying to rid himself of it. He could feel its greasy spider legs pulling itself deeper inside of him.

Then another spider entered his mouth, following the first.

He fell to his knees, back arching in dry heaves, trying to spew them from his system. But it was to no avail. They held to his insides, going deeper, clawing at his insides for purchase.

Then everything switched. Gone was the pure white of Sefid. Boy Scout felt himself slow and his body become someone else's... something else. Something ancient.

Visions—no, memories—began to spin by.

A family chased by a saber-toothed tiger on a flat brown plain. The tiger took down the girl child, ripping into her bowels.

A man on horseback, firing an arrow directly into Boy Scout's point of view, then disintegrating as a ray of white-hot energy was returned.

Alexander the Great's Macedonian phalanx— fifteen thousand Macedonians with sarissas holding off the Persian swords and allowing the phalanx to mow through enemy units.

The Sacred Band of Thebes—he recognized it right away from history books, now from the point of view of a warrior battling through them.

Sensual sex with an Indian woman of incredible

beauty, her lips the color of brown sugar and tasting of mangoes.

An up-close view of a knife fight with another man, his own hands a blur of razor-edged steel, then still as they stopped in his opponent's chest.

And fire in the sky, burning incredibly bright, but feeling joyous at the sight of it.

Boy Scout gasped with the power of the memories—surely the instigating action that had brought the travelers within him, each one the moment of their death. He held his head was between his knees as he hyperventilated.

When he finally straightened, McQueen was standing, concern plastered on his face.

Preacher's Daughter was beside him, a hand on his back.

When Boy Scout was finally able to straighten, the scent of mangoes and the stench of death in his lungs, he shook his head emphatically. "Wow. Where did that come from?" He paused, gathering his breath. "Listen. The White? That's the last thing I want. I was hoping to do what Sister Renee said to do, but this astral projection is not easy. Too many thoughts. Too many memories."

Preacher's Daughter bit her lip and observed him carefully as she returned to her seat. "I'd say that there might be a way to reduce those distractions through stimulants, but the others might attempt control." She held up a finger, clearly working something out in her head. "Let me try something."

"Go ahead," Boy Scout said.

She cleared her throat and said, "*If you understand what I am saying then stand on one leg.*" Then she waited.

"*Very funny,*" Boy Scout said.

She grinned widely. "*What did I say?*

"*You said if I understand what you are saying then stand on one leg.*"

She clapped her hands together once. "*Do you know what this means?*"

"*What are you talking about?*"

"McQueen, what did we just say?"

"I have no earthly idea. Boss, when did you learn to speak Afghani?"

Boy Scout's eyes narrowed.

"*Boy Scout, we are talking in Pashtun right now and you don't even know it,*" Preacher's Daughter said.

"*But that's imposs*—" He switched to English as his eyes widened. "How am I doing this?"

"You must be able to tap into the consciousness in your brain. Because the traveler is in you, you can speak the same language it can speak. If it was a rocket scientist, you could also probably build rockets. If you only knew how to take advantage of these things inside you, you might be able to be better and more effective than you are now."

"As good as it could be, as much knowledge as they impart to me, I want them gone," he said firmly.

She nodded. "I understand. But at least you can take advantage of it in the meantime. Conversely, those inside of you should be able to speak English. You share all the knowledge in consciousnesses within you."

Boy Scout closed his mind and reconstructed the images of the phalanx and the saber-toothed tiger and the man on horseback and everything that had flashed through him yet again. Then he thought of the suicide bomber and the man in the pile of dead bodies pretending to be dead and the view of the boy left on a train platform as the train pulled away. The last left him with a feeling of such grief he had to struggle not to sob.

"I feel—I feel as if there are only four inside of me, but there seems to be memories of more. These four can't possibly have all the memories I'm trying to account for."

"That's because you have something much more powerful inside of you," came the voice of a woman he recognized.

He opened his eyes and beheld a vision he wouldn't have believed.

Poe entered behind the woman and closed the door.

"This is Charlene," he said, pronouncing the first part of her name like something you might do to a steak—CHAR-lene. "She says she knows you."

Preacher's Daughter stood. "But that's impossible."

Then everyone started talking at once.

Chapter Twelve

China Lake Command Center

SHE STOOD ABOUT five and a half feet tall, even on her three-inch glittering heels. The candy-apple red hair piled on top of her head like a 1960s sorority girl perfectly matched the hue of her lipstick. She was beautiful in the way women are when they spend five hours a day preparing themselves. She wore shorts that were about as tight as they could possibly be and barely covered what needed to be covered for her not to be arrested. A skin-tight T-shirt, with a glittering Julie Newmar-era Catwoman silhouette with the words *I Am Not That Kind of Cat Lady* printed on it, hugged a small waist and medium-sized breasts and was somehow the same hue as her lipstick and hair.

"Hello," she said, managing to break through

the cacophony of voices. "You guys have met me but I don't remember it. Problem is, I remember you but I don't know how I do."

Boy Scout, McQueen, and Preacher's Daughter all looked at each other and the cacophony broke out once more. Finally, it was Poe who yelled for everyone to be quiet. When they did, he said, "Maybe someone can explain to me what's going on. You first," he said, pointing to Preacher's Daughter.

She seemed about to say something, but glanced at Boy Scout for approval.

He nodded but kept his eyes on Charlene, the look on his face the same he'd have had had he met someone else from a dream.

"While we were in a fugue state and still in the cistern we traveled to Guadalupe, Arizona, and met this woman so that we could get access to Narco. She was able to read Boy Scout's mind and explain what the girl with the goat we were all dreaming about really was. She seemed to be the real deal, then we all woke up and realized that she was only a figment of our imagination."

"For a figment, my feet sure are hurting." She sat down on one of the chairs and pulled out a package of Virginia Slims. "Mind if I smoke in here?"

"I actually do," Poe said.

"Maybe they wouldn't hurt if you didn't wear those FMPs everywhere," McQueen said.

"Said the gay hipster like he knows."

McQueen laughed. "You called me the same thing in the fugue."

"Narco knew me better than most." She flashed her eyes at Boy Scout. "I felt it when he died. Maybe you can tell me how later."

Boy Scout shook his head. "This is so surreal."

"Says the guy with four entities who was taught by a possessed nun how to astral project," Preacher's Daughter said.

"Oh." Charlene's eyes widened. "That sounds interesting. I wasn't aware of the nun. Who is she?"

"Let's figure out what to do with you before we begin parsing out information," Poe said.

She turned and gave him a cold stare. "There's very little you can do *with* me, Maurice. You should call your mother. She's been out of rehab for a month and desperately wants to talk to you. Plus, your cat is pretty pissed because you've left it at a friend's."

Frowning, he mumbled, "I actually gave the cat to them."

"Then you need to explain that to the cat." Turning to the rest of the crew, she added, "And as far as parsing out information, I'll be the one doing the parsing because you sad lot don't know what the hell you're doing."

McQueen whispered, "She's really unbelievable, isn't she?"

"Positively a force of nature," Boy Scout replied softly.

"Are you sure I can't smoke in here?" she asked the room in general.

Fifteen minutes later and on her fourth cigarette, she finished telling them how she'd felt their need, understood that inside Boy Scout resided a being of tremendous power, and how she'd arrived on base from the Phoenix area despite her car breaking down in Blythe. Apparently, she convinced a truck driver on his way to Los Angeles to drive her two hundred miles out of his way because she was able to tell him where to find his brother, who had gone absentia the previous year. (He was working in a hospice in Costa Rica after having a mental breakdown and had forgotten who he was.) By the time the driver dropped her off near the front gate of the weapon's center, he'd arranged for a flight from LAX to Juan Santamaria Airport in Costa Rica.

With Boy Scout's nod of approval, Preacher's Daughter began to tell the story of Narco and how he'd been both in and out of reality. She told Charlene how they'd rescued him from Sheriff Joe Arpaio's work detail using camels with boom boxes and pictures of the sheriff on them to distract the sheriff's deputies, only to find out that they'd been in a fugue and none of it had actually happened, including them meeting *her*. Preacher's Daughter also shared the moments when Faood had sent them into a fugue just to show them what the dervishes were doing and how they were actively trying to get Rumi's soul to come home. Finally she related the events when he'd actually died, defending them in a vicious final fight they'd had against a dervish QRF force, which had turned the cistern into a slaughterhouse. The QRF had used a block of explosive like a grenade, except the explosive power was more like five grenades.

As Preacher's Daughter spoke, Boy Scout remembered Bully lying face down next to the entrance, her head sheathed in blood, and Narco, sitting as if he'd just gotten tired and plopped down, his head lolled back at an impossible angle, his eyes endlessly open, a piece of sharp stone protruding from his neck.

A feeling slung through his chest, twisting his heart. The sudden emotion was so powerful it almost reached his face, but he wouldn't let it. Instead, he sat there with nothing more than a frown as Preacher's Daughter explained reality to Charlene.

After a moment, he excused himself and went to the bathroom. He left the light off and sat down on the toilet seat, his head in his hands. A wave of survivor's guilt swept through him and he tried desperately to ignore it. But like Charlene was to the universe, some things were virtually impossible to ignore. No matter how Boy Scout felt about his abilities, the truth of the matter was that he was the cause of other people's deaths. His decisions, his actions, his failures—all had led to the deaths of those who'd trusted in him to keep them alive.

And now he had two left—Preacher's Daughter and McQueen. He didn't know what he'd do if they died. He'd never once considered killing himself, but for a brief, sizzling moment he knew that if both of them somehow died, he might just do it.

Three, five, ten minutes later—he couldn't be certain how long it was—he heard a knocking sound.

Glancing towards the door, he said, "Go away." The knocking came again, this time echoing strangely.

"I said go away," he said miserably.

Still, the knocking came.

He jerked himself up, grasped the door knob, and jerked it open.

The doorway was empty.

The knocking came again.

He let the door close as he backed up and again sat on the toilet seat.

Except he must have missed the seat... because he fell farther and farther and farther, his body in freefall in a dark universe that was made of knocking. Loud knocking. Soft knocking. Rapid knocking. Slow knocking. Knocking of all shapes and sounds assaulted him until he wanted to scream. And he would have, but he had no mouth. Instead, his body was gone and all that remained was the idea of himself.

And then he saw her. Or at least he *thought* it was her.

A figure floated next to him, a glowing silver in the void, looking more like a ghost than anything that could possibly be human.

He tried to back away, but without a body, he was unable to move.

"Boy Scout," the figure whispered, the words almost hollow in the darkness.

The figure reached out to him and he tried to scream but he had no mouth.

It touched him and in doing so, crystallized into a ghostly facsimile of Sister Renee.

"Is that you?" he whispered.

"Yes," she said. "But we have a problem. The being inside you has taken over and you have been pushed back inside of your own mind."

"For how long?" he asked, thinking of the enormity of her claim.

"Hours," she said.

And Boy Scout felt the true horror of it.

Chapter Thirteen

Astral Plane

"WELCOME TO THE astral plane," Sister Renee said quickly. "There are conventions here that you need to learn. For instance, everyone is generally anonymous until you *interact* with them. Then features snap into place. The more you know the person the more the features make sense. If you don't know the person, the features are a basic male-female visage, like a generic avatar."

Boy Scout thought about this. "So, I see you as you are because we've interacted on the physical plane and then we touch."

"Yes and no. We don't actually touch because we aren't actually here. We *interact*. No words are perfect for what we do here. We don't stand, for instance, we float—except we aren't really floating either." She nodded. "It's all words, as imperfect as they are."

Boy Scout looked around. He saw a group of huddled figures nearby but nothing more. Beneath him lay lines of white-hot power that ran in multiple directions. Dots of light were also nearby, but with little detail. In the sky, if he could call it a sky, was a globe of darkness darker than everything else. But other than those features, there was nothing.

"What you see beneath us are ley lines. They're invisible in the material plane, but clear here. The dots are living beings—animals, reptiles, people, but not plants. And in the Up you can see what some refer to as the dark sun. Be careful of that. Do not go too far into the Up or you will find yourself unable to break away from the dark sun's gravitational pull."

"What happens if I do?"

"We don't know. No one has ever been able to return."

"Point taken." He tried to inspect himself but couldn't see anything. He couldn't feel anything either. It was as if he wasn't even there and he said as much.

"You can't perceive your own energy, just the energy of others."

"And those over there?" he asked, pointing but not seeing his hand.

"Those are the things inside of you."

He felt a hush descend upon him. There were four of them and it looked as if their heads were pressed together in a private conversation.

"What are they doing?" he asked.

"They won't know where they are or what this place is. Because they are attached to you, when you enter the astral plane, they enter as well."

"Is this... is this how it was with your... your..."

"My possession? It was, but much more, much worse. But I didn't have travelers. I only know what Father Emmett told me about them."

He stared at the blurry shapes for a moment, wondering which was the warrior, which was the Berber, which was the little boy, and which was the suicide bomber. Of course, any being capable of creating an alternative life for him to live inside of his own head must have some kind of supernatural power, or at least abilities greater than his own.

He stopped himself, the anxiety washing through him in a cataclysmic rush.

Finally, he asked, "How did I get here?" He was unable to turn away from the figures.

"I brought you here."

"But how?"

"You practiced trying to leave your body. Know how I know?"

"How?"

"Because you unlocked your chakras and never locked them back. You have got to lock them when you are done or things can get to you... entities can come inside. Not that you don't already have that problem, but it's important to remember. In this case it allowed me to help you, otherwise you might never have known your body was moving on without you."

Your body was moving on without you.

"That's such a terrifying concept," he said.

"What's terrifying is that you didn't even know your body was hacked. You might never have known. But I knew it all. I was witness to the hostile takeover of my body and watched as it did things at the behest of the demon, me unable to do anything to stop it. And that was also terrifying."

Anger surged through him. "Know what's terrifying? *This*. Know what else? Six months in a cistern thinking I was living a life instead of soaking in a thousand years of other people's piss and vomit. Going into a building stacked with a bunch of other guys, only to watch two of your best friends get shot in the face or eat a grenade or explode into a spray of crimson fucking mist because they just happened to be in the wrong place at the wrong time." He paused, then added, "Listen, I appreciate that some fucked-up shit happened to you, but we can't continue trying to one up each other. I'll just give it to you here. Being possessed by a named demon wins you the *my life was the worst fucked-up* award. Now relish it and move on."

She stared at him, her face impassive, then nodded. "Of course, you are right."

"Good, because I don't like this whole thing. In fact, I want back into my body."

"That's going to be quite easy at this point."

"What do you mean?"

"The reason you see the four is because when you came out, they did as well. They are attached to you and your essence can't go anywhere without them. Basically, I show you how to reenter your body and everything goes back to the way it was."

"If it was so easy to do, then why didn't you do it to yourself?"

"Because I had a no-kidding demon inside me who'd spent eons perfecting the ability to stay inside someone else's body. These things inside of you are probably as surprised as you were about where they ended up. They might not even realize what's going on. Back when you were in The White, you were a light in the darkness and they just ran to it."

"The thing who took control of me knows what's going on. Is it still *inside* of me."

"I think it is. I can't see it, which worries me. It

means it's done this sort of thing before. One of those has control over it or is being controlled."

He thought about it. The fourth entity. He knew there was something different about it and he said as much.

"I think you're right. You know, we could go over right now and touch it to find out what it is."

The thought petrified him, but he was willing to do it as long as she was here with him—how silly was it that a Ranger wanted his hand held by a nun who couldn't be a hundred and twenty pounds, soaking wet.

"But you're not ready," she said. "Like I said, there are conventions you need to follow or you might find yourself never able to get back into your body. If that thing knows even a little of astral combat, then that's more than you know, so no... we shouldn't touch it."

"Then get me back inside, please."

"Okay. Here's how you do it. Reach behind your head. Yes. Just like that."

He reached back to where his head should be and felt something that was both cold and hot at the same time. It had length like a rope.

"Did you feel it?"

He nodded.

"That's the *sutratma*, or the silver cord. It is the connection back to your physical self. Think of it as a long spool of almost impossible to break thread that connects you to who you are."

"*Almost* impossible to break? What happens if it breaks?"

"Then you stay here. No *sutratma*, no body."

"Jesus." He felt how thin it was and how flimsy it seemed. "It seems pathetically easy then to get stranded here. "

She shook her head. "It can't be severed because it really doesn't exist. But it can be ripped out of your head if someone knows what they are doing. Ecclesiastes 12:6-7: *Before the silver cord snaps, and the golden fountain is shattered, and the pitcher breaks at the fountain, and the wheel falls shattered into the pit. And the dust returns to the earth as it was, and the spirit returns to God, Who gave it.*"

"The Bible talks about astral projection?"

"Of course. Now concentrate. Think of your third eye chakra. Touch where the silver cord touches the base of your skull. Imagine you falling backwards back into your body. Clear your mind of everything and concentrate on nothing but that third eye. That is your doorway. That is your way back home. The third eye. Your body. The silver cord. And whatever you do, keep your damned chakras closed."

He remembered the first time he'd HALO'd out the back of a C141 at 30,000 feet. They had a tradition of walking backwards off the ramp and falling backwards into the sky. *Letting the heavens embrace you*, as they called it. Boy Scout did just that. He imagined himself on that ramp, walking backwards towards the rush of wind and darkness, ready to let gravity and the elements grab hold. Only this time, it was to be his third eye that would grasp him.

He backed away, his eyes closed as he imagined falling.

And let it happen.

Chapter Fourteen

Camp Pendleton Command Center

"WELCOME BACK, SLEEPY head," McQueen said, kneeling beside him.

Boy Scout's head roared with a headache like none other. He wanted to get up, get something for it, maybe a bottle of scotch, but he remembered what Sister Renee had told him. He slowed his breathing and closed his eyes, closing each of his chakras from the crown to the root, imagining each of them like a lock that was snapped into place with only him having the keys. It wasn't easy to visualize. But he forced himself. Finally, when he opened his eyes, Preacher's Daughter was there as well, standing over McQueen.

Then Boy Scout noted what they were wearing–full out combat kit—as if they were ready to go out on assault.

"Are you okay?" she asked. "One moment you were leading us out the door, the next you were flat on your face." She grinned. "You'll probably have a black eye."

Boy Scout struggled to a sitting position and felt his right eye, which was beginning to swell. "This just in. I'm tired of being used. I'm not a fucking Buick and I don't want anyone driving me." He glanced down at his chest and saw his own combat kit—chest rig, body armor, ammo carriers full. "And why the fuck am I wearing this getup and what third world country are we about to invade?"

McQueen's eyebrows pinched as he frowned. "Maybe you just hit your head, boss. You should lie back down."

"I definitely hit my head." He held out a hand. "Help me up, please."

Both McQueen and Preacher's Daughter held out a hand and helped him to his feet.

When he stood, he experienced a moment of dizziness, but that soon passed. "What time and day is it?"

They looked at one another, then back to Boy Scout.

"Jesus, do I fucking stutter? How much time has passed since we've been at China Lake?" he demanded.

"China… Boss, we're not at China Lake. We're at Camp Pendleton. We left China Lake two days ago."

He groaned and rubbed his head. "How long have we been here?"

"A day," McQueen said. "Maybe less."

"And how long were we at China Lake?"

"Three days," Preacher's Daughter said.

"That means I've lost three days," he said, staring at the ground. "And I don't suppose Charlene turned up."

"Charlene?" Preacher's Daughter asked.

"You mean that red-haired girlfriend of Narco's from the fugue?" McQueen asked. "Are you sure you're feeling all right? You know she's not real, right?"

Boy Scout was feeling anything but all right. Part of him wanted to scream. After all, how could he be sure that this was reality and not some entity-induced fugue? Or worse, what had been waking him up in the middle of the night? What if they'd never left Afghanistan and were still stuck in that miserable cistern?

"It appears that an entity inside of me has been in control for the last three days. If it hadn't been for Sister Renee, I wouldn't even be here." He spied a chair and sat heavily. "Now, tell me why we're here, what were we about to do. And where is Poe?"

McQueen's eyes widened. "Oh, shit, boss."

Preacher's Daughter snapped her fingers. "I knew something was off with you."

"Next time that happens, tie me down and bring me back."

"Bring you back how?" she asked.

"I haven't figured that out yet."

They spent the next thirty minutes detailing what he'd been having them do over the last few days. He was amazed to discover he'd ordered them from China Lake to Pendleton and hired Noaks on as their personal transportation export. Poe had cleared the way for him to land on the marine base and have access to the airfield, which Noaks was very psyched about. He used this opportunity to replace some older parts in his helicopter that the marines had in inventory.

Boy Scout had ceased to be in control of his body when he'd tried to astral project that first time, which made him less than eager to do it again. That said, the entity had fed him some correct information, probably while figuring out how to create an alternate reality for Boy Scout. All the information Poe had provided about facial recognition and ALPRs was true and accurate. Where things started to run in a parallel reality began with the introduction of Charlene. Everything from that point on never happened.

The timeline was off as well. What he thought had only been an hour or so turned out to be three days. Evidentially the entity could manipulate his perception of time, which was not a good thing at all. Or maybe time was a construct of the physical world, and once separated from it, time ceased to have an effect on him.

Just as he was wrapping up, Poe came in, a perplexed look on his face. "Come on. We're already late."

Preacher's Daughter gave him a look that said, *this is not the situation you think it is.*

McQueen said, "About that."

Boy Scout said, "We're not going anywhere."

Then he spent five minutes giving good Lieutenant Poe the CliffsNotes version.

The man's only response when it was all over was, "Fuck me. I never had any idea."

Boy Scout curled his lip into a snarl and said, "You barely know me. These galloots didn't have any idea either." He perched his chin on the steeple of his fingers. "My question is why did it want us to move here? Why are we kitted up? What's the op?"

"The dervishes have clustered at their consulate on Wilshire Blvd," Poe said. "You figured—I mean, *it* figured that it would be a good opportunity to take them all out in one place."

Boy Scout stared at his crew with wide, unbelieving eyes. "And you all agreed? I can run tractor trailers through the holes in that logic. Jesus on a pogo stick." He turned to his second. "McQueen? Seriously?"

The big man stared at the floor.

"And don't give me shit like it seemed like a good idea at the time." He turned to Preacher's Daughter. "And you—you're the smartest one of us. Why did you agree to it?"

"You seemed to know what was going on." She began to tick her fingers. "You knew they were going to regroup. You knew when it happened. You also wanted to get them all together and try and kidnap one of them during the raid." For one of the only times he'd ever seen her, she looked flustered. "Dammit, we just trusted you."

"And who was going to conduct the raid?" he growled.

"We were," she said. "The four of us."

"And Noaks, I suppose." Boy Scout shook his head. If it didn't already hurt, he would have slammed it against the wall. Now it was his turn to tick off questions on his fingers. "Why would we attack a force of equal or greater size than ours when they are in a fixed position? Why would we put all of our assets together? Why would we attack a protected diplomatic mission which is essentially Turkish soil? Why wouldn't we try and separate them and capture them one or two at a time and interrogate them? Huh? McQueen?"

"Now that you put it that way, you make a lot of sense."

"Now that you... Okay, listen to me and heed my words. You two need to think and wonder if I am the Boy Scout you know at all times. You need to realize that I have things inside of me and I can't be trusted. Everything I say, look at it critically. Apply the Military Decision-Making Process. MDMP." He looked round at his mollified crew. "Do you understand me?"

They merely stared at him.

"Fucking nod or break dance or something."

All three nodded.

He stood. "Okay, now we need to figure out why it wanted us to attack the consulate. Poe?"

Poe nodded.

"Can you get on your assets and find out if there have been any deliveries to the consulate lately. Look for a large box. Something like a twelve-foot coffin."

"Sure... uh... are we looking for a vampire?"

"Worse."

"Do you really think they have another one?" McQueen asked.

"I'd bet your paycheck on it."

"I'm not getting paid right now, boss."

"Then I wouldn't lose anything if I'm wrong, but I don't think I am."

"Do you think the thing inside of you wants the *daeva*?"

"I think it might be afraid of it. That's why it wanted me to try and kill it, and might not have cared if I died trying."

"Why would it be afraid?" she asked.

"Because I think the thing inside of me was a creation of the *daeva*. I remember when it spoke to me. It didn't even know who made us. One minute they had their own race of beings, the next we were there. It said that we were shadows upon the world, bringing darkness wherever we went."

Chapter Fifteen

Camp Pendleton Command Center

BOY SCOUT NEEDED his own information. He found a computer terminal, and after getting the right logins from Poe, searched the internet for what he knew would be there. He'd actually been to the bird market in Kabul before and had run surveillance routes through the closely confined quarters of the birds, their sellers, and those who were part of the fighting circuit. He'd also heard about a bombing that had occurred in the late 2000s, but didn't know the specifics. So, he used the Great Oracle of Google to assist him. It was all in knowing which words to use, and sometimes in what order. His first few tries didn't provide any information, but did get him to an article about the Taliban using real birds and fitting them with bomb vests.

He almost laughed out loud. If only they knew how to weaponize homing pigeons, that would have been the perfect weapon.

After another five minutes, Boy Scout found a short article. The attack wasn't listed as terrorist-originated, but an Afghan-on-Afghan crime. Boy Scout knew the truth of it from the memory he shared. Six people had died in the attack. A village elder, his driver and bodyguard, a vice-principal of a madrassa, two bird sellers, and the boy. No motivation was listed in the article, but one witness said that the killer had been a troubled boy from the elder's village.

The boy's name had been Mohammad Poya. The way Afghan boy names were constructed meant that the first part of the name was the subordinate name and was usually that of a famous person. The second part was the proper name, and how the boy was generally addressed. A quick check told Boy Scout that Poya meant *one who is consistently searching for something*. He had no last name, which was no surprise. He was a simple kid from a mountain village. So that would be Boy Scout's approach to him.

He fired off a quick email to Sister Renee to let her know his plan, then returned to his room.

He thought about telling his team, but he knew they'd be against it. This was just something he needed to do.

He settled himself on the floor again, naked, sitting on a towel to soak up the sweat as he unlocked each of his chakras to release his energy. When he got to his Third Eye chakra, Boy Scout hesitated. He knew he wasn't ready for what he was about to do, but he didn't have the time to plan and practice. He needed to get it done quickly. The problem was it was like building an airplane in mid-flight. If he wasn't successful, he'd crash headlong into the ground, or in his case, maybe never be able to return to his body. Instead of quitting, though, he took a deep breath and willed himself to leave by his third eye. In a whoosh, he found himself once again in the black and white world of the astral plane.

It had been easier than he'd expected. Maybe having been here created muscle memory, engendering his mind to release his essence.

He glanced to where the dark sun pulsed in the Up, then searched the Down. Three pinpoints of light moved nearby. He guessed those were his team. More pinpoints of light were nearby, including two lines of them moving at speed. Since he was on a marine base, he guessed it might be a running formation. Then again, it could be people on a bus. Part of him wanted to discover which was which, just so he could become smarter about this new environment. He also realized that he was putting off doing what he'd come here to do. When he found the four huddled beings, he willed himself to move until he was right next to them.

They all looked the same, glowing white featureless mannequin faces bent forward until their heads were touching.

He knew better than to join them. Interacting with all three might just drive him crazy. So he picked one, reached out with his hand that was not a hand, and touched it.

A sizzle of electric energy shot through him as the being turned towards him. The features of a middle-aged man, North African, replaced the simulacrum. The face was free of emotion at first, and then washed into anger.

"You. What have you done with me?" it asked, speaking Berber.

Boy Scout was filled with the images of *horses charging over a sand dune upon an oasis lit by a lone fire. The cries of warriors like coyote song in the night. Screams of panic by those on foot.*

"I haven't done anything," Boy Scout responded in the same language. "You were lost in The White and came into me when I visited."

Riding down a mountain trail in a line of armored SUVs. The second SUV explodes. Pieces of metal and men raining down on the hood and windshield. A finger bounces off the window.

Its expression went from anger to concern, then to confusion and thoughtfulness. "The White. Yes. I was in a place with all white. Many of us were. It was like a nightmare and I couldn't wake up. Then I saw something like an exit and I raced for it."

A dinner on a blanket under the stars. Lamb stewed with goat's milk cheese. Tea with cardamom. A breeze carrying the sweet salt of the Mediterranean.

"That exit was me," Boy Scout managed to say, struggling with the contact.

Sitting around a table at a bar, his entire team back together, Narco standing on one side of the table telling a joke that they all laugh at.

Images came furious with the contact. Boy Scout fought not to become overwhelmed by them, thinking of them as curtains on a window to be pushed aside so that he might see past them. Not just those of the Berber, but his own, broadcast without his will, surfacing like mysterious bobbers in a lake he didn't know he was fishing.

"But what is this place? And who are these others?" Surf crashing against the shore. Seagulls fighting for morsels. "Two of them want to talk, but another controls them." He paused, then asked, "What am I seeing? What are these things you ride in?"

"We call them vehicles. Powered by invisible horses."

A rifle range back when he was in basic training. Twenty-four new recruits in foxholes sweating under the noonday sun and firing blindly at 300-meter targets as perspiration smears their vision.

"Why is it that you aren't controlled?" Boy Scout managed to ask.

"I can feel the history of those around me," the Berber said. "Sometimes their memories. I can feel you and the strangeness of you."

A baby cries in the other room as he snuggles with a woman, both of them naked. A jar of honey rests on the floor next to them, much of it spooned on her breasts.

"But I can't feel the other who controls. I don't want to feel the other."

Boy Scout paused, wondering what it was he needed to know. The Berber was interesting, but ultimately, he wasn't who Boy Scout needed to get to. But did he really want to interact with this other? Was he ready for it?

He suddenly found himself in a horde.

A hundred horses gallop across the sand. Cries of men raze the quiet of the night like scythes through corn. He carries a curved sword. A rifle rests in a scabbard on his roan horse. An encampment of white tents beneath tall palms lies before him. Legionnaires in sand-colored kepis are arrayed before the horde. Suddenly smoke erupts from their line, followed by the sounds of rifle shots. A bullet sizzles past him. The man in front of him sags and falls into the churning feet of his horse. He fights to control his horse that is struggling to clamber over the fallen man, the idea of hurting a rider foreign to the beast. Then he is past the broken body, now hacking into the line of defenders as he crashes through men and into the tents.

He feels a pain at the back of his head but ignores it as he continues, hacking and slashing at anyone on foot. Kepis fly as their heads are mauled. Still, the pain increases, but he fights on.

His enemy is the French imperialists who would take his country and make it their own. The sands of his ancestors will never belong to anyone else. He is Berber and he is proud.

The pain blinds him but still he swings, his sword arm pumping up and down like a furious—

Once again in a world of black and white he is confronted by the astral ghost of the Berber, whose face is planted against his own, arms behind him and tugging at the base of Boy Scout's silver cord.

"Don't," Boy Scout whispers, out of breath from the charge. "Stop," Boy Scout murmurs, part of him still swinging the sword.

He reaches up with his arms, but they pass through the Berber, his form somehow insubstantial.

He who was once Boy Scout is becoming Berber. He feels a tremendous pressure as memories begin to flood in and replace the ones he had. Who he is blends, two becoming one, one becoming none. He feels himself begin to float away and cries out weakly that he wants to go home. But there is no more home, only a vast plane of darkness and an even darker sun that pulls at him.

His essence is peeling away and he cannot stop it.

He knows what is happening, but he does not understand what to do.

He has no frame of reference.

He has no technique.

He is once again in the oasis and fighting.

He cries out in a language he should not know.

He sings the song of victory in a voice that isn't his own as the last Frenchman falls from a vicious sweep of his sword.

Then he dismounts, his booted feet hitting the sand where his ancestors have bled for centuries.

Chapter Sixteen

Astral Plane

SOMETHING GRIPS HIM and he spins.

Standing on the sand in front of him is a woman dressed in a black and white gown.

He raises his sword to bring the blade down on her, but pauses. There's something familiar in the way she stands, in the manner in which she holds her head and appraises him.

"Who are you?" he says in Berber.

"Fight!" she commands in English.

"What are you?" he asks in the same language.

"Your only hope."

Then she reaches out and puts her hand inside of his face.

He can feel the fingers grab something, but there is no pain.

She pulls her arm back and he suddenly feels light.

The oasis fades and he's once again in a universe of black.

"Imagine this is The White. Whatever you invent is real."

"But this is black," he says with all the effort he can muster.

"White, black, there is no difference." Her hand became a flat piece of something shiny and she struck him with it. "Buck up, Ranger."

At that word, Boy Scout returned to his essence and immediately understood what was going on. The other—the Berber—was hijacking him. But Boy Scout had little energy to fight. Somehow, someway, the Berber had siphoned everything from him. He could see the other man latched onto his astral projection, glowing brightly like a light-infused parasite.

"What am I?" he asked Sister Renee.

"You are an astral shadow and are fading fast. You must find energy. You must fight it while I try and hold him off."

Then she soared towards the Berber and was soon locked in battle, both of them furiously moving, their bodies shifting and changing into things that could punish and defend.

Boy Scout felt himself diminishing. He saw the other three beings that were inside him and moved towards them like a moth to their flame. He felt the warmth of their life energy, one more powerful than the others. He avoided this and sought the one with the least energy, hoping to borrow some of it, maybe to take it as his own. He felt desperate, himself a phantom eager to possess something that didn't belong to him.

He reached out and touched the illuminated being before him and immediately smelled the scent of oranges. He smiled wide on a face with no mouth as he inhaled the scent of the sweet citrus through a nose he did not have. It was nothing more than a memory, but the sensation of it being real was enough to make him want more. He grabbed fistfuls of orange-scented dreams—walking down a mountain lane, carrying a baby goat, rolling in a sea of flowers with other boys, giggling at the wonder of it all. He took them. He took them all.

He barely heard the whisper of the boy, Poya, who asked, "What is happening?" He was so hungry for more oranges and flowers and goats that he grabbed faster, his arms now windmilling through the essence of what was once a simple Pashtun boy turned suicide bomber turned accidental traveler, until the boy was no more. He didn't wink out—he simply ceased to be. The essence which had made the boy, the light that bound all of his memories and idea of self, now became part of Boy Scout.

Before he could stop, his essence touched that of the other—the strange one who would control—and Boy Scout discovered that there were two essences. Images of a wet gray English garden were juxtaposed with those of a land where men walked beside greater men—men who were twice the size of those who would be normal, voices booming as they commanded the lesser to do their bidding. And then Boy Scout realized that his vantage was from on high which meant that—

The other turned to him and fixed an astral gaze upon him.

Boy Scout felt the buzz of power as the other began to turn it on him, pulling out memories of oranges and eating a hamburger after fourteen days of eating MREs, both sweet and delicious snapshots in culinary time. Boy Scout managed to kick away, severing the contact with the other, knowing that this was too much and that he could never hope to defeat the duality that was this iconic essence. Although it was destined to be a battle in the future, the battle at hand was the one on which he must concentrate.

He spun away and surged towards the clash raging between Sister Renee and the Berber. For all her talents, Sister Renee seemed dimmer than before. Had the Berber taken some of her light? An image of a little girl possessed by a demon powered

Boy Scout to action. How could he not protect her, even as she was protecting him? Now armed with the power of the boy, he could do damage, but would it be enough? So instead of fighting, he surrendered, imaging himself falling back into the body that no longer existed. If this Black was truly like The White, then anything was possible.

And like the missing piece of a ten-thousand-piece puzzle, he snapped into place and was once again Boy Scout. But now he was stronger. Not only did he have what remained of his power, he also had that of the boy.

The Berber felt the change and his look of victory slipped to fear.

Sister Renee shot Boy Scout a glance and grinned fiercely, so much like Preacher's Daughter that it hurt his heart. He wanted nothing more than to return to the present and the real—and the path to that reality went through the Berber.

Sister Renee's hands were around the wrists of the Berber, whose own hands were deep inside of her chest.

Boy Scout instinctively knew what the entity was doing and shoved his thumbs into the Berber's astral eye sockets. Instead of using them to create damage, he treated his thumbs as straws and began to draw in the essence of the Berber.

Feeling the drain, the Berber removed one hand

from the chest of Sister Renee and reached for Boy Scout.

A third arm sprang from Boy Scout's chest as he willed it into existence. The new hand grabbed the Berber's and all of Boy Scout's new fingers became more straws, drawing in the essence faster.

The Berber stared at the new hand, unable to fathom where the third arm came from. It was clear that he never realized he could completely change his body into something different.

Seeing this, Sister Renee did something similar, creating six tentacles that shot free from her own chest, the ends shoving themselves into the chest of the Berber.

The effect was instantaneous.

The Berber became smaller and smaller as his essence was sucked away, ingested by both Boy Scout and Sister Renee. And as he became smaller, they grew brighter, until neither were able to see the other through their combined halos of brightness.

And then he was gone.

Memories of honey and sex and violence mixed with those of oranges and birds and fields of flowers, all wedged between Boy Scout's own memories. He wondered if he might soon forget which memories were whose. In taking the essence of the Berber and the boy, he had also taken what had made them individuals—he'd taken their *selfs*.

"Go back," Sister Renee said to him.

Boy Scout stared at her, then looked back toward the other two. Only there weren't two—there was only one, and it shined so brightly that even the dark sun was invisible. Ahmad's Friend, the unknown Afghan soldier from the Battle of Kabul, was gone, probably ingested the way they'd ingested the other two. But while they'd done their deed in self-defense, that duel had been done because it, the last remaining entity, was merely hungry.

So what next?

There was now this single dual entity inside of him. Did that mean the thing would come for him next? For now, he couldn't worry about that. He felt immeasurably tired.

"Hurry," Sister Renee urged. "I will watch you, then return myself."

Boy Scout reached around the back of his head and felt the place where the cord was affixed to his astral self. He once again imagined himself backing down a ramp and falling backwards into a brackish night sky over one of the many countries he'd HALO'd into. And as he fell back, he returned to his body, slamming into it as it fell back onto the floor. He barely had the energy to lock his chakras before the realization of what he'd done hit him.

He'd killed a child.

He'd also killed the Berber, but that was different.

The Berber had died in battle, while the boy had been a victim of Boy Scout's hunger.

Yes, the child had been a suicide bomber and had killed others.

But he was *Boy Scout*. He'd never willingly harm a boy, but his desperation to survive had made the decision for him: the boy or him.

The smell of oranges came to him and he thought of his mother—*the boy*'s mother—and how her fingers had always had the hint of the citrus upon them. Then Boy Scout curled into a fetal position and did what he hadn't done since he was a child: he cried like one, soul-deep sobs mixed with the gentle weeping of the sorrowful.

Chapter Seventeen

Camp Pendleton Command Center

Boy Scout met his crew the next morning. He hadn't eaten the night before and had told everyone to go away when they'd offered to take him out or bring him something. He was starving, but he hadn't felt like eating. Instead he filled his stomach with black coffee and self-loathing as he told them his plan. As it turned out, Poe was able to track a delivery to the consulate. He couldn't be a hundred percent sure what was delivered because it came in a covered delivery truck; he was, however, able to track via customs that a cargo container recently passed through from a Turkish flagged cargo carrier, and that the container had been guarded by Turkish diplomatic security carrying heavy weapons.

They'd asked him what had gone on, but Boy Scout didn't want to talk about it. He was too busy processing what had happened and what sort of karmic hit he'd taken. He realized that taking the life of an entity that had already died wasn't the same as if the person were alive. He just didn't like the desperation he'd shown. It was as though he hadn't had a choice. His own essence had made the choice for him, and like a vampire he'd sucked the boy dry. That he and Sister Renee had done the same to the Berber was different. Not only had he been an adult, but he was also an aggressor who would have gleefully killed either or both of them if he'd been able.

No, this memory was his to deal with and his alone.

"If we're going to raid the consulate, we need some better intel," he said. He turned to Poe and asked, "What have you got on security, personnel, etc.?"

"I have the layout with a date of information within two weeks ago, so I feel comfortable that it's accurate. I have a list of all permanent employees, as well as cleaning services and food and beverage deliverers."

"We need one. Have you run their financials?" Boy Scout asked.

"For the permanent employees, yes. There are

two who are in way over their heads. One is about to have her house foreclosed on."

"Any chance we can help her out?" Boy Scout asked.

"Legally?"

"You're the federal government, you tell me."

"I suppose we can help her. Special Unit 77 has a large pot of discretionary income."

"Okay, you and Preacher's Daughter work that angle."

McQueen sat forward in his chair. "And us? What's our plan?"

"We're going trolling for dervishes."

"What's that mean?"

"Any way we can tip them that I'll be at a certain location at a certain time?"

"They're monitoring Noaks's computers and phones," Poe said.

Boy Scout tapped the side of his head with his forefinger as he thought about the best way to approach this. "Fire off a simple message to Noaks that says I need to get some supplies at Del Amo Mall and we'll meet him at the Goodyear Blimp Air Base at 1500. Make sure you get him clearance to land. Use all of your Special Unit 77 mummery. National security, counter terrorism, whatever you need."

Poe raised an eyebrow. "You do realize that you're not in charge. We're partners."

McQueen sat back and crossed his arms. He might have been smiling beneath his bushy Fu Manchu but no one would ever know.

Preacher's Daughter shook her head.

Boy Scout turned and directed his gaze on the lieutenant. "What did you say to me?"

Poe paused, then chuckled. "I said, you do realize that you aren't in charge."

"How do you know what I realize?" Boy Scout said. "I've run a VIP and diplomatic security detail in the harshest environment on the planet for over three years. This is what we do. We investigate and get information. We get people to talk. We get what we need to protect, and then we do just that. You're my fucking IT department. You're my financial advisor. You provide what we need and the mission gets done. You start wishing you're in charge, the whole plan gets derailed while we stroke your ego like the ears of a cat."

Poe opened his mouth to say something, but Boy Scout cut him off. "I'm not done. These are *my* people. They trust *me* to keep them alive. *We* don't know you, Poe. In fact, I have a hard time trusting damned near everyone on the planet except these two right here. You want to be in charge? You want to be the big boss man and run your own operation? Then prove you're capable."

Boy Scout paused, then added, "Now you can

talk." During the entire monologue, he'd never raised his voice and he'd never gotten heated. Just like the best sergeants he'd had in Ranger School, it was those who weren't yelling who'd made the greatest impact.

"I did save you," Poe said.

"From what? We saved ourselves from the monastery. All you did was take us from China Lake to Pendleton. Thanks for the ride."

"I have assets that can be—"

"Then we'll use them. If anytime during a mission briefing you have a better idea on how to accomplish it, or if you have assets you believe can assist, by all means bring it up. Both Preacher's Daughter and McQueen know they can provide operational advice. Now, can we get on with it?"

Poe stared at Boy Scout for a moment, his mouth tight, the rest of his face implacable. Then he nodded sharply. "We'll discuss this later," he said.

Boy Scout glared at him for a moment, realizing that much of his anger was misplaced, then turned back to the room in general, releasing the young lieutenant from his gaze. "Where were we?"

McQueen was the first to speak. "You and me were going shopping at the mall and Preacher's Daughter and the lieutenant were going to go pay off some loans and make one woman happy enough to want to give us the information we'll need to go in and capture a supernatural being held hostage."

"Right. We're also going to need an assault team for tomorrow." Boy Scout looked at the three in the room.

McQueen said, "Don't look at me. I'm a bouncer at a gay bar. If you want a bunch of queens to throw their shoes, I know where to find them."

Preacher's Daughter shook her head. "I keep to myself. You know that."

Boy Scout looked once again at Poe, this time his gaze softer, eyebrows raised expectantly.

"I suppose I can round up some of my *assets*," he said, with emphasis on the last word. "They going to see actual action, or are they decoys?"

"Decoys, I think."

"That makes it easier. I'll have something ready."

"Good. Then let's rendezvous back here at 1900 hours."

Poe went to the door and held it.

Preacher's Daughter stood and shook her head at Boy Scout and McQueen. "Don't you boys go and get yourselves in trouble."

"We'll be fine, sister," McQueen said. "Go and make that woman's day."

Preacher's Daughter: "Feeling like Ed McMahon all day long."

"No one is going to get a reference from a guy who hasn't been on television for twenty years," McQueen said.

She stuck her tongue out. "You did." Then she skipped out the door.

Poe followed behind her.

McQueen and Boy Scout sat for a time in silence, neither moving.

Finally, McQueen said, "What's going on, boss?"

"Why do you think something's going on?"

"You've lost a spark or something. Dunno how, but I just know. You told us to let you know if you changed. Let me just say you've changed."

"I lost my spark when the dervishes took us. I lost my spark when Narco and Bully and Criminal were killed. I haven't had my spark for some time."

"No. There's something more. There's also a sadness about you—something new."

Boy Scout looked at McQueen. He'd led the man into so many bad situations he couldn't count them all. He and Preacher's Daughter were really all that were left of those he truly loved. They were his family. And McQueen knew more secrets about Boy Scout than anyone. Like the fact he'd actually murdered an Afghan lieutenant colonel because the man was hiding behind an old Pashtun custom and forcing himself on a little wheelchair-bound boy. Boy Scout knew that he'd do it again in a heartbeat, but it didn't stop him from realizing that he'd murdered—the right or wrong of it couldn't undo the stain on his soul.

McQueen had also told Boy Scout about the terrible thing he'd done to a man who'd made fun of him, how he'd lost it, thinking that one act of rage would get back at the man for what he'd done. Instead, the deed had wrapped itself around McQueen's heart like a length of barbed wire and would squeeze it forever.

"What was his name?" Boy Scout had asked, when McQueen had finally unleveraged his heart in the ancient complex of cisterns in northern Afghanistan.

"Why do you want to know?" McQueen had asked, fighting back tears.

"I think it's important that you say it out loud."

"Is this a form of therapy?"

"Maybe." Boy Scout had leaned forward. "Maybe I just want to know. You know, a detail. Like the red house or the nasty smell. A detail."

McQueen exhaled. He'd glanced at Boy Scout several times before he spoke. "His name was Billy Picket and he'd been my best friend until he found out I was gay." Then McQueen slammed his face into his hands and bawled.

Details.

Cleaning out the closet.

And to discover that the man McQueen had raped had been his best friend.

Neither Boy Scout nor McQueen were model human beings.

Neither wanted their worst deeds known to the universe.

For all the good they'd done in their lives, he wasn't sure that they'd made a difference in the face of those two acts. And now the boy suicide bomber. That the kid had murdered people was beside the point. Boy Scout could still taste the innocence and the longing the boy had had at his core. Did the boy know he'd killed others? Probably not. He was merely avenging the death of his mother and the universe would probably treat him with more favor than it would ever give Boy Scout or McQueen.

So, Boy Scout told McQueen what happened.

When it was over, McQueen cupped his cheek and said, "My friend, even when you're the worst, you are the best of us."

Boy Scout needed to hear someone else say this, but each word was still a nail in the coffin of his self-respect.

Chapter Eighteen

Sunnyvale

THOSE FROM LOS Angeles tend to geographically separate the city into three districts: everything north of the 10, everything east of the 405, and everything west of the 405.

North of the 10 was LA City proper, Beverly Hills, Hollywood, Glendale, Burbank, Eagle Rock and points north.

East of the 405 was Compton, Inglewood, Gardena, Hawthorn, Downey, Lakewood, Bell Gardens and points east.

West of the 405 was where many wanted to be. The 405 itself rose out of the land like a great wall, separating populations by class, race, ethnicity and weather as the raised highway propelled traffic from south to north, around the great curve and lost itself somewhere north of the 10. West of the 405 the weather was often ten to fifteen degrees cooler because of the onshore breezes offered by the Pacific Ocean. The towns of Malibu, Santa Monica, Manhattan Beach, Redondo Beach, Torrance and Rancho Palos Verdes had homes that gradually shrank in square footage as they increased in value with each block west towards the Pacific, until those along the beach, which looked like any other condo complex in the world, were the homes of those who'd been able to bite off a piece or two of LA's golden apple.

When people say Los Angeles, most think of one sprawling metropolis of strip malls, corner stores, fast food, joints and homes. Sure, there's the iconic palm trees, the Hollywood sign, the Santa Monica Pier and others, but for all intents the idea of Los Angeles was, and will always be, inspired by the television shows set there.

NCIS: Los Angeles.

CHIPS.

Curb Your Enthusiasm.

Californication, one of Boy Scout's favorite shows.

Entourage.

And *Buffy the Vampire Slayer.*

Buffy the Vampire Slayer was filmed in Torrance, where they were heading. Just like the streets of

San Pedro had been transformed into the streets of San Francisco for the TV show *Charmed*, Torrance had been transformed into the mythical city of Sunnyvale. With its tree-lined streets of Craftsman model homes behind wide lawns, it didn't embody the concrete and hopelessness felt by much of the locals east and north. For LA residents, except those west of the 405, Torrance didn't feel like LA. It felt like Sunnyvale, which was why Buffy's house lay on one of those tree-lined streets, and Torrance High School became her high school, as well as that of the cool kids in *90210*. It was why director and creator Joss Whedon chose that location. Not only did he need somewhere people could relate to, he needed a place near enough where he could film *Buffy* on the cheap. After all, who was going to watch a show about a vampire slayer who had to go to high school before saving the world.

As it turned out, pretty much everyone.

Boy Scout remembered binging all the seasons during a particularly boring six-month tour in Iraq where they'd been kept locked away on the FOB. Of all the characters on the show, Boy Scout had been most interested in Giles. The idea that there was a larger organization watching over the events and that the fate of the world wasn't solely resting on the sloped shoulders of a pretty blonde high school girl made him feel better. On the drive to the mall, he reflected that Special Unit 77 was a similar unit. So far all he knew of it was from Poe, but he hoped somewhere there was some adult supervision over the event that had made Boy Scout and his team accidentally unleash a squadron of *daeva* on Los Angeles—something like the Watchers Council.

McQueen drove a white Ford Explorer they'd signed out of the USMC motor pool, tapping the wheel as he listened to Nicki Minaj on the radio.

Something occurred to Boy Scout as he thought about Torrance and *Buffy* and the mall. Something that on the surface sounded ludicrous but could possibly be of serious help. If he couldn't share his thoughts with McQueen, then who could he share them with? Knowing he might be made fun of, he decided he might as well ask anyway.

"Mind if I ask you a question?" he asked McQueen, reaching to turn down the radio.

"Sure."

"You ever watch *Buffy the Vampire Slayer*?"

McQueen gave him a quick glance. "That's not what I expected you to ask."

"I guess not. Still, it's on all the time. It had a seven-year run. The show influenced a generation."

"You taking a general poll or is there a reason for the question?"

"You know that *Buffy* was filmed in Torrance, right?"

McQueen shook his head slightly. "Only the first three years, then except for B-roll, they got the backing they needed from the studio."

Boy Scout turned in his seat and appraised McQueen. "So, you *are* aware of the show."

"Aware is not the correct word," McQueen said, grinning. "I saw all the shows repeatedly. I read all the comic books. I used to own a lot of the merch. I even read the spinoffs. Christopher Golden's and Nancy Holder's books were terrific, but I absolutely loved Yvonne Navarro's take. I thought she hit it out of the park when she had Buffy and dinosaurs. I mean, who does that? But when she took that part where Willow turned evil and then was good again and turned it on its head, that was a moment of literary genius. Navarro's three books on Evil Willow were the absolute best of the lot. I still have them somewhere. Took them on two tours to Iraq and one to Somalia."

Boy Scout realized his jaw had fallen open and closed it. "You'd consider yourself a *Buffy* expert, then?" he asked.

"I wouldn't think of me as an expert," he answered. "But I wouldn't bet against me in a *Buffy* trivia game. Why the interest? What's so important about *Buffy* that it relates to what we're doing?"

"It might sound crazy, but I was thinking TTPs."

"Techniques, tactics and procedures? Are you feeling well, boss?"

"Listen, I know it sounds crazy, but hear me out. If I want to get an infantry squad and take a hill, where would I learn how to do that?"

"Uh, Fort Benning?"

"Right. And I'd consult the manual—*FM 7 – 8, The Infantry Rifle Platoon and Squad.* The marines have their own version. If I want to fire a cannon or do tank combat, there are manuals for that. If I want to conduct a counterinsurgency on a country or positively affect their internal defenses, I can go to SOCOM and find an FM or an instruction that tells me what the great military minds have come up with, hopefully based on best practices."

"Where does *Buffy* come into this?" McQueen asked.

"Tell me this: what manual of instruction or field manual would you go to in the event you needed to fight the supernatural?"

McQueen clenched his jaw as he nodded to himself. He switched lanes twice, checking the mirrors occasionally for surveillance. When he spoke, his words were measured, but tinged with a thread of sarcasm. "I'd think that Special Unit 77 would have such documents, seeing as they've been around for so long." He sighed, then turned the radio completely off. Until now, Minaj's lyrical rap about what she was doing with champagne and a man's genitals was just on the edge of hearing. "But you're right. There's nothing out there that we know of. If there was, I'd be eager to read it. The problem is none of the real stuff is currently available to us. Your solution to follow the guidance of a bunch of Hollywood suits who've never even held a weapon, much less fired one?"

Boy Scout agreed, but still pressed on. "My thinking is this: after seven seasons, they've sat around enough writing rooms, game-playing how best to take down certain supernatural creatures. They had to do some research."

"Or make the shit up."

"Or make the shit up... but I can't help believe there was a lot of research done that shouldn't go to waste."

McQueen gave him a questioning look. "Like I said, your solution is to follow the guidance of a bunch of Hollywood suits who've never even held a weapon, much less fired one. You want us to consult *The Watcher's Handbook* before each mission."

Boy Scout slumped in his seat and stared at the traffic. "You're right, of course." After a moment, he shook his head and stared out the side window. "I'm so off my game."

"I can see it now," McQueen said, a big grin taking over his face. "Before every mission we ask ourselves *What would Buffy do?*"

Boy Scout closed his eyes, feeling about as uncomfortable as he'd ever felt.

"We could even get it tattooed on our forearms—WWBD—to remind us to think of our favorite episodes and what TTPs she used to dust the creature of the day."

"You're not helping."

"You do know that back in the day it was five thousand dollars a dust, right? So when two vampires got dusted in one show, that was a big deal. They called it a double duster."

"You're still not helping."

McQueen's voice had raised in pitch as he held himself on the verge of outright laughter. "Or even better. I could find out where the showrunners have gotten to and we could hire one of them as our J2 intel section."

"There's a line and you've crossed it."

But McQueen was really on a roll. He raised his head and laughed. "Who are we in comparison? I think Preacher's Daughter is like Anya, the vengeance demon. I'm not sure if she's Anya before she lost her powers or after, because she can definitely be badass. And what about you?"

"What about you?" Boy Scout asked, turning the question back on his friend. "Who do you think you are?"

McQueen cocked his head and scratched his cheek. "It's hard to say. Not too many big, gay hipsters in the series. I wonder who I'd be. But in all seriousness, if we were like Buffy then she'd be you. You'd be Buffy, boss. Leader of the team and baddest of us all."

"I'm not exactly a slayer."

"I don't know about that. I've seen you in action."

Boy Scout suddenly realized what McQueen was doing. His over-the-top diatribe was designed to bring Boy Scout out of his self-created shell. Jump kick him back to who he should be. Make him angry, then get him past it. Against his own masochistic wishes, it was working.

McQueen snapped a finger. "Maybe we should change your call sign from Boy Scout to Buffy. What do you think, Bryan?"

"I think I'll stick with Boy Scout."

"It would also be far easier to call Preacher's Daughter Anya. A lot less syllables."

Boy Scout said nothing.

"Do you think she'd go for it? Maybe I should call her and ask."

"You mean ask the vengeance demon to change her name?" Boy Scout replied.

"Good point."

They drove in silence for awhile, passing the

place they'd rendezvous with Noaks later, one of the Goodyear Blimps parked in a great open field.

Finally, McQueen said in a low voice. "I'll admit that there is some merit there. As the expert," he said, taking his hands of the wheel for a moment to give air quotes, "I'll let you know if anything comes to mind."

"That's all I ask," Boy Scout said.

"And if that doesn't work, I think I've also seen every episode of *Scooby Doo*. Those Hanna-Barbera cartoons were aces."

"Fuck you, McQueen."

"Yes, boss. I'll get right on it."

Twenty minutes later they were pulling into the mall and Nicki Minaj was still singing about men's genitals.

Chapter Nineteen

Del Amo Fashion Center Mall

DEL AMO MALL, or more rightly Del Amo Fashion Center, rested in the heart of downtown Torrance and was everything you wanted in a mall and more. With a leasing space of almost three million square feet it was one of the largest shopping malls in America. But where bigger ones went up, many sporting carnival-type rides, Del Amo concentrated on the most natural of American human rights: the right to spend money. With three tight levels and nearly two hundred and fifty stores, a shopper could become lost inside and never have to leave. Having been a fan of the *Dawn of the Dead* franchise, Boy Scout had assessed Del Amo as a possible hideout in an end-of-the-world scenario and had found it wanting. Not for everything it had, but for its too many entrances and the fact that it rested squarely in the middle of millions of people. A far better redoubt would be some small, midwestern mall with three or four entrances, off the interstate, and in the middle of nowhere.

But everything that made Del Amo a poor place to defend during a zombie apocalypse allowed it to be a prime spot to detect surveillance. The uninitiated might wonder how one would spot surveillance in such a massive property with tens of thousands of fellow shoppers milling about, browsing, hanging out, and doing the various consumer dances relative to popular culture. But there's an attitude of inattentiveness the average shopper assumes upon entering one of the Great Temples of Capitalism. They look forward and not backward. They search ahead and rarely care what's behind, because once surveyed and dismissed, there's no need to return. The evolutionary hunter-gatherer mentality dictates that their desires might be met in the next or the next or the next store, even if they aren't even sure what it is they're looking for.

Some go to malls to buy a specific item, then leave.

Some go to spend time with friends or loved ones and inevitably buy things they may or may not need.

Still others go to hang out with friends or find new ones, the food court being the locus for most of these social activities.

And still more people frequent malls as retail therapy, erasing the bad events of the day or replacing one's poor idea of self with something new and shiny that fits them perfectly in the moment, allowing them to achieve a momentary mental triumph as who they were and what had happened was temporarily erased by the purchase of a two-for-one blouse, a new pair of shoes, or a Starter Jacket with their favorite team logo. Who they were wearing these new things is not the same as who they had been before they bought them.

Then there are the exercisers. They were recognized by their complete disdain for capitalism, using the interiors of such malls as their own free gyms. Headbands, Sketchers, eyes forward, body straining, eager to urge a year or two more on a structure that had become inevitably more fragile as the decades were heaped upon it.

These categories made up more than ninety percent of those who regularly go to malls. This didn't include those who go there to work, those who go to provide security, and those who go to hunt. Hunters came in all shapes, from those looking to remove a handbag from a busy mother, or a wallet from a distracted husband, to those eager to exploit capitalism without the desire to perform legal commerce.

Then, of course, there were the hunters like Boy

Scout and McQueen. Hunters who pretended to be victims only so they could become better hunters. By now, the dervishes should have been able to have persons in place and ready for them, with others probably on the way. The problem the dervishes had was the same one that Caucasian Americans have when operating in Muslim or Asian countries—they stuck out. Not as much so in Los Angeles, but enough that the attentive prey could discern the differences. For instance, each of the men hunting them would be of military age. Each of them would be of Turkish or Middle Eastern descent, which created a specific facial biometric profile. And most importantly, each of them would be hunting rather than shopping.

For their benefit, McQueen and Boy Scout each carried a slender P238 in an ankle holster and wore the special glasses they'd field tested against the dervishes at the monastery. On the edge of retro-ridiculous, the shades looked more like something a grandfather or Elton John might wear, their thickness a little unnecessary. In fact, the frames were so thick they made the army issue Birth Control Glasses, or BCGs, seem stylish by comparison. But the team couldn't operate without them. The series of flashing lights hidden in the frame structure were designed to catch the attention of their eyes just enough that they couldn't concentrate on a specific thing—this was the secret of being able to ignore the hypnotic dance of the dervishes. It was ironic that the technology for the glasses was based on EMDR, or eye movement desensitizing and processing, which was being more frequently used to help veterans overcome the trauma associated with PTSD. Now it would be used to help veterans overcome those who would seek to add to their PTSD.

With their glasses on and the pistols tight against the ankles, each of them slipped into the mall using different entrances.

Boy Scout entered using the door nearest Crate and Barrel on Hawthorne Way.

McQueen entered near AMC Theaters on Fashion Way.

The idea was for them to drag whatever surveillance they had to the food court and then see what transpired. They had an idea, but they weren't about to assume that would happen. If nothing at all happened, then they'd meet and enter the theater as two persons and take down their surveillance teams in the dark.

It was only when Boy Scout entered that he remembered why he hated malls.

The crowds set him on edge. His tinnitus hissed higher as his blood pressure raised. The problem with so many people was that he found it impossible to track and assign threat levels to everyone. Add that he was no longer in full combat kit and he might as well have been naked. Hispanic and Asian families seemed to be the majority. The few Caucasian men he saw were dressed in gangbanger shirts and cholo shorts, Lakers or Dodgers shirts, or any variation of Nike apparel. Boy Scout had thought about changing their appearances, but that might tip the dervishes that they were worried about surveillance. Instead, they dressed as they always did: black polos, tactical kakis, Merrill shoes, and belts strong enough to drape all sorts of weaponry from. They looked like off-duty cops or military contractors.

Boy Scout walked along the corridor, head slightly down as if he were thinking more about what he was going to buy than paying attention to his environs. He clocked surveillance immediately. A military-age dark-skinned male wearing a red track suit with black stripes down the sides of the legs, standing against the wall and reading texts from his cell phone. As Boy Scout passed, the man began to tap on his phone.

A few seconds later, Boy Scout made a right turn into Dick's Sporting Goods. He went first to the bag section and spent fifteen minutes selecting a bag to carry everything else he'd buy. He settled on a red Osprey Go Bag. Then he went to the clothing section and grabbed three sets of pants, three shirts, a new belt, six pairs of socks and a set of new Merrill shoes. All the while, he kept the man in the track suit in his sights. This wouldn't be the threat. He was merely the tracker.

Finished, Boy Scout exited south into the mall proper and grinned as he paused at the US Army Recruiting Office, posters of men and women in action plastered on the windows.

Then he resumed window shopping, meandering around the south mall before entering Macy's from the east side. Inside the department store, he went up a level, then down two levels, before returning to the main level and exiting the west entrance. While inside he spotted a second dervish, this one wearing the same brand and style of track suit except in blue. Boy Scout was disappointed. It was like they weren't even trying, which demonstrated how certain they were of their TTPs.

He exited Macy's into the food court, which had the usual suspects such as Chipotle, Sbarra, Pita Pit and various pizza and burger places. What surprised him and had him salivating was Pink's Hotdogs. He'd had no idea that the oldest hot dog stand in America had a satellite stand in the mall. He'd been to the original Pink's off La Brea many times, ordering dogs that no self-respecting mid-westerner or northeasterner would ever have. So staid were New Yorkers and Chicagoans about their various dogs that they wouldn't even consider trying something so un-geographically tasteful.

Pink's named many of their dogs after famous movie stars or Californians. Boy Scout's go-to dogs included the Huell Howser Dog, which had two dogs on a single bun with mustard, onions, and chili, and the Martha Stewart Dog, which was a nine-inch stretch dog with relish, onions, bacon, chopped tomatoes, sauerkraut and sour cream. He laughed when he noted a new Lord of the Rings Dog, which had BBQ sauce and onion rings as if they came straight from the Shire.

After much hemming and hawing, he settled for an Emeril Lagasse Bam Dog, another nine-inch stretch dog with mustard, onions, cheese, jalapenos, bacon, and coleslaw. It was the jalapenos and coleslaw that did it for him. When they gave him a tray with the dog and a Coke, he took it to a table where McQueen was already seated.

McQueen was eating an Asian bowl with Kalbi chicken, zucchinis, onions, and jalapenos, mixed with kimchi rice and topped with seaweed and a fried egg. Waiting on the table was a boba tea from Bibigo Fresh Korean Kitchen.

McQueen was about to eat when he saw Boy Scout's dog, the coleslaw almost covered in fresh, steaming bacon. He glanced up at Boy Scout like a puppy and all but licked his lips.

The funny thing was that Boy Scout had been looking at McQueen's Bibigo box in the same way.

Without a word, they switched trays.

While Boy Scout retrieved his Coke, McQueen grabbed his Boba Tea.

They ate in silence for a moment, then Boy Scout asked, "How many do you have?"

"Three. Two followed me and one who was waiting by the brick pizza oven over there," he said, flashing his eyes in a direction.

"I counted two," Boy Scout said. "Are yours on the track team as well?"

McQueen chuckled. "It's like they're not even trying. Give one a wife beater and some cholo shorts and some black Nike high tops and I'd never know."

"Right?" Boy Scout sipped his coke and realized that the glasses were giving him a headache. "Do you think they'd actually try it here?"

The final third of the hotdog disappeared in McQueen's mouth. Around chewing the food, he said, "If they do, they're desperate and you have to wonder why."

Boy Scout saw a flash of white and lowered his eyes. "Don't look now but Mr. Desperate himself just walked in wearing a dervish dress."

McQueen started. "Do you really think they're going to do it?"

"It would be suicide. I already see security has pegged this guy as trouble and are vectoring towards him." And they were, one larger than life African American woman and a thick Hispanic man, neither with more than mace and a walkie talkie with which to defend themselves. The other dervishes weren't moving, instead standing where they were. And then as one, they all turned and faced the other way. "Oh shit. Here it comes."

The dervish wearing the traditional conical felt hat and a white dress leaped atop an empty table in the middle of the food court.

At first guess, Boy Scout surmised that there had to be two hundred people mingling, eating, or passing through.

The dervish raised his arms and a woman screamed.

The African American security guard ordered him down.

Then the dervish began to dance, twirling in the way only dervishes could, head knocked to the side as they entered a place where they were closer to god. But these dervishes had discovered that with a few more steps, they could create in the human mind a need to sleep. And like they'd all practiced, everyone who was watching sagged to the ground, their mind spinning and lost in the grooves at the end of a record. Those who didn't go down right away turned to see what was going on and, in one mesmerizing moment, were also down.

And on the dervish twirled, until the only people standing were two blind men near Sbarro, and Boy Scout and McQueen. The latter ran towards the whirling dervish, taking him down in a flying tackle that would make any professional linebacker an instant Pro Bowl selection.

The crash was followed by the other dervishes turning and realizing the almost perfect effectiveness of their plan—*almost* because the two they had actually targeted were up and violent.

Boy Scout tore into two of the dervishes with short chopping rights, hitting each of them where the jaw met the skull. Both fell like the other patrons and Boy Scout began running towards another. He glanced back and saw McQueen had an arm under the shoulder of the whirling dervish and was escorting him into the movie theater.

Then he heard his name called.

"Bryan? Stop!"

Boy Scout twisted for the sound.

A seventh dervish stepped from behind a support beam wearing clothes identical to Boy Scout's. *Faood.* Boy Scout recognized him immediately as the one who had been with them at the cistern, the one who had explained everything to them, then disappeared with the others.

Boy Scout mouthed the man's name.

Faood nodded. "You have it wrong. We need you."

Boy Scout shook his head. "We don't have it wrong." He gestured to the hundreds of fallen. "Is this what you think is right?"

Faood smiled. "They are not hurt. They will be fine." He started to walk toward Boy Scout. "It's the glasses, isn't it? What's in them, lights?"

"I've seen what your kind can do. My team was killed for it. Narco, Criminal, Bully... all killed because of you."

"Not me, my friend." Faood continued moving toward him. Several of the other dervishes were also vectoring in. "I am here as a friend. I am here because we need to work together."

Boy Scout saw their plan and knew he had to leave. They were almost in place and where they'd have him. He thought about reaching down and pulling out his pistol, but there was still the issue of the surveillance cameras.

"Has it spoken with you yet? Did it explain who it is?"

Boy Scout backed away. He wanted nothing more than to rush Faood and bash in his head, but he needed to fight another day. He thought of a dozen things to say, but none were as good as the ones John McClane delivered during the battle for

Nakatomi Tower, so instead he shut the hell up, turned and ran. By the time he was running out the west entrance to the food court and slipping past Aéropostale, the people in the food court were beginning to recover, those entering now screaming as they probably believed terrorists had hit the mall with a strange new weapon.

Boy Scout was able to race out the west exit before anyone could stop him. He slowed to a walk, forcing himself not to turn around, the last words of Faood playing through his mind. He knew he'd have to tell Preacher's Daughter about what had happened here. He needed her religious history expertise, and he needed to tell her about the giants, and ultimately, about the boy whose mother's fingers once held the memory of oranges.

Chapter Twenty

South Los Angeles

BOY SCOUT UBERED to the Home Depot in South Torrance. He went inside through the contractor entrance, cruised the aisles for a few minutes, stopped to marvel at a kitchen setup, chatted with an employee about various granite choices, then left through the garden center. He walked to the Costco a few blocks away and met McQueen, who was sitting in the driver's seat of a white panel van. A pair of marines had driven it up earlier, and when McQueen had arrived at the mall, they'd exchanged keys. The dervish was trussed in the back, his scowl almost comical.

"Did he have a cell?" Boy Scout asked.

"He did."

"Did you exploit it?"

"I did. Got his call history as well as all the emails he'd downloaded."

"What'd you do with the phone?"

McQueen shook his head. "What do you think this is, amateur hour? I tossed it in the back of a pickup with Tijuana plates."

Boy Scout climbed in the back and inspected the dervish's bonds. McQueen had done a good job. "Did he give you any trouble?"

"I might have had to give him a little punch or two. Funny how if you hit the stomach hard enough all effort of trying to escape just vanishes."

"Does he speak English?" Boy Scout asked, squatting beside the dervish.

"He knows all of our best curse words."

Boy Scout looked into the man's eyes. They radiated hate. "Did he give a name?"

"Not one that I heard."

"Well, then," Boy Scout said, his face inches from the dervish's. "Shall we begin?"

The dervish stared at him a moment, then smiled. "Are you going to torture me in the parking lot of a Costco? I think there's a metaphor for your people in that."

Boy Scout rocked his head back and laughed. "A metaphor for my people. Did you hear that, McQueen? He can speak English."

"Except for his accent, you might even think of

him as being born here," McQueen acknowledged.

The remark about his accent earned McQueen a glare from the dervish.

"Why are you trying to find me?" Boy Scout asked, opting for asking the direct question before he began trying other means. But the dervish clammed up and merely stared at the floor.

Boy Scout pulled out his phone, touched the microphone on the Google bar and said, "Tell me about whirling dervishes."

His phone began to speak. *"According to Wikipedia, The Mawlaw'īyya / Mevlevi Order is a Sufi order in Konya (modern day Turkey) (capital of the Anatolian Seljuk Sultanate) founded by the followers of Jalal ad-Din Muhammad Balkhi-Rumi, a thirteen century Persian poet, Islamic theologian and Sufi mystic."*

"Pause," Boy Scout said to his phone. Then to the dervish, "You know I met Rumi. We spoke, him and me, in The White. I bet you've never spoken to him. I bet you've waited your whole life to hear his words and he chose me to talk to. I wonder why that is.

"Continue," Boy Scout told the phone.

"The Mevlevi order was founded in 1273 by Rumi's followers after his death, particularly by his successor Hüsamettin Çelebi who decided to build a mausoleum for their master, and then

their master's son, Baha al-Din Muhammad-i Walad. He was an accomplished Sufi mystic with great organizing talents. His personal efforts were continued by his successor Ulu Arif Çelebi. The Mevlevi believe in performing their dhikr in the form of a 'dance' and musical ceremony known as the Sama, which involves the whirling, from which the order acquired its nickname."

When the phone finished summarizing the Wikipedia article about whirling dervishes, Boy Scout pocketed it. "So, let me get this right. Your order created and then perfected a dance that allows you to get closer to Allah. It's a sacred form of prayer that you display during a dancing ceremony. And now some of you have taken the sacred form of prayer and weaponized it."

The dervish shook his head slightly.

"Why would you do such a thing? It's one thing to discover that if someone watches you dance and you add a few steps, it affects the human brain in such a way that it renders people unconscious. But then to intentionally decide this would be an opportunity to do evil? What would Allah think of this?"

The dervish shook his head harder, then spoke slowly and evenly. "It is Allah, our lord, who blessed us with this. He did it so that we could bring Rumi back. It is his will."

"It was his will to kill all of those you had trying to get into The White by using the *daeva*?"

"It was his will to find Rumi. How he is found is based on our own limitations."

"Don't you think if Allah wanted Rumi he could get to him himself?"

The dervish paused and stared. Finally, he nodded. "Yes. We have discussed this."

"And?"

"Allah does not give directly. He wants his people to earn what they desire. To work hard for it."

"Your idea of earning what you desire is to kill all those thousands of people?"

"You will never understand."

Boy Scout nodded. "You're right. The problem with your methods is that you've stirred up the supernatural pot."

The dervish raised an eyebrow. "I don't know this pot."

"You sure as hell don't," Boy Scout said, his voice raising as he poked the dervish in the side of the face. "What you and yours did was to put me in a place over and over until entities came into me. This White was there long before you started mining it. You have no idea the beings that live in that place and now, because of you, I have one inside me just ready to take over. What do you think will happen if it takes me over?"

"It will burn you up inside," the dervish said flatly.

Boy Scout rocked back on his heels. "You know what this is, then."

"We do."

"What is it?"

"A dweller of Iram, lost to time."

"Where is Iram?" Boy Scout asked, wondering if it was a place he could go.

"Iram is a myth. The Quran speaks of it as a lost place that constantly moves."

"Who lives in Iram?" McQueen asked.

"Djinn. The Lost Tribe of Aad."

Boy Scout opened his mouth to ask a question, but the words wouldn't come out.

"Djinn as in magic, lives in a bottle and grants wishes?" McQueen asked.

"That is your Disney djinn. These are not those. These are giants who were able to do things no one thought possible."

"Giant djinn? Boss, are you hearing this?"

"I'm hearing it," Boy Scout managed. "And you want this Djinn of Aad."

Now it was the dervish who leaned forward, straining at his bonds. "Yes. We do. We can get him out of you. We can make it so that he does not harm you. Let us help you and all will be forgiven."

"You almost had me until that last bit. What's to forgive?" Boy Scout asked.

"For killing my people back in Afghanistan."

"For killing your people? What about mine?"

"You killed far more of us than we of you," the dervish countered.

"Only because we are much better at killing people. You need to remember that."

Boy Scout climbed into the front seat.

"Where to?"

"White Point Park. Take us around Rancho Palos Verdes."

"213 south of Lomita is closer," McQueen said.

"I know. I have my reasons."

"What are you going to do with me?" the dervish asked, swallowing at the end to keep his voice even.

Boy Scout frowned as he belted himself in. "I'm not sure yet. We'll just have to see."

McQueen pulled into traffic and headed down Hawthorne Avenue, up into the hills until they ran into Rancho Palos Verdes Drive.

Rancho Palos Verdes, or RPV as the locals called it, was the southern bookend to Malibu in the north. Like Malibu, RPV was a high-priced zip code. But unlike the cliff and beach side Malibu, RPV was hundreds of feet above the Pacific Ocean. Still heavily forested, the mountainous peninsula boasted large homes with astonishing views. One of the reasons Boy Scout decided to travel through the area was because there were enough choke points that he'd have to be blind to miss surveillance.

While McQueen drove, Boy Scout texted Preacher's Daughter.

BS: How's your day.

PD: Made a new best friend.

BS: Did you now. Good for you. She going to help out?

PD: I think she will.

BS: Need to make sure she's not playing you.

PD: Oh please. ;p How was yours?

BS: Ask Poe if there are any police reports about Del Amo Mall.

PD: What specifically?

BS: You'll know.

PD: Hold on.

Boy Scout placed the phone in his lap, leaned his head back, and closed his eyes. He was bone tired. His body wasn't used to so much action. Still, doing something was so much better than sitting in the darkness in the Hermit's Cabin. Thinking of his time at the monastery, he wondered how de Cherge and the men he'd wounded were faring. He wondered if knowing that the entity who'd done the damage was no more would raise their spirits.

The phone vibrated.

PD: Holy shit, what did you do? DHS has the

place surrounded and they think there's a terrorist bio hazard going on.

BS: A dervish danced in the food court.

PD: I bet that went well.

BS: Yeah. About two hundred people hit the ground.

PD: Then what?

BS: Tell you more later. Just want to make sure there's no APB for us.

PD: Poe says the internal CCTVs were inop for half an hour after the event and during the event.

BS: Wasn't us, was it?

PD: Poe says no. But there is a video of a dervish table dancing that went viral on Facebook. I'll send you the link.

Boy Scout waited less than a minute for the link to show. When it did, he clicked it and watched. Sure enough, someone had caught the beginning of the dance, before succumbing to it, the view from the image shifting downwards as the phone's owner passed out.

For a second he worried that he might succumb as well because he was no longer wearing the glasses. But after a few seconds he realized that there was no crossover. Good thing, too. Otherwise, the whole YouTube-watching universe would be passed out at their keyboards.

The rest of the video was noise and the view of

someone's chest. But Boy Scout had seen something that made him nervous. He went back to the start of the video and stopped it every second until he came to what he'd thought he'd glimpsed. And there, as the owner was almost on the ground, grinning like two idiots wearing Elton John glasses, was him and McQueen, plain as day. If someone was smart, they'd do biometric matching and find out who they were and then ask themselves why everyone else passed out but they didn't.

Fuck.

Chapter Twenty-One

Camp Pendleton Command Center

THEY LET THE dervish go near a bluff overlooking the Pacific. Boy Scout didn't want to bring him back to the camp. Not only might they have to explain kidnapping to the nice marines at the guard shack, but they didn't want to let the dervishes know their operating location. It was with a snarl and a curse that they pushed him out to roll on the grass, his white clothes wrapping about him. Then it was down South Pacific Avenue and over the Vincent Thomas Bridge, made famous because director Tony Scott chose it as the place to leap to his death.

Soon they were once more on the 405, then the 5, cruising in the HOV lane, heading back to Camp Pendleton. They arrived at their offices just after the prescribed time, only because McQueen insisted on stopping by Popeye's Chicken first.

"You might run a tight ship, boss, but when a guy's gotta eat, a guy's gotta eat," McQueen had said as he pulled into the BX parking lot.

With the aroma of freshly fried Louisiana-style chicken surrounding them, they entered the offices. Poe and Preacher's Daughter were sitting there, as was a third person. No one in the room looked particularly pleased, which was not the reception Popeye's fried chicken usually received.

McQueen had a leg in his mouth and a bucket and bags of sides in his hands. He lowered them onto the table, then leaned against a wall and concentrated on eating the chicken.

Boy Scout laid the tray of drinks down and gave Preacher's Daughter a look.

She rolled her eyes slightly but said nothing more.

"What's going on, Lieutenant?" he asked.

"This is Special Agent Joe Ripple of the FBI. Looks like we bumped into an ongoing investigation."

The new man was an African-American with a plain face, a scar on his lower lip, and blue eyes. His hair was cut tight against his head and he wore a dark gray suit with a black tie and white shirt. Black Florsheims hugged his feet. Boy Scout could see the slight bulge of his shoulder rig under his jacket.

"When you say *bumping into,* what is it you mean?"

The suit stood and flashed his badge. Normal people would offer to shake hands but FBI special agents weren't normal people. "Special Agent Ripple," he said, his words clipped and officious. "And you are?"

"You can call me Boy Scout."

"Another one. This one over here," he said, thumbing towards Preacher's Daughter, "says her name is Preacher's Daughter."

"That's right," Boy Scout said.

"Let me see some ID," the agent said.

"Don't have any."

This made the agent pause.

"And you there," he said to McQueen. "What's your name?"

"Man Eating Chicken."

The suit turned to Poe. "Lieutenant, I thought you said you'd all be cooperative."

Poe glanced at Boy Scout and McQueen, his face impassive. "These three are UC," he said, using the law enforcement jargon for under cover. "You can understand why they don't want to break role. Now that everyone is here, let's iron this out."

The FBI agent sighed dramatically. He walked to the other side of the room so that everyone would be in front of him.

"The reason we're here is because of Ms. Francis Fernandez."

"Nice lady," Preacher's Daughter said. "What about her?"

"She's been in our sights for over a year," Ripple said. "I understand you had a meeting with her."

Boy Scout nodded slightly towards Preacher's Daughter, who was watching him.

She shifted in her seat and said, "You know we did. I saw your surveillance van and clocked the other guy on the corner. You probably already have her phones wired."

Ripple frowned. "We do. As soon as you contacted her we wanted to find out why."

"Why didn't you just ask?" Boy Scout asked.

"I didn't want to divulge that she was under investigation."

"And now here we are," Boy Scout said. "What do you have on her?"

"I don't want to divulge the nature of our investigation, I just need to tell you to back off."

Boy Scout raised an eyebrow. "Back off? You say it like you can do something about it."

Ripple paused and leaned back slightly, hands on hips, appraising Boy Scout.

Boy Scout took advantage of the pause and said, "This is a military operation governed by Title 50. Not your jurisdiction."

Ripple laughed. "Everything is my jurisdiction. I'm with the FBI."

"Not on a military base," Preacher's Daughter said. "On this one it's NCIS."

Poe shook his head. "Nice try. This is a presidentially mandated mission in support of the Global War on Terrorism. Special Unit 77 is a special military unit that operates at the behest of the president. Only he can tell us to *back off*. If you want to give him a call, I can Google *the White House operator* for you."

McQueen waved the remains of his chicken leg in the air. "Make sure you Google the .gov address because the .com address is a porn site." He laughed to himself. "Found that out the hard way."

Everyone stared at the FBI special agent until he finally spoke.

"Maybe I got off on the wrong foot."

"Ya think?" Preacher's Daughter said.

Ripple gave her an angry glance. "We have the opportunity to work with Ms. Fernandez on an ongoing investigation into smuggling operations being conducted by diplomatic personnel associated with the Turkish consulate."

Ripple stared at Boy Scout as if his words had the magical quality of changing the man's mind. Then he added, "These smuggling operations could include weaponry, bomb-making materials, or worse."

Ripple waited once more.

When no one seemed to be speaking, it was McQueen who opted into the conversation.

"You see what happened, boss," said McQueen, tossing the dead drumstick in the trashcan, "the special agent here has been thinking about using her as his own action agent for some time now. The problem is that he waited too long and we came along and probably offered her the deal that he was going to offer. Now he wants us to unoffer the deal so he can offer it and she'll then be beholden to him. Did I get that about right, Special Agent Ripple?"

Ripple gave him dead eyes. "Our investigation is ongoing."

"If there was an investigation, then there was a charge or an indictment pending, right?" Preacher's Daughter asked.

Ripple merely stared at her.

"Otherwise, what you were conducting was a fishing expedition, hoping you might find something to use as leverage. My guess is paying all of her bills wasn't in your budget."

Boy Scout walked over to the chicken bucket and dug out a wing. "But it is in ours." He took a bite of chicken. "I'll tell you what. We might be able to work together. Our two missions might just dovetail."

Ripple sat down in his chair.

"Want some chicken?" Boy Scout asked, offering the box.

Ripple glanced at the box, began to shake his head, then grinned. "Sure. Why not?"

They all ate in silence for the next ten minutes. Poe, Preacher's Daughter, Boy Scout, McQueen and Special Agent Ripple paid attention to their chicken, their eating broken intermittently with the slurp of soda through a straw. When there was nothing left but bones, McQueen boxed everything up and threw it away. Meanwhile, Preacher's Daughter passed out hand wipes.

When everything was cleared except for the drinks, Boy Scout leaned over the table.

"When did you go to Quantico?" he asked.

"Summer of '99," Ripple said.

"Were you in the service first?"

"USMC for four years. Then college."

"Desert Storm?"

"Mortar man. Company K, 1st Battalion, 25th Marines."

McQueen whistled. "Bet you made the Iraqis' life a living hell."

"And you?" Ripple asked.

"I was a Ranger. McQueen over there was Special Forces."

"And the lady?"

"The lady can speak for herself," Preacher's

Daughter said. "I was intel. Mainly because the other options weren't open to me."

"Rangers take girls now," Ripple said.

"You mean women." She smiled tightly. "I did my time."

Everyone was silent for a moment. Memories of serving ran through Boy Scout's mind. Jungle trails in Thailand. Burning oil fields in Desert Storm. Clearing buildings in Mogadishu. Hiking a goat path in the Hindu Kush. Moments like these when military folks got together to compare their backgrounds always brought back memories. He glanced at the others, Ripple included, who were staring off into space, probably mired in some military memory, good or bad.

"And now it's Special Unit 77," Ripple finally said, getting up. "We definitely got off on the wrong foot. Listen." He took out a business card and offering it to Boy Scout. "Please, call me."

Everyone else stood as well.

Boy Scout offered a smile and a half salute. "Will do, jarhead."

Ripple paused, then nodded his head and walked out the door.

After about ten seconds, Poe let out a breath as if he'd been holding it the entire time.

"You all should take your show on the road," he said.

Preacher's Daughter glanced at him. "What do you think we're doing?"

"You ran him through the ringer and I don't think he even realized it."

"If he doesn't now, he will once he thinks back on it," Boy Scout said. "The FBI might be officious and prone to following the rules, but they're not stupid."

"What do you think is going to happen now?" McQueen asked.

"I think we're going to be able to see what was in that box." Boy Scout turned to Preacher's Daughter. "But that's for later. Right now, I need your help."

"With what?" she asked.

"Some religious stuff. Specifically, what do you know about the members of the Lost Tribe of Aad?"

Her face went still. "Why do you want to know about them?"

"Because I think I have one inside me."

She sat down hard, speechless.

But she was never speechless, which immediately made Boy Scout more worried than he had been. In fact, he hadn't been worried at all. But now...

Now he was flat on scared.

Chapter Twenty-Two

Camp Pendleton Command Center

MᴄQᴜᴇᴇɴ ᴡᴇɴᴛ ᴛᴏ work out and Poe said he had to check in, whatever that meant, leaving Boy Scout and Preacher's Daughter alone in the room. She sat and listened as Boy Scout told her about his conversation with the dervish, as well as the brief but powerful connection he'd had with the entity inside of him and how he'd seen giants in the vision. He explained his astral travel with Sister Renee and how he'd almost died because he neither had been prepared, nor had he paid attention.

When he was finally done, he sat, out of breath and just dead tired. Before she could speak, he added, "The worst of it is that I'm terrified of the thing inside of me. I feel like it could take me over at any moment. It's like I'm walking around constantly ducking because I know it's going to happen at any moment. We've all had our share of PTSD, but this is probably the worst I've ever felt—worse than dying, because this thing would become me."

"Loss of self is always worse than loss of life. When you told me what Sister Renee went through, I couldn't help wonder how horrible it must have been to have someone in control of your own body, with you just as passenger. When it took control of you before, I couldn't even tell it wasn't you."

"And I didn't even know it." He laughed soberly. "It's like I need a safe word."

"Rumpelstiltskin."

"Right. Like that would even work." She gave him a half smile.

"So," he said, the word long and breathless. "What about that lost tribe?"

"Have you ever heard of Iram of the Pillars?" she asked.

He shook his head. "Not before this."

"What about Sodom and Gomorrah?"

"I've heard of that."

"I figured. So, we have the Old Testament Christian Bible and we have the Qur'an. They are more similar than most people know. For instance, did you know that Jesus is mentioned more in the Qur'an than Mohammed? And Mary is mentioned more times in the Qur'an than in the New Testament."

Boy Scout shook his head.

"The Qur'an includes most of the prophets in the Bible—Adam, Enoch, Noah, Abraham, Lot, Ishmael, Isaac, Jacob, Joseph, Job, David, Solomon, Elijah, Jonah, Aaron, Moses, Zechariah, and John the Baptist. Jesus is spoken of as a prophet of God and not the son of God. What I'm getting at is there are a lot of the same stories, but told differently. Such is the case with Iram of the Pillars and Sodom and Gomorrah. Both were cities with sinners who wouldn't follow the word of God, and both places were smited—uh smoted, smitten, whatever—by an angry god."

She held up a finger and took a deep draw from her drink.

"But that's the Sunday school story. Palimpsested beneath these tales is an older one that many Biblical and Qur'anical scholars won't touch. How good are you on your Bible teachings?"

"Uh, *do unto others as you would have them do unto you.*"

"The Golden Rule. Not bad. What about Genesis?"

"*In the beginning there was light?*"

"Nice try. *In the beginning God created the Heaven and the Earth.* This seems simple but is significant. We believe that God lives in Heaven. That's why everyone looks forward to it when they die so that they can finally see God. So riddle me this, Batman: how did God create the place where He lived unless He came from somewhere else? He had to come from somewhere, and if He'd just finished creating Heaven, where was that somewhere?"

Boy Scout raised an eyebrow.

"But let's say he created those. That's Genesis 1:1. Let's skip to Genesis 1:27, where it says *So God created man in his own image, in the image of God created he him; male and female created he them.* This shows that we man and woman were created by God and in his image. But we are not the sons of God. He had his sons already around. We can prove that by skipping ahead to Genesis 6, verse 1-5."

She closed her eyes and recited, "*When man began to multiply on the face of the land and daughters were born to them, the sons of God saw that the daughters of man were attractive. And they took as their wives any they chose. Then the Lord said, 'My Spirit shall not abide in man forever, for he is flesh: his days shall be 120 years.' There were giants in the earth in those days; and also after that, when the sons of God came in unto the daughters of men, and they bare children to them, the same became mighty men which were of old, men of renown. The Lord saw that the wickedness of man was great in the earth, and that every intention of the thoughts of his heart was only evil continually."*

She held up a finger, "But wait, there's more. This is the moment when God decided to trash everything. This is what leads up to Noah. *And it repented the LORD that he had made man on the earth, and it grieved him. And the LORD said, I will destroy man whom I have created from the face of the earth; both man, and beast, and the creeping thing, and the fowls of the air; for it repenteth me that I have made them.* Why do you think that God, after all the trouble he went through to make everything, suddenly decided to kill everything?"

"Because the sons of God had children with the daughters of man?"

She touched her nose with a finger. "Bingo. Boy Scout gets the prize. Let's unpack that. God created man and woman but there were already beings that were created by him before the start of the Bible. This means that they did come from another place."

"Like aliens?"

"Shush that nonsense. We only know of four dimensions. Quantum scientists posit that there might be up to eleven. Topology mathematicians have a unifying theory that deals with the concepts of the shape of things. Bottom line is that we don't know shit about our universe. What everyone overlooks in the Bible is the sensation of there being sons of God already there and that these sons of God were able to create giants through their mating with daughters of man."

"What does that have to do with the Pillars of Iram and the Lost Tribe of Aad?"

"The Lost Tribe of Aad are the giants. The Pillars of Iram are where they were supposed to have lived until God got rid of them. Except the Bible never talks about it. If it did, it would highlight the fact that God came from somewhere else and brought his own sons with him. So they did a whole bunch of hand waving and had the animals came two by two nonsense and then Noah and the entire Earth was covered in water, et cetera, et cetera, et cetera. I'm afraid you can't have it both ways."

"How come this isn't public knowledge?" he asked.

"Oh, it is. But no one really cares. They say it's all conspiracy theories. There are plenty of sub-Reddits about this. 4Chan has rooms where people get together, but no one dares talk about it in public. I knew a guy once who wanted to publish an academic paper about this while he was in seminary and all but got kicked out for even trying. In the end, he threw away all of his work, but not before I read it." She laughed. "I mean, it's so ridiculous. People think it's okay to believe the Earth was created in six days by a supreme being, but it's not okay to ask where that supreme being came from *before* he created the Heaven and Earth."

"And all this time I thought you were Christian."

She placed a hand to her chest as her eyes widened. "I *am* Christian. I believe in Jesus. But I also believe in giants and other things in the Bible that mainstream Christians would have you ignore." She took another drink as she shook her head, a few strands of hair falling free of her pony tail. "Now there are those who claim to have found the Iram in modern Yemen, but the jury is still out on that. I'll get behind it when I see better evidence than I've seen on the web."

"So then who do you posit are the sons of God?" he asked.

She nodded. "That's the million-dollar question, isn't it? Do you remember what the *daeva* told you?"

Boy Scout remembered it very well. For a reason he still couldn't understand, he'd reached out and cupped the *daeva*'s cheek, the same way he used to do with McQueen, and had been immediately transferred to a street in Saigon where a monk had just set himself on fire. Boy Scout smelled the burning skin mixed with car exhaust, a man's body odor, and a curry dish being made on the street in an immense metal wok. The fire sparked, whipped, and roared in a voice of its own. A car honked. A woman screamed. Flashes from cameras lit the scene. The monk burned before him, stoic and unmoving, staring at Boy Scout with all the volition of an angry god. But he had been only the mechanism. It was the *daeva* who was speaking.

"Why is it you kill us?" it asked.

"Why is it you kill us*?" Boy Scout asked in turn.*

"You are with the others. You use us—torture us with your dreams. Like this thing. How could you do this to yourselves?"

"It's my understanding that he did it in protest... something political."

The burning monk grinned. "He did this and you don't even know the reason why."

"This was not from my time. This was from before."

"And still you fail to learn from history."

"What are you really?" Boy Scout asked. "What made you?"

"The better question is who made you. We looked away, then looked back, and there you were... shadows upon this world bathed in the

light of creation. And like shadows, you bring darkness wherever you go."

"Shadows upon this world bathed in the light of creation," he muttered, giving voice to the memory.

"What if the *daeva*s were the sons of God?" Preacher's Daughter asked. "This makes a certain sense. Both Islam and Christianity take many of their stories from Zoroastrian religion, which is thought to be one of the oldest organized religion. These *daeva* are creatures of Zoroaster, according to Faood."

Boy Scout said, "I saw him, you know. At the mall. He was with the dervishes who came for me."

"Faood was there? What did he say?"

"He said he was there to help me. It's funny, there was a part of me that wanted to believe him."

"What you have inside of you is dangerous. Maybe he wants to take it."

"But is that the best decision? Will they weaponize it? What will they do with it? I feel like this decision is the most important I've ever made and I don't want to fuck it up."

"I'm with you. I'm just worried about you."

"Me as well. So, what to do? If what we're speculating is correct, I have the consciousness of one of the giants—a son of God—inside of me and he wants it back."

She twisted her mouth and cradled her chin with her hands. "Has anyone considered what the entity wants?"

"It's not as if I can just go and ask it."

She tilted her head. "Why not?"

Chapter Twenty-Three

Camp Pendleton Command Center

WHEN POE CAME back later, Boy Scout pulled him aside. They found a room with a desk and two chairs. Boy Scout gestured for Poe to take the place behind the desk. Boy Scout sat in front of it.

Poe wore an eager, amused expression. He still wore his uniform with starched creases that looked like they could cut.

Boy Scout had always associated a starched uniform with FOBBITs, those who never left the forward operating base. It was the sort of gear admin folks would wear, rather than the grunged-up, digicamed ACU. But with Poe, he wasn't sure. The man kept everything very close to his chest. He hoped that was about to change.

"I wanted to thank you for all the help you've

provided," Boy Scout said.

"We have similar interests, you and I," Poe said.

"I gotta wonder, though, how much of your assistance is really oversight?" Boy Scout asked, laying out the question most on his mind.

Poe sat back and smiled. "A lot of it. I had to submit a report with recommendations before I could even begin to help you."

"Who'd the report go to?"

Poe hesitated, then said, "An office inside the Pentagon that reports to a subcommittee of the House Armed Services Committee. That's about all I can say."

"So an elected congressman or woman who was selling real estate last year has access to information about supernatural events?" Boy Scout asked. "That doesn't seem like good OPSEC."

Poe shrugged. "The military has civilian oversight. You know that. It's how it works. Still, from what I hear after asking the same question, those selected for this subcommittee have additional vetting and the Pentagon put triggers in place that would ensure the information not be disclosed in the event of a leak or someone trying to monetize the information."

"Triggers. I can imagine what they could be."

"Yep. And the members of the subcommittee are fully aware of them."

Boy Scout paused before he asked his next question. "How much support are you able to provide?"

"We've already provided a lot. More than you know. Your glasses, for instance. We gave McQueen the idea on Reddit. We planted enough Boolean search words to ensure that he was destined to run across it."

"I won't tell him that. He was proud of the discovery and thought it might be his own idea. What else?"

"A lot of more subtle things. That's really our specialty. Subtlety."

"No direct confrontation?" Boy Scout asked.

"Not if we can help it. That's why I could provide a military unit as backup or as a distraction, but not for direct action against an objective."

Boy Scout scratched his chin, realizing he needed to shave. "You're not just a lieutenant, are you?"

Poe kept his mouth set, but his eyes smiled. "I am what I need to be. No one tends to bother a lieutenant. After all, lieutenants don't know anything and can't really do anything."

"Hiding in plain sight."

Poe just stared back, the answer as obvious between them as a five-hundred-pound gorilla. If Boy Scout had to guess by his age, if Poe was truly in the military, he was at least a major—if not a full-blown colonel. His respect for the man soared, and he couldn't help realize it had been muffled for the very reasons Poe had stated.

"Are you really in the army?"

"Yes."

"Well, there is that, at least." Then he asked, "What do you think about Special Agent Ripple?"

"I think it's an opportunity," Poe admitted. "If you let the FBI take the lead, your part of the mission would be invisible."

"Sounds like oversight."

"You asked me the question. I gave you the answer."

"We could use them as direct action just so we could get inside and see if there's really a *daeva* in the box."

Poe shook his head slightly. "It's a touchy thing. All consulates are considered sacrosanct and off limits. The last thing we want happening is for that to change. After all, what we do to them, they could do to us. I mean, I still think it's possible. We just have to have a locked tight mission plan."

"How do you imagine his plan taking shape?" Boy Scout asked.

"That's a tough one. Fast, in and out, under cover of night. Or if not directly, then perhaps a ruse such as a biochem spill or a terrorist threat where it necessitates the FBI or the CDC entering and providing them support." When Poe had said CDC, he'd made air quotes. "But let me ask you this: if it turns out to be a *daeva*, it's not like you can just walk out with it. What's your plan when you find it?"

Boy Scout realized he'd been leaning forward in his seat, and now he sat back heavily. "That's the million-dollar question, isn't it? I have this thing inside of me that appears scared of the *daeva*. I'm not sure what it will do if I go near a *daeva*. Will it take control? Will it do something to me? I don't know. I just remember that the *daeva* was the key to getting into The White, and it's the only way I know to get there."

"Didn't it take a long time to get into it? Six months, during which you thought you were actually living in Los Angeles?"

Boy Scout sighed. "Yes. That is an issue. But when I went back into the fugue, I was able to re-enter The White easily."

"But not always. Remember the car chase when Narco shot Sufi Sam and took off?"

Boy Scout eyed Poe suspiciously.

"Preacher's Daughter told me. I'd asked for some details."

"Yes. That was when I thought I was shot and dying."

"But it never happened. You were in a fugue state."

The sound of a bleating sheep cracked through his mind. He blinked as a memory enveloped him.

By the look of the bodies, Narco hadn't even slowed down. He'd plowed right through a herd of sheep that had been blocking the narrow track to the cistern. At first, there were just dead bodies, but soon they could see sheep with wounded legs. One looked as if its spine had been crushed, but it was still alive, bleating weakly.

If the complete disregard for the animals were indicative of the inhuman creature that had its talons in Narco, then they were truly up against a being that lacked any shred of human empathy. For as much as Boy Scout wanted to get to Narco and save him, he wouldn't disregard the sanctity of life unless the lives of his team were at risk. So Boy Scout had to slow the Land Cruiser to a crawl at times, just so they could weave their way through the minefield of dead and dying animals.

A scrub bush held the bodies of six mutilated sheep in various positions. Boy Scout's eyes fixed on the ignoble slaughter and he slowed to a complete stop as he tried to make sense of it. He couldn't breathe. He felt a tightness in his chest. The scene was alarming and he realized that the reason it affected him was because it was so reminiscent of a notable passage from Blood Meridian by Cormac McCarthy. 'By and by they came upon a bush that was hung with dead babies. These small victims, seven, eight of them, had holes punched in their underjaws and were hung by their throats from the broken stobs of a mesquite to stare eyeless at the naked sky.' *Although these Afghan sheep were far from the babies killed by the Comanche war party in the book, there was an equity of the tragic, a validation of innocence. The murder of the lambs and sheep were no less recreant than those of the babies.*

He inhaled as the image faded. His hand went to his chest where he'd been shot soon after, but there was no wound because it had all been in his mind.

He breathed through his nose for a moment, ignoring the look of concern on Poe's face. "Historically, does Seventy-Seven have any insight into the *daeva*?" he asked, remembering the conversation he'd just had with Preacher's Daughter.

Poe shook his head, his expression not dissipating. "Not really. That area has been a black hole to us. Our mandate has always been to protect the homeland. We've been known to project forward when we need to, but those missions are infrequent at best." He raised a finger. "That said, we did get a load of data from the Black Dragoons. I've made it all available to Preacher's Daughter. She's been sifting through it."

"If there's something to find, she's the one."

"One smart soldier, that's true."

Boy Scout detected more than admiration in the comment, but left it alone.

"Here's my issue. I want to get this thing out of me, but I'm concerned for its existence. As strange as that seems, I'm filled with the need to ensure it survives."

Poe's face hardened. "Do you think this influence comes from the entity itself?"

Boy Scout hadn't thought of that, but it made sense. After all, he was sure that it didn't want to die. Was he being influenced? A creepiness filled him as he realized that his actions might be influenced by the thing inside of him. He couldn't help believe that Sister Renee might have some input. He didn't want his actions influenced like they had from the move to Pendleton. If they were, he couldn't be a leader to anyone. Everything he did might be suspect, unless he did the opposite of what he believed in. If that were the case, his instincts—which had been honed after more than twenty years of military service—were suddenly useless. Which meant *he* was useless and nothing more than a font to contain the conscience of an entity that once might have been a giant—a giant that had just sent him a message in the memory of chasing Narco in the fugue.

They were truly up against a being that lacked any shred of human empathy.

Then the obvious question was: did the giant have human empathy? As a son of God who had loved the daughters of man, could it be reasoned with? Did it try and send him a message? Or was it all in his mind? Hope suddenly colored his worry.

He stood. "Thanks, Poe. I think I need to make a phone call. I might have a way of helping myself."

Poe nodded and Boy Scout was out the door.

Chapter Twenty-Four

Astral Plane

BOY SCOUT CALLED Sister Renee and asked her for another meeting in the astral plane. He thought she sounded strange on the telephone, almost like she was drunk. Several times she slurred her words, but she agreed to join him. He was so eager to see her that it took him more than forty-five minutes to slow his breathing and clear his thoughts enough to unlock his chakras and pop forth into the astral plane.

The first thing he noticed was the dark sun. The second was the entity. Each seemed to be the antithesis of each other, yet each represented an unrelenting danger. He'd been told not to allow the gravitational pull of the dark sun to draw him in. For a brief moment, when the Berber had almost killed him, it had. Boy Scout wondered what was on the other side. Was it truly a dark sun, or was it a black hole, pulsing as it drew everything in, a gateway to yet an even different dimension?

Then there was the entity, now twice the size it had been, as if it was showing off that it had become a giant. It glowed, pulsing as though with each inward breath it became lighter, then darker on the exhale. But that couldn't be right. One didn't breathe in the astral plane, they just *were*. What would happen if he touched it? Would he learn everything he wanted to know, or would it suck him in, eating him from the inside out as he'd done the boy? Or would it be both?

Yes, each one represented an irrevocable future, and it was his fear that he'd be forced to choose.

"Where were you?" Sister Renee asked.

He turned and saw her aspect, noting that it wasn't as clear as it should have been. It seemed as though he was seeing her through frosted glass.

"It took me time to get into the right mode," he said. "Are you okay?"

"I've had better days." Then she asked him, "Does it ever get any better?"

"Does what get better?"

"The killing. You've killed so many and I wonder how you deal with it."

He flashed to the Afghan colonel with the garrote around his neck.

"I see the person I killed every day," she continued. "Sometimes she's sitting on the couch next to me. Sometimes she's standing at the window of a restaurant staring at me from the outside. Sometimes I don't see her but I know she's there."

"Wait—what killing? What are you talking about?"

"There are things I haven't told you. Things Kamaris made me do before he took complete control."

"What things?"

"It was like he was trying to dehumanize me—to tenderize me, to make it easier."

"What did he make you do?"

"I killed a cat."

"You killed a—what are we talking about? Sister Renee, are you okay?"

"One moment I was petting it while sitting on a bench on one side of the yard, the next I was holding it underwater in a bird bath. I didn't even remember moving, yet there I was, holding it under as it clawed at me."

Boy Scout was unprepared to help her. He'd been so keen on getting help from her that he hadn't even considered she might be in trouble. The slurring of her words. He wondered if she was self-medicating.

"But that wasn't you. It was Kimaris. It was the demon who took control."

"Then there was the old woman."

"You killed an old woman?"

"We were standing on a train platform, her and me, in Istanbul. I had an intense hate for her when I saw her. The slowness of her movements, the crookedness of her body, the smell of her as if she were already dead. We were waiting for the train and she'd just looked at me and gave me a toothless crone smile. When the train came, I pushed her off the platform."

She pushed a woman in front of a train.

"What makes it different is that I remember doing everything. I remember hating her. I remember wanting her to go away. I remember pushing her. Before, when Kimaris took me over, I never knew what was going on. So, tell me, was it me, or was it the demon? Am I an evil person at heart? Is that why it took me over? Why it chose me?"

"What did Father Emmett say?"

"I never told him."

She never told him. He wondered if that would have made a difference in Father Emmett being taken over. He wondered if the demon had made Father Emmett kill something or someone.

"All this doubt is what it wanted," he said. "It wanted you to think it was you. I think you were right. I think that demon was beating down your spirit, making it easier to take you over, to get its hooks into you."

Her aspect looked like she was praying, but through a frosted window.

"There's a fantasy author and military historian named Myke Cole who wrote an essay about PTSD. He says it's like the weather. Anyone can experience it anytime, anywhere. Like the soccer mom going to pick up her kids from practice, and she sees a dog get hit and killed by a car. It might not affect her at all, or she might not be able to drive down that road again. She didn't do a thing, just witnessed. But now her mind has problems filing it away, so it leaves the experience front and center."

"Like the weather, huh? Then I'm a fucking tornado."

The curse startled him, but he continued. "The idea is to find ways to deal with what you've seen."

"What do you do to keep sane? How do you keep from slitting your wrists?"

Worry grew. "Sister Renee?"

If anything, her image was even more blurred as if she were being erased.

"Sister Renee, what did you do?"

"I made the woman go away."

"I'm going to call de Cherge."

"It's too late."

"What did you do?"

"What I should have done a long time ago."

"What about the church? What about Heaven?

If you killed yourself—"

"What about Heaven? What is it? Is it what's on the other side of the dark sun? Is the astral plane purgatory? I thought about this for a long time, and then you came along."

"Me?"

"Yes, you. A simpering giant of a man who can't deal with the fact that he has *travelers*."

He bristled at the comment, but let it slide in the face of what he was discovering. "I think I have one of the sons of God inside of me."

Her aspect looked up. "I knew it was something powerful—something substantial."

"Then why did you kill yourself? Or are you—"

"Oh no, I am very dead. Split my veins from stem to stern, as they say."

"Then why?"

"I can't help you from where I was, but I can help you here."

She'd sacrificed herself for him? "But the dark sun," he said. "Without the cord it will draw you to it."

"For the last bit, I will need you to help."

He wanted to go back in time to the meditation grotto. He wanted to never have spoken to her. If she hadn't known his plight, she never would have done whatever terrible thing she did. Still, he asked, "What is it you want me to do?"

"Take me to the entity."

"And then what?"

"I will touch it. I will merge with it."

"You're going to what?" he asked.

"I saw what you needed. I saw what I needed. I made a choice. Should I continue living life as a victim, or could I die and become a champion? I survived Kamaris, so there was no way a human entity could deceive or even conquer me."

"What's to keep you from wanting to take me over? What's to keep you from wanting to live my life?"

"My sense of right and wrong."

"What's to keep it from consuming you?"

"The power of the Lord that flows through me."

"But what if you're wrong?"

"Then the pain will still be gone. Now take me." She reached out and touched his essence. Boy Scout felt the deadness of her, like a static-filled leech. The sliminess of the blood made him want to vomit. But beneath it all was a hatred so powerful it seemed like it could jump-start a star.

Chapter Twenty-Five

Astral Plane

So much passed to him from her.

The woman she'd pushed off the platform, turning and grinning.

The cat in her hands, ragged and dripping.

Looking in a mirror, madness in her eyes as she stayed locked inside of herself. Kimaris in charge, his grin on her face like the final lick on an envelope before it's sent away.

A straight razor cutting narrow marks over and over, counting the days, providing a scorecard for all to see that the demon was winning.

But it was like Kamaris knew it was going to leave. Why count the days unless there would come a day when it was no longer be necessary to count? The thought struck him like a starburst in a rocket shower—one spark of wonder amidst a fireworks show of information. And then he felt her impetus.

He moved towards the entity and she moved with him. Where before her aspect had been that of a figure seen through the fog, now it was as if she'd been scribbled in by a mad child. She was coming apart. He felt the need to hurry, and in that need he moved too close.

As he approached, the entity reached out and grabbed her. And, of course, it knew what she planned. It was inside of him and probably saw everything he did. It had probably been waiting. Probably luxuriating in the idea of a new essence with which to merge. For one brief moment, Boy Scout saw the image of an Englishman wearing something out of a Kipling novel, his pudgy face sporting a mustache that all but hid his mouth, eyes encircled by round glasses.

Two words echoed through the connection, *Oh my*, and then he was gone.

Boy Scout tried to pull back, but was caught in the connective current.

Sister Renee's aspect began to unravel as the scribbled lines of her took on a life of their own. But there was a control afoot and as they unraveled, they moved around the entity as if to bind it. Strings of her essence wrapped around the entity until it was almost hidden beneath the strands that were Sister Renee.

"Now this is different," she finally said.

"What is? What's going on?" Boy Scout demanded, unwilling and unable to remove his connection to her—to it.

"I didn't know what to expect. I thought it might be darkness, but it's not. It's pure light."

A thought worried through him. "What do you mean, pure light? Is it all white?" he asked hurriedly. "Is everything white?"

"The floor, the ceiling, the universe, everything."

"You've found the *Sefid*," he said. But how?

"Is this The White you told me about?" she asked.

"Yes. Somehow you found it. I thought only the *daeva* could, but that actually makes sense. If they created this thing, then maybe that's another avenue to The White—a dimension separate from our own that only they have continuous contact with."

"It's as if... Wait, is that darkness up ahead?" Wonder slid to worry. "What is that? Is that the sound of a monkey?"

Boy Scout remembered when he'd first encountered the creature in The White. He'd been able to escape it because it he'd had time to form.

"Hurry, Sister. Imagine your body forming beneath you. You need to run. You need to get away."

The mating call of a monkey came from somewhere behind him.

The memory of spinning towards the sound. He'd been so dizzy he might have fallen, only there was no ground. He was now upside down in front of the nightmare creature running towards him. In the split second he took to take it in, he saw a giant spider with more than a hundred legs coming toward him. Instead of central eyes, it had a face that was constantly changing into everyone he'd ever known.

Again came that sound of a monkey, impossibly loud, echoing, emanating from the lips of his mother's best friend, Rebecca. Then from the mouth of his drill sergeant, Sergeant First Class Reddoor. Then from the mouth of a girl he'd dated three years ago, Connie. The same sound, but different faces.

"I can't," she said. "Oh, Boy Scout. What have I done? It's her face. It's the woman I killed. Why is she making monkey noises? What is her face doing on this giant—?"

Then nothing.

He checked his connection, but he was still holding onto their comingled essences.

"Sister Renee?" He tried again. "Sister Renee?"

Not knowing what happened to her, his mind went to what he knew best—what the creature had done to Boy Scout and how it had played the memory, in vivid high definition, of when the world exploded inside The White and the entities had entered into him.

The mating call of a monkey came once again, but this time much softer. Then another and another. There seemed to be dozens of monkeys. Then he saw them. The spider creature had blown to bits as well, but instead of reforming into a whole, it was now hundreds of smaller spiders, all rushing towards him. He'd barely started to reform his own body when three of them crawled up his essence. He batted at them, but he only had a single hand. He struck one and it flew off, shattering into even smaller spider monsters that came back at him. One got onto his back and he tried to reach for it. That was the moment when one skittered onto his face and climbed down his throat.

He gagged, trying to rid himself of it. He could feel its greasy spider legs, pulling itself deeper inside of him.

Then another spider entered his mouth, following the first.

He fell to his knees, back arching in dry heaves, trying to spew them from his system. But it was to no avail. They held to his insides, going deeper, clawing at his insides for purchase. Then everything switched. Gone was the pure white of Sefid. *Boy Scout felt himself slow and his body become someone else's... something else. Something ancient.*

Was this what was happening to Sister Renee? How could it? She didn't have a mind or a body.

"Boy Scout," came the words as if they were trying to free themselves from the bottom of a well.

"Yes. Sister Renee. I'm here. What's wrong?"

"I was so wrong."

"How were you wrong? What's happened?"

"Oh, Boy Scout," she said. The words seemed to come from far away. "This thing—this—"

He waited for more, but she'd stopped mid-sentence. "What is it?"

Then she was there, and shouting, her voice a universe made of noise.

"BOY SCOUT. GET THIS OUT OF YOU. THIS IS FAR WORSE THAN ANY DEMONS. THIS IS THE FATHER OF DEMONS AND IT WANTS YOU BACK."

Then silence.

Boy Scout tried to pull away, but his astral arm wouldn't move. He tried again, pulling and heaving, but the more he tried, the more held fast he became. He was desperate to figure out a way to keep himself from being consumed. Gone were the wrappings of Sister Renee. Any vestige of her was no more and the entity burned brightly from within like Boy Scout had when he had consumed the boy.

Boy Scout didn't want to be next.

He didn't want to be this thing's meal.

It was then that he knew exactly what he had to do.

He imagined himself falling backwards off the ramp of a C140 at 30,000 feet. Down, down, down, he tumbled, until he felt himself slam into something solid with enough force to shatter himself into a million pieces.

Chapter Twenty-Six

Camp Pendleton Command Center

"WHAT'S THE SAFE word?"

He opened his eyes and tried to sit up, but realized that his right arm was dead—paralyzed.

"No no no no!" This time he managed to sit up, and he brought his left hand to his head and began knocking on his skull. "Let her go, damn you! Let her go!"

"Boy Scout, is that you?" Preacher's Daughter asked. "What's the safe word?"

"No—you've got to save her. You've got to—"

McQueen grabbed Boy Scout's hand and held it so he couldn't keep hurting himself.

Preacher's Daughter knelt in front of him. "Boy Scout, is that you? What's wrong with your arm?"

His gaze sharpened and he finally realized where

he was. He hyperventilated for a moment, then sighed. "Sister Renee is gone."

Lore glanced at McQueen. "I know. De Cherge called."

"Boss, what's wrong with your arm?" McQueen asked.

"I have no—I think the entity hurt it." He shrugged his shoulder and the arm flopped like a dead fish. He looked up at his two team mates. "She tried to save me, but she couldn't," he said. "She—she—I think the thing inside of me *ate* her."

"Then she's inside of you?" McQueen looked from Lore to Boy Scout. "I don't get it."

"Help me up," Boy Scout asked.

McQueen stood and hauled Boy Scout to his feet.

"I don't know if I do either, but I need to make a call."

"Who you gonna call?" McQueen asked.

"Ghostbusters," said Preacher's Daughter.

Boy Scout shook his head. "Not funny. I'm calling Faood. I think he's the only one who can possibly help."

"Why him?" she demanded. "I'm not forgetting he tricked us. Bully, Narco, Criminal. He killed them."

"He didn't kill them. Is he responsible? Fuck, yes. But he didn't kill them. The machine killed them." He stumbled.

"There is no machine, boss." McQueen held his

hand out to steady Boy Scout.

"The machine. The fucking machine. The mechanism that the dervishes have created that taps into things they shouldn't even be fucking dealing with."

"A virtual machine, McQueen," Preacher's Daughter said. To Boy Scout she asked, "What is it you think Faood can do?"

"Blow it up. Or if not him, tell me how to do it. But first, I need to call him." He sighed and hung his head. "I need to clean up. If you don't mind, maybe you can leave me alone."

"Not until you tell me the safe word," Preacher's Daughter said.

"We never agreed on a safe word," he said, not looking up, his mind already on the problem.

She paused. "That's true, but I recommended one to you. Do you remember?"

He said nothing, just stared at the floor.

"I asked if you remember."

"I do remember," he said, loud then soft as he repeated the words.

"Then what is it?"

"Rumpelstiltskin," he said. "Rumpelstiltskin." He finally looked up. "Can you leave now?"

She stared at him, a worried frown on her face. Then she nodded and left, dragging a reluctant McQueen with her.

When the door slammed, Boy Scout stumbled over to his bed and sat heavily. He grabbed his right wrist with his left hand and inspected the arm. He couldn't feel a thing. It was like it wasn't even there, except he could feel the weight of it pulling on his shoulder. Part of him wondered if it was permanent. Another part wondered if it even mattered. An interesting idea, since he'd always been concerned about the nature of his body, the primary tool of a Ranger and protector.

Chapter Twenty-Seven

Oceanside, California

BOY SCOUT DIDN'T actually have Faood's number, but in the end he managed. He left Camp Pendleton and found the fishing pier in Oceanside. Couples young and old walked hand in hand up and down the pier. Several hardened fishermen camped out in their favorite spots, surly looks on their faces. Using a burner phone with no GPS chip supplied by Poe, he called the Turkish Consulate and asked to speak to Faood. When he was asked about the last name, he said, "Just tell someone that Boy Scout wants to chat."

While he waited, listening to Turkish pop music play in the background, he could only think of Sister Renee. She'd been a fun-loving girl until the entity came out and snatched her life. She'd always been told it was a demon—a major demon nonetheless. In fact, it had named itself. Had it merely used the language of its victims, pretending to be what they thought it was? Was there any difference? Without the Hollywood smoke and sulfur version of Hell, was the thing inside of him merely a demon with another name? He wondered vaguely if those who'd created the first Latin Bible knew the truth of it. Demons and the threat of Hell sure made it far easier to control the masses. After all, with the eternal soul as a fungible resource being fought for by two competing sides—in this case Heaven and Hell—one needed to make sure that their eternity wasn't among long-limbed, fire-breathing demons.

He chuckled to himself.

Even as he thought it, he knew he'd just described a *daeva*.

He moved his shoulder and his arm flopped. Still no feeling. Was it permanent?

"Mr. Starling, is that you?" came Faood's familiar voice.

"I'm Boy Scout right now."

The voice on the other end of the line hesitated. Then, "Of course you are. You're on mission."

"That I am."

"To what honor do I accept this call?" Faood asked, his word order strange but lyrical.

"I want to speak about the *daeva* you have at the consulate."

Again hesitation. "I could say that I don't know what you're talking about, but you'd not trust my words to you so I will just say, what about it?"

"I need to get into The White."

"Of course, you do. This is why we brought it."

"Your methods of looking for me have been interesting," Boy Scout said, thinking of the dead security guards dressed as monks at the monastery. "Not exactly a welcome wagon."

"When others are in charge, they tend to make poor tactical decisions."

"Is that your way of saying that now you are in charge and everything is hunky dory?"

"I'm not familiar with this hunky dory."

"It means cool. Fine. Without problem."

"Then, yes," Boy Scout could almost see Faood nodding. "Everything will be hunky dory."

"What is it I have inside of me?" Boy Scout asked, the question he'd been asking the universe ever since his last time in The White.

"Ahh, that is the question, isn't it? What is it you think you have inside of you? Or if your woman lieutenant is there, what is it she thinks is inside of you?"

So Faood remembered Preacher's Daughter. Hell, he should remember them all.

"She thinks it's a *son of God,* whatever that is."

"*Whatever that is* is a good way to describe it. My guess is she is right. We don't actually know because the only historical references we have are various religious scriptures."

"Which can't be trusted," Boy Scout said. Then he asked, "When did you discover them?"

"Early on in our search for Rumi. We call them *yazatas.*"

On intuition, Boy Scout asked, "How many times have you been into The White?"

"One hundred and sixty-seven."

Boy Scout couldn't help but whistle aloud. The number made his visits seem paltry, like a whine.

"Do you have one inside of you?"

"Yes."

A simple word like nuclear or bomb. "What does it do?"

"You can learn to use it. The problem with the *yazatas* we find in the *Sefid* is that they've been there for so long they don't know what they are."

"It doesn't know? But it eats. It consumes."

"Other travelers. Yes. I have to feed it."

"Then why keep it?" Boy Scout asked.

"Because I can live forever and no one gets hurt."

Boy Scout let the hand holding the phone fall to his side. He watched as a fisherman reeled in a large flat red snapper. The fisherman's scowl turned into joy as he hauled it up and into a waiting bucket of ice. All the while the words *I can live forever* were being power drilled into the inside of his skull. He licked his suddenly dry lips and breathed for a moment. Then he put the phone back to his face. "Why have you told me all of this?"

"There are those who want you for what you did. There are those who want you for who you killed. There are those who want you for what's inside of you. I don't want any of those. I have another idea about you and our relationship."

"We don't have a relationship."

"Not yet. But we should."

"Why should I ever trust you?"

"Because I've never lied to you. Everything you've ever asked, I've answered."

Boy Scout remembered the words they'd exchanged in the cistern.

"It was Rumi who discovered you could travel," Boy Scout said.

"Travel to learn. Travel to discover. Not to be what we've become. We Sufi memorize thousands of Rumi sayings. He was truly marvelous with words. Want to know my favorite one? Forget safety. Live where you fear to live. Destroy your reputation. Be notorious."

"Notorious," Boy Scout repeated. *"That's a hell of a word. Is that what made you come around?"*

At Faood's confused expression, he added, *"Change sides. Did you want to be notorious?"*

"Many things I didn't like, but yes, this saying is central to who I am."

"I once wanted to be a teacher," Boy Scout said. *"Then I became a killer. Think there's ever a time I could be a teacher again?"*

"Intellect takes you to the door, but it can't take you into the house," Faood recited.

"Was that Rumi again?"

"No. That was from Shams Tabrizi, Rumi's teacher."

Intellect can get you to the door, but it can't get you into the house. *"So you say that what I do is necessary then?"*

"Everything is necessary. Nothing is necessary. It depends on your design. Listen, these are merely sayings. We have thousands of them. Sayings can mean many things to different people. The meanings of sayings are not owned by those who say them."

"Then why offer me the saying to begin with?"

"Every word is a doorway. Every thought is an egress. Doors are everywhere. There is no shortage of doors. What's important is deciding which one to go through."

"Are you saying you can't go back?"

"Once you are who you are, you can't become someone who you were," Faood said. *"Be who*

you are and become what you want to be."

"You know how that sounds, right?" Boy Scout asked.

Faood blinked and asked, "Like what?"

"You sound like a fortune cookie."

Faood grinned. "You mean I sound like the paper inside a fortune cookie. Ever wonder where that paper comes from?"

"A factory? A machine?"

"Ever wonder why that fortune comes to you?"

"It's random."

"Is it now?" Faood nodded. "Yet the fortune always seems to fit. Interesting."

Sparked by the memory of their earlier meeting, Boy Scout said, "Intellect can get you to the door, but it can't get you into the house."

"Ah, you remember what I told you. Tell me, Boy Scout, are you at the door, then, or are you in the house?"

"What if I am afraid to go into the house?"

"Then you don't have adequate intellect. Is that the right word? Adequate?"

"That's probably the right word, but I don't think it applies. I have the intellect but I lack data. I don't know enough about the side effects of having something like this inside of me."

"Think of this," Faood said. "You can think more clearly. You heal faster. You know what others are thinking, not by reading their minds, but by intuition. There is no downside."

Except that the *yazata* ate Sister Renee.

But that gave him another question. "What happens when they figure out what they are?"

"Then they are the most dangerous things in the universe."

"How do I keep them from figuring it out?"

"Feed them souls."

And there it was. All he had to do to live forever was to *feed them souls*.

Boy Scout wondered how *that* wasn't hurting anyone. "What is this relationship you have in mind?" he asked.

"The others in the cistern were following an old tradition. They play a game of chance with human lives. I belong to another group. All of us have *yazatas*. All of us can live forever. Myself, I am two hundred and sixteen years." He chuckled. "But who's counting."

"You talk as if living forever is the greatest prize."

"Is it not?" Faood asked, in a way Boy Scout could tell the man was smiling as he said the words.

"I've always wondered if the quality of one's life might be greater than the quantity, but I've never been in a position to experience it."

"Always the warrior."

"It seems so. This group of yours, do the others know?" Boy Scout asked.

"They do not. They are busy searching for Rumi."

"He doesn't want to be found. He told me as much."

"We know this and no longer look."

"Instead you feed the beast," Boy Scout put in. "One hundred and sixty-seven times, you said. All those times to get travelers or souls or essences or whatever the fuck they are so you could keep the beast inside of you fat, dumb and happy. I don't call that a quality of life. I call that being a zoo keeper who feeds the animals their own."

"But you are then a zoo keeper who lives forever. Feeding it something that has gone lost is not so wrong."

Boy Scout thought about Sister Renee and how she'd been absorbed. She hadn't been lost. She'd sacrificed herself for him. Was he going to keep feeding this beast inside of him? Did he even want to live forever? There were nights and days when the events of his past became too much, overwhelming, sometimes leaving him unable to breathe. Did he want more of those days? Or in the middle of them was a final silence more likely something he wanted to achieve? A permanent silencing of the sights and sounds and smells of what seemed like a lifetime of war.

Chapter Twenty-Eight

Camp Pendleton Command Center

AFTER HE HUNG up and tossed the burner into the trash, Boy Scout went inside the nearest bar. He entered a bar and had a cold beer. He didn't want to get drunk. He didn't want to self-medicate. All he wanted was to just get away from the others for a time. Baseball games were on all three of the televisions above the bar. He hadn't paid attention to sports in more than a decade, but he could remember when he was young how it all but consumed him. He'd loved playing baseball. He'd been a second baseman on his high school varsity team. His batting average had been .289, which should have been enough to get him a scholarship, or even a look by pro scouts. But his utter inability to hit a breaking ball doomed any hopes he'd had to play in the majors.

Which was probably just as well.

As Boy Scout drank, he noticed that the finger of his paralyzed arm had begun to twitch. The same arm that had thrown out batters at first base and home plate like he'd been made to do just that. Baseball. He hadn't thought of the sport in so long. So he sat back and watched two innings of the Red Sox versus the New York Yankees. He didn't know any of the players but watched the infield play, sparking memories of when he'd done the same on a smaller stage.

Then, when the beer was gone and his arm was all but his own again, he got up and left the bar, found the Expedition, and returned to Camp Pendleton

McQueen was back and laying out weapons and ammo.

Preacher's Daughter worked industriously at her workstation.

No one said a word when he entered, which he found unusual. He stood watching them for several moments, remembering the times each of them had come into his life.

Preacher's Daughter, the US Army military intelligence lieutenant who'd had a taste of special operations... but just a taste because back then women couldn't be operators. The army had lost a good one the day she'd chosen to leave them and search for more violent pastures.

Randall McQueen, the only one of them who didn't really have a call sign. When asked if he wanted one, he'd said his name was perfect the way it was. After all, he was just a generic gay guy, or as he liked to say when he'd had a little too much hooch, a McDonald's Queen, shortened to McQueen. He'd found acceptance in the special forces teams, brotherhoods tighter than most families. He hadn't said much during his initial interview, but the way he'd carried himself had spoken legions about his capabilities.

Both their loyalties and friendships were rock solid.

They'd go into a drop zone covered in searing napalm for him, if Boy Scout asked. And he'd do the same for them. But Boy Scout was beginning to think that they'd be better off without him. After all, they couldn't help him with astral projection or astral combat. Sure, they could Google shit for him and give him advice, but they had their own lives to life.

Preacher's Daughter glanced at him and then his arm. "Your arm—it's better."

He nodded. "Whatever effects I had from touching the *yazata* didn't linger long."

"*Yazata?*"

"It's what Faood called it."

"Let me see what we have in the database." Her keys flowed over the keyboard. She lowered her voice. "Otherwise, are you okay?"

He grimaced. "It's just been a long couple of days."

"I was referring to Sister Renee," she said.

"I know what you were referring to. She had darkness inside of her. What she did, she did for a reason. She didn't want to be a victim. She didn't want me to be a victim either. She tried to be a hero."

Preacher's Daughter stared at the ground. "I wish she hadn't done it. We don't need any more heroes."

"I feel the same way." He now had the memory of pushing the woman off the platform, just as he had the memories of the woman's fingers smelling of oranges.

Poe entered the main room, moving fast. When he saw Boy Scout he stopped.

"Take care of what you needed to?" he asked, referring to the phone.

"I did. Faood does have the *daeva* at the consulate," he said.

Poe flashed his gaze to where McQueen was checking weapons.

Then it clicked.

Boy Scout's eyes narrowed. "You knew? But how?"

Poe inhaled as if it was going to hurt him to say something, but Boy Scout beat him to the punch.

When he spoke, he enunciated each word carefully. "You listened to my conversation."

Poe's lips pursed and he shook his head minutely. "Wasn't me. It was 77 Central. They monitor all Special Unit 77 coms. I should have told you."

"You gave me a phone for a private conversation and you knew it wasn't going to be private?" "Come on, Boy Scout. Can the self-righteousness. We have an existential threat of unknown origin on American soil. It's my job to protect against things like this."

"Special Unit 77 wants the *daeva*. Why now?"

"Members of the subcommittee made it known that they want us to capture the specimen for study."

"Specimen. Interesting term for a Zoroastrian deity."

Poe shook his head. "This is a military unit, regardless of what we look like. If you want to be a part of it, then start acting military, Boy Scout."

"What's that supposed to mean?"

"What's the first thing you do as a leader when your people are targeted?"

"Protect them first, then remove the threat."

"And that's what we're doing. Are you going to go back to your room and meditate on this, or do you want to be part of the tip of the spear?"

If there had ever been any doubt about it, that confirmed Poe was definitely not a lieutenant. A first lieutenant would have pissed his pants rather than confront Boy Scout like that. Boy Scout had seen it happen on two occasions, one when he'd returned to discuss a vehicle failure with the motor chief after he and his team had to run seven miles in full gear from the site of the piece of shit Hummer, another when an officious lieutenant wouldn't give him the extra ammo he needed for his team.

"I asked you a question, Boy Scout."

"I heard you, Colonel. Count me in."

Poe frowned, but humor reached his eyes. "Good. Then bring your team up to speed and be ready. We leave tomorrow morning at 0600 hours."

Then he exited out the door and was gone.

When Boy Scout turned back to his team, both Preacher's Daughter and McQueen were staring at him.

"Enjoy the show?" he asked.

"Immensely," said Preacher's Daughter. "Just missed having popcorn." Then her face got serious. "Why'd you call him colonel?"

"Look how old he is. Do you really buy the oldest lieutenant in the army schtick? There's no way he's a lieutenant," McQueen said. "He carries far too much *wasta*."

She nodded to herself. "Which was why I sucked

at military intelligence. You spoke with Faood, according to Poe, and discovered that the *daeva* is there."

Boy Scout pulled up a chair and relayed most of what the conversation had been about. He concluded with, "You've got to understand, talking with Faood in many ways is like talking to Rumi. He's full of all sorts of odd sayings that can mean many things."

"Lay one on me," McQueen said.

Boy Scout pondered, then said, "Forget safety. Live where you fear to live. Destroy your reputation. Be notorious."

"Hey, I like that one." McQueen rocked back in the office chair. "Be notorious. Like a T-shirt or a bumper sticker. Give me another one."

"Intellect can get you to the door, but it can't get you into the house," Boy Scout said.

McQueen stopped rocking. "That's harder. What's it supposed to mean?"

"It means we need more data," Preacher's Daughter said. Then she went still and snapped her finger. "You just reminded me of something I read."

"You actually read?" McQueen asked. "I mean, other than *Better Homes and Gardens* and *Oprah*?"

"Are you getting fat, McQueen?" she asked. "I think you might be gaining weight. You working out enough?"

His smile dropped as he chewed the corner of his mustache.

"Anyway," she said, rolling her eyes from McQueen to Boy Scout, "speaking of doorways, there's this thing that scientists call the doorway effect. They based the title on research done at the University of Notre Dame. The idea was to try and explain why the brain partitions information a certain way. For instance, when you carry something from one room to the other, once you leave the room you came from, there's a better than average chance you'll forget why you were going to the other room or what you were supposed to do with the object in your hands. Because the subjects were tested in the room and then after they left the room, scientists were able to determine that moving through the doorway had an effect."

Boy Scout leaned forward with interest.

"Distance didn't have the same effect as the doorway," she continued. "Subjects were tested after walking the same distance with the only differing operand being a doorway and, in every case, going through the doorway affected the ability of the subject to remember. What is it about a doorway that causes the mind to partition or replace a human's random-access memory? This suggests that there's more to the remembering than just what you paid attention to, when it happened, and how hard you tried. Instead, some forms of memory seem to be optimized to keep information ready-to-access until its shelf life expires, and then purge that information in favor of new stuff, like a computer would have RAM."

"Aren't you talking about ROM?" McQueen asked.

She shook her head. "That's *Read Only Memory*. Think breathing, the heart beating, etcetera. The body's ROM is what it needs to merely survive. By being *read only* it can't be overwritten. Imagine if it was and suddenly you stopped breathing because the code would no longer be there."

"Deleterious," McQueen said, nodding sagely.

"Deli—" She laughed. "Deleterious indeed? Were you just playing Scrabble or something? More like devastating. If that happened you might not have enough time to even say *deleterious*." She sighed. "Where was I before Mr. Scrabble joined in?" She snapped a finger. "Right. So ROM covers everyday functions. RAM is short-term memory that gets you through the day, and the hard disk is where memories are stored. So again, what is it about a doorway that makes the brain decide to overwrite the mind's RAM?"

"The mind is a strange machine. My PTSD proves it," Boy Scout said. "There are those who have done far less than I have whose minds can't deal with that they've seen and done. Do you think that the more doors you've gone through—metaphorically—the easier it is to deal with everything you've seen?"

"Certainly the more experiences one has, the better their mind should become in organizing the information," she said. "For instance, a person who has never traveled might find themselves completely lost in a large airport because they have no frame of reference—no information on the hard drive. But me, or you, or even our fat gay hipster over there—"

"I'm not fat," McQueen said.

"Wouldn't have a problem, even in an airport in a foreign country without any signs in English. Know why?"

"Because we can bring our experiences to bear and use them to figure out the current configuration," Boy Scout said.

"And this is all done by the mind accessing the hard drive and placing the needed information in the RAM."

"I am not fat." McQueen repeated. "This is muscle." He flexed his arms and sucked in his stomach. He seemed disappointed that it wouldn't suck in more.

"Sure it is, dear," Preacher's Daughter said.

"How does this apply to the doorway effect?" Boy Scout asked.

"I was thinking about the entities inside of you. They knew who they were and what they were back before they passed into The White. Then they passed into you. That's two completely different doorways. The White was a universe that could be molded by those within. The reason we called it The White was because it was featureless until we did something to it. I bet that's the same thing with your mind and I don't think they know where they are."

McQueen nodded. "Like the airports. These entities had never been in an airport or the mind of a middle-aged semi-broken former Army Ranger, so their minds don't know how to explain it to them. And I'm not fat."

"As they go from one door to the other, they forget what they were going there for," Preacher's Daughter said. "We know that the boy was a suicide bomber and never meant to enter The White in the first place. What his mind must have done to try and come to terms with his environment must have been quite the mad scramble. And you are too fat."

"That's something that's been bothering me," Boy Scout said. "Those things that entered me in The White were in the shape of spiders, something either created by my mind or the mind of something else. In essence though, they didn't exist. Yet they had a complete mind—ROM, RAM and hard drive—that entered into my already filled mind. Why don't I feel like ten pounds of shit in a five-pound bag?"

Preacher's Daughter gave him an iffy smile. "Now we're getting into quantum physics. How can two things occupy the same space? How can your mind transfer from your body into a netherplace? I think there's probably the science to explain it, only we don't know it."

"I'm not sure it's all science," McQueen said. "Explain the *daeva* using science. Remember what the *daeva* said to you? It was around long before humans ever walked the Earth. How does science explain that?" he asked Preacher's Daughter.

"Maybe the *daeva* don't live in our same reality. Boy Scout and I talked about it, but I really have no idea. Like I said, this is quantum physics. Supernatural is merely something our brains can't parse naturally. Like the airports or your brain, Boy Scout."

"Nothing natural about his brain," McQueen muttered.

"With the *yazata* we have an interesting concept," she said. "If it takes on the aspect of the being it last eats, in this case you mentioned something about an Englishman, then each entity it absorbs is another doorway. Consider that it has probably lived for thousands of years. If it needs to be fed regularly it might have absorbed thousands of souls, each being a different doorway or identity. I'm sure early on it knew what it was and who it was, but over time, after absorbing so many others, it's probably more a collection of all these other parts than its original identity."

"What you said was just spooky smart," McQueen said.

"It sure would explain why it doesn't know what it is. But if what you're saying is correct, there's still an echo of Sister Renee inside of here," he said, pointing to his head. "And if I let it consume another soul, she will be gone forever."

"That seems to be the case. You might not be able to avoid it if you want to survive, Boy Scout."

"I don't even want to think about crossing that bridge. Damn if this isn't becoming a horror novel. If I had the ability, I'd look up and tell the author to stop it right now."

"I don't automatically think that just because we can't explain something, it has to be out of a Stephen King novel," she said.

"Said the woman who marked her entire body with religious symbols, then wrapped herself in cellophane and tinfoil," McQueen said.

She pointed a finger at him. "Hey, that was a dream. That never really happened."

"You didn't know it at the time," he said.

"Welcome to quantum mechanics," Preacher's Daughter said. Then she added, "And you definitely *are* too fat."

Chapter Twenty-Nine

Hollywood Boulevard

THE PROBLEM WITH a direct assault on the consulate was the dervish's ability to put people who watched their dance instantly to sleep. The assault team could show up wearing McQueen's glasses, but then the dervishes would know that the assault team knew about their ability, and thus had to be connected with Boy Scout. If the assault team showed up without them, they'd be susceptible to the dervish's powers. All of that was beside the point anyway, because a direct assault would create a diplomatic nightmare.

Working with Special Agent Ripple, Poe had devised a plan that was equal parts subterfuge and chance, and for loss of a better idea, Boy Scout had gone along with it. There was no doubt that the dervishes still wanted Boy Scout and his team, but using them as bait again in such short a time span seemed farfetched. Still, the idea had merit, so they conferred with Boy Scout. In the end, he went with their approach, asking only for a single concession.

Which was how he now found himself standing on Ray Bradbury's star on the Hollywood Walk of Fame, wearing nothing but regular clothes and an earpiece for coms, thinking about the movie *The Illustrated Man*, based on three of the author's short stories and starring Rod Steiger. The idea of the film was that Rod Steiger's tattoos represented startling versions of the future, each with its own terrible realities. Although the movie wasn't very good—inculcating some of the weirdness that movies of the 1960s seemed to have had—the image of the tattoos shifting and acting on their own always creeped Boy Scout out.

Honestly, he hadn't thought of that movie or the author for years, but being so near the star brought it all back in a wave. Even when he'd sat in the chair of a tattooist outside of Fort Benning twenty years ago, seeing the tats on his tattooist and the flash on the walls, he'd started to wonder if maybe they would move if he dared to stare hard enough. Which was why he'd gotten up and left, had never gone back, and had never gotten a tattoo, even when his friends begged him to do so. He just didn't want the reality to change. He wanted the world as he saw it to be just that.

Which was incredibly ironic considering his current circumstances.

Boy Scout had come to find out that the world was nothing like he thought it was. What he saw was carefully chosen outer garments and make up. Villagers in Iraq weren't mere villagers. Fishermen in Somalia weren't mere fishermen. And Afghan colonels who professed to be good men were really pedophiles hiding in plain sight, at least in the case of Sharif. And now Boy Scout wasn't actually Boy Scout. He was a man harboring a soul-eating *yazata* and a woman had killed herself to save him, only to fail in the process.

Boy Scout shook his head to clear his thoughts, then took inventory of his surroundings.

All around him were stars, monuments to those who'd been famous. Some were lost to time despite their stars and some commemorated for specific events. But the stars remained as memories for what they once had been. Even so, were the stars really who they'd been? Or were the stars merely avatars of who the world thought them to be, five-pointed mnemonics to jumpstart memories of where they were, when they were, and what they were doing back then.

And, of course, there was Hollywood Boulevard.

The street was as busy as it ever was.

Cars cruised bumper to bumper at less than ten miles an hour, slow enough for the odd pedestrian to jaywalk between them.

Starbucks had a line out the door, as if it were the only place coffee could be had.

A TV star he recognized dodged into the Hollywood Suit outlet across the street—evidently the advertisement of *Three Suits, Three Shirts, Three Ties, Three Socks for $399* a draw even the elite couldn't pass up.

Tourists of all ilk ogled the windows, occasionally stopping on one of the stars on the Walk of Fame to photograph themselves or loved ones, then relate a story about how the honoree had changed their lives or made them happy or had been a role model.

An older couple with liver-spotted hands and feet enclosed in black socks and sandals posed near a hooker and pimp to take pictures on a no-shit camera instead of a cell phone.

A group of twenty-something women, half-sloshed from mid-afternoon adventures on the strip, walked arm in arm down the sidewalk across the street, singing the theme song from *Gilmore Girls*.

A young man wearing a pressed black shirt and pants hurried down the street, late for some waiter job and probably dreaming he'd be discovered and able to star in a movie alongside Brad Pitt or

George Clooney.

The sidewalks teemed with foot traffic, some local but most clearly from out of town. If Boy Scout had really wanted to lose himself in a horde of people, he could have chosen to stand in front of Kodak Theater or Mann's Chinese Theater. There, in addition to the masses trying to match their footprints and handprints with the famous, were men and women dressed convincingly like Superman, Batman, Lady Gaga, Spider-Man, Wonder Woman, Rocky Balboa, and Tyrion Lannister, among others.

But there he wouldn't have as clear line of sight as he had now.

Which was why he was able to see Faood strolling towards him from almost a full block away. When he saw the man, Boy Scout turned and noted that there were dervishes now poised on the corners of the street to his right, each dressed in a long traditional white dress and wearing a conical hat in the event they needed to put people to sleep.

"Faood approaching," McQueen said through his earpiece.

"Way to go, Captain Obvious," Preacher's Daughter said.

Boy Scout reminded himself to discuss the merits of radio discipline later.

Faood was dressed to blend in with the tourists.

He wore a T-shirt with an image of two cats in suits dressed as Mulder and Scully and the words *The Truth Is Meowt There* scrawled below it. The shirt was tucked into high-end jeans and he had Jordans on his feet. A gold chain hung from his neck and an expensive watch adorned his left wrist.

"You look like a middle-aged gangbanger," Boy Scout said when Faood approached.

They fist bumped like old friends.

"Then goal accomplished," Faood said. "I see you're not wearing your magic glasses."

"They clash with my look."

"What you going for, middle-aged government military contractor?"

"Hoping to pull it off." Boy Scout glanced at the other dervishes who, even in full kit, seemed able to completely fade into the human mosaic of Hollywood Boulevard. "I see you have your dervishes in place to knock everyone out. Aren't you worried about the traffic? You might cause some accidents."

"Drivers should keep their concentration on the road. What is it they say? A distracted driver is a dangerous driver."

"That is what they say," Boy Scout said. "Cute, what you did back at the mall."

"We thought our plan was solid."

"But so public. You must want me so bad."

"That wasn't my op. The man who planned that has been recalled back to Turkey."

"Can't tolerate failure."

"No one can."

"I don't know about that. But if he'd applied MDMP even a little, he would have discovered that in such a public area with so many witnesses, there'd be too many obstacles to overcome."

Faood nodded. "I'll make a note of that. So where are your men?"

"Close."

Faood leaned against a telephone pole and checked his phone like any normal person would. "Should I be worried?" he asked.

"My people will stay put as long as your people don't do anything."

"Stay put?"

"It means they won't kill your dervishes."

"Oh. Good phrase."

"Back to your Del Amo Fashion Center escapade," Boy Scout said. "The problem with such a public performance is that it's hard to contain the evidence of the event. Although you were able to successfully purge the contents of the mall's CCTVs, you couldn't stop individuals from taking videos before they were rendered unconscious. Seven videos were subsequently uploaded to social media once the owners awoke and discovered that they had the footage."

Faood's eyes widened slightly.

Boy Scout nodded. "Yup. Being high and mighty and living forever can make the best of us out of touch with modern social communication methods. Can't do shit in this day and age without it being on social media." He held up a finger. "I bet you'll like this twist to the story, though. Based on the video evidence, the FBI is investigating a possible chem-bio attack conducted by unknown persons staying in the Turkish Consulate."

Faood was in full-out frown mode now. He glowered at the pavement.

This next part Boy Scout delivered carefully. He leaned into Faood and said, "You'll love this part even better. The FBI is putting together a package for the Ninth Superior Court to enable them to break diplomacy because of the threat of you using weapons of mass destruction against the American populace. My guess is that within the next twenty-four hours they'll be able to enter the consulate and take into evidence whatever they encounter." He repeated. "Whatever they encounter."

Faood lifted his head and stared at Boy Scout. "Why are you telling me this?"

"Self-preservation." He glanced around. "You see, I can't get the help I need if the *daeva* is in a federal vault. Ever seen the ending sequence to

Raiders of the Lost Ark? Once it goes in there, I'll have no chance of ever seeing it again."

"They would do this?"

"Gleefully." He paused. "Proudly. And then they'd accept the rewards for saving America from a Chemical Biological Threat."

"How do I know that this isn't all a setup?" Faood asked, gesturing at the street and surroundings. "This story of yours—do you have proof?"

"You don't know that. But I figured that you'd be less willing to make a public spectacle again." Boy Scout shrugged. "As far as proof, that will come with a warrant. We're trying to beat that."

"You're asking me to trust you," Faood said flatly.

"Like you once asked me to trust you."

"And see where that got us." Faood put his phone away and stood up straight. "I knew the moment they brought you into the cisterns that this would turn out poorly."

Boy Scout ignored the man's self-pity slip. "Will you be able to help?"

Faood frowned. "There are elements I cannot control."

"Should I be worried? I thought I could trust you."

"You can, but know that if anything happens to me, I won't be able to contain them." Faood tilted his head toward the dervishes.

Boy Scout looked around. They hadn't moved.

They all stood still, heads cocked, ready to dance. "What would they do?"

"They want you and the others who survived. They want to kill you. More."

Boy Scout laughed. "Torture? That's ridiculous."

"You killed too many of our best," Faood said, shrugging.

"It was fucking war," Boy Scout snarled. "And you brought us to this. It was you who put us in a position to have to fight. Without you, there would be no deaths and my three people would still be alive."

"I understand that, but you only lost three. We lost twenty-seven."

Boy Scout shoved his finger into Faood's chest as he said, "Tell the others that so many died because we are better at killing. If they want more, we'll do the same to them."

"Bold words," Faood said, swiping Boy Scout's hand away.

"Backed up. Proven. If we were a stock, I'd say to invest because our superior ability to kill and survive is a safe bet."

Faood stared at Boy Scout for a long moment. "I will let them know. I anticipate you already have a plan."

"It's totally up to you. I need access to the *daeva*. I don't want the *yazata* in my mind. I need it gone.

Maybe we can find another place to conceal it so it can be used."

"They're not going to want to move it from the consulate."

"They're going to lose it if the judge allows the FBI to break diplomatic seal. The argument for weapons of mass destruction is a game breaker. WMD is a magic word—the modern *open sesame*—and it can open any door. You can trust me on that. We can either do it in plain sight, like in a hotel room anywhere in LA, or we can find a more remote location."

"Do you have a remote location in mind?"

"We have a friend who has a house in Malibu, right off the ocean. We could meet there."

"Malibu? *Lifestyles of the Rich and Famous* Malibu?"

"The same."

"Will your people bring weapons?"

"As protection. I expect yours to do the same. As long as we remain adults, nothing should happen."

"My people will need convincing."

Boy Scout shrugged. "That's up to you. The only reason I'm doing this is for personal reasons. Frankly, what the FBI is doing is the right thing. If they knew I was here, they'd be really pissed. I try not to piss off major three-letter government agencies."

"I have twenty-four hours, then?"

"Less. The FBI will move in as soon as they have the warrant."

Faood glanced at his watch which turned out to be a Breitling. Evidently being a dervish had more perks than Boy Scout realized. "Then I need to move."

Boy Scout held out a piece of paper. "Here's the address."

Faood glanced down, then took it. "You had the Malibu place planned all along."

"We had to do it somewhere."

Faood glanced at him one more time, then headed back the way he'd come.

"Think he bought it?" McQueen asked through his earpiece once Faood was a block away and the dervishes had left.

Boy Scout began to walk in the opposite direction that Faood had gone. "He did. Everything ready at the house?"

"We got it locked down."

"And Ripple?"

"I heard," Special Agent Ripple said from behind Boy Scout. "You did good."

Boy Scout could hear the grudging respect from the other man. They'd argued hard about the specifics of the meeting. The agent had wanted him to go armed and to have backup. Boy Scout insisted that not only he not have backup, but that his people be prepping the meeting house and the FBI not be anywhere close to this operation. It was bad enough that they traveled in pairs in sedans and wearing suits. Boy Scout took this moment to remind Ripple of his promise.

"Remember, this is a complete MilOp. We don't want you or your men anywhere near. And no surveillance."

"I heard you."

"I'm serious about that."

Ripple didn't respond, but that didn't mean he hadn't heard.

Boy Scout continued heading west along Hollywood Boulevard, then a petite red-head stepped in front of him.

"I don't know if you know me, but I'm Charlene Johnson," she said.

The woman's appearance sent Boy Scout reeling. Was this real? Had the *yazata* taken over? The world spun for a moment. He backed up, stumbling a bit as he did. He managed to collect himself and realized he was holding his breath.

"Preacher's Daughter, are you there?" he asked desperately.

"I'm here, boss. "

"What's the safe word?"

"The safe word?"

Charlene's eyes scrunched in confusion, hearing him speak but not to her. "Your name is Bryan but they call you Boy Scout."

"Wait. Am I hearing who I think I'm hearing?" Lore asked.

"I'm afraid so. Am I awake?"

"Rumpestiltskin," she said, as if it were a magic word to keep them all safe.

"Boy Scout, is that you?" Charlene asked. "I mean, we've never met, but we have sort of. It's pretty hard to explain."

He reached out and touched her shoulder with the tip of the forefinger of his right hand.

"Are you real?"

"I think I am," she said. She touched him in the same way he was touching her. With a grin she asked, "Is this how they greet each other from your planet?"

"Fuck me," McQueen said in his ear.

Boy Scout nodded.

"Oh, I see. You're talking to your team." She withdrew her hand, straightened and smiled. "Please say hi to that tomboy and the fat gay hipster."

Preacher's Daughter laughed a good one in his ear. "I told you that you were fat," she said to McQueen.

Chapter Thirty

In-N-Out Burger

OTHER THAN THE words, *Follow me,* Boy Scout didn't even speak until they were seated at In-N-Out Burger. They were the only ones with no food and had taken the last table, causing several customers with trays heaped with fast food to give them dirty looks. But whether it was Boy Scout's size or his barely controlled look of terror, they didn't bother and instead just grumbled on by.

Even after several minutes to collect his thoughts, he had more questions than he had answers. That wasn't right. He wasn't even smart enough to know what questions to ask. Instead, he had a great chasm of *what the fuck* that needed to be filled with something. So he stared at her, ready for her to explain, seeing that she was eager to say something.

But she didn't. She just sat and stared at him, a half smile on her face.

Finally, he asked her, "How?"

Her face lit up. "How did I get here? Or how did I know to come to you?"

He frowned more deeply. "Are you real?"

She playfully pinched her arm. "I'm as real as you are."

He pinched his own hard enough to feel pain. "Is this part of a dream? Are we in a fugue?"

Her smile dropped. "I see the problem. Here, let me hold your hand."

He tentatively offered her his hand.

She took it in both her hands and closed her eyes.

He watched as her face twitched. Her eyebrows raised at one point. Her mouth opened in surprise, only to close and morph into a frown. She shook her head slightly and began to hum. After several increasingly uncomfortable minutes of this, she clucked her tongue and let go of his hand. She sat back and stared at him, then stood and said, "I'll be right back."

Boy Scout watched her go, not knowing what to say.

When she returned, it was with a tray that held two orders of fries, two double cheeseburgers, and two diet cokes. She placed the food in front of him, then began to eat her own.

He didn't touch his food. He wasn't hungry. He just wanted to know what was going on.

She was about halfway through her burger before she put it down and wiped the corners of her mouth with a napkin. When she spoke, her words couldn't have surprised him more.

"Tell me about Sister Renee."

"Sister—How?"

Charlene raised her eyebrows indicating he should answer her question.

He cleared his throat, totally flummoxed at the turn of events. "Sister Renee was a nun I met at Our Lady of Atlas in Exile, a monastery in the San Bernardino Mountains. She taught me astral projection and gave her life in a futile attempt to save me from the *yazata* inside of me."

While he spoke, Charlene nodded and chewed on a bite of burger. When he finished, she said, "That's about what she told me. What she wants to know is why you've abandoned her."

"Why I—She's dead. The entity inside of me consumed her essence."

"Bits and pieces. She's still there. She's just not herself nowadays."

Not herself nowadays. Bits and pieces. The understatement of the year. "What else does she say?"

"She wants you to visit her."

"In the astral plane?" He couldn't believe he was even having this conversation. "Are you certain that you spoke with her and not the *yazata*? It can take on aspects of what it most recently consumed." Which was Sister Renee. He couldn't suppress a shudder.

"That beast inside of her? Is that what you call it? I try to avoid it as much as I can. It craves power. It feels like a battery that's almost empty of its charge." She touched his arm. "Whatever you do, don't feed it. Don't let it get back its power. It will burn you from the inside out." She pulled back her hand and dipped a fry in ketchup, then jammed it into her mouth.

"I did not abandon her," he said.

She raised her eyebrows to express her doubt.

"I didn't. She was eaten," he said.

"She's still there. She wants to talk to you."

He stared at her for a long minute. "Can't you just tell me what she wants?"

"She needs to say it to you herself. She's worried about you."

He glanced down at his food. He still felt absolutely no inclination to eat. "You came once before, but you weren't here. An entity inside of me brought you into my dreams so that it could try and convince me that what I was doing was real. So part of me doesn't even know if this is real or if

I am locked inside of a dream thinking I'm doing something."

"What do you think is going on?" she asked.

"That's the point, isn't it? I can't be sure. Every waking moment I'm alert to the fact that something might not be real and I wouldn't even know it. I just power through and act the part and hope that this thing I'm calling life isn't really a dream pretending to be me."

"Like in that old movie *The Matrix*. Everyone is being used as a biological battery and they think they're living certain lives. Only a few know otherwise."

"But the difference is once they wake up, they don't fall back to sleep unless they're captured."

"But are they really captured, or is that part of yet another dream?" she asked.

He gave her a horrified look.

"The point is that you can only play the part in the way you're able. If this is a dream, then be the best you can be and do what needs to be done."

He leaned forward and whispered, "Is this really a dream, then?"

She leaned forward as well and whispered, "If it is, we're living the same dream."

"Then all of this is real?" He glanced around.

"As far as I'm concerned." She sat back. "Then again, my idea of what's real isn't the same as yours. For instance, I knew you'd dreamed me the moment it happened. It was such a peculiar feeling being in someone's dream and being aware of it. I can still remember our conversation about the girl and the goat and the sky that burned."

"You seemed so real to me, as well."

"That was a bad time for you. I felt your weakness. I felt your sadness. They had you locked away but I see you escaped."

"Mostly," he said, finally leaning back and accepting that he'd have to at least pretend he wasn't in a dream. He touched the side of his head with his fist. "I left with some souvenirs."

She nodded. "The boy, yes. I can still smell the oranges on his mother's fingers. What a wonderful memory that was. The others were violent men, though. I can see where you'd want to be rid of them."

"I felt bad for the boy, as incongruous as it sounds. He was a suicide bomber who killed innocent people."

"Are there really any innocent people?" she asked.

Boy Scout looked around the restaurant and saw families with children and older people, all living within what might be just been a dream set aside for only him. "In Afghanistan, innocence is by degrees. No one is truly innocent," he said. "Even children are guilty of being children. After all, they'll eventually grow up and became the antithesis of what they wanted to be, their fates carved by the actions of all the weaknesses in the men who came before them."

"What you say lacks any sort of hope."

"They should have a sign at the airport in Bagram that says *Abandon All Hope, Ye Who Enter Here*."

"The words at the gate to hell."

"According to Dante," he said.

"Did you forget that you are a Boy Scout?"

"That's just a call sign."

"Is it? Are you not a Boy Scout? Do you not live to serve others and make their lives better?"

"Like I said, just a call sign."

She waggled a finger as she ate a fry. "Nothing is just a call sign. Do you think Preacher's Daughter could have any other call sign than the one she has? You *are* Boy Scout. You live and breathe it. It's part of your DNA."

He stared hard at her. Elfin features beneath a mound of stark red hair. "Who are you?"

She gave him her patented grin. "Just your average psychic hairdresser who can do nails, acupuncture, and speed load magazines for 9mm pistols. That last thing, I learned from Narco," she added. "I felt when he died. I knew it was coming, but it still saddened me to see it actually happen."

"You know when people die?"

"Honey, I know when everyone dies."

His eyes widened.

"Don't even ask, because I'm not going to answer. Why I have the information, I'm still trying to figure out. When I was little, I tried to change fate, but if there's one thing I've learned, it's that fate cannot be changed. Once it decides, that's it."

"Maybe by knowing it negates the ability to effect change," he said.

She cocked her head as she thought about what he'd said.

But then he shook his head. "There's no reason to try and change things then. No reason to fix things—to try and save people."

"Sure, there is. People die all the time out of sequence. Some early. Some late. What I see is what happens when no one does anything to impinge future events. We each have our time, but there are those forces who would hasten our deaths for their own mortal reasons. This is why the world needs you. This is why you are a Boy Scout. You can't change who wins at the end of the game, but you can influence how well everyone plays and ensure that the game is played fairly." She grinned again. "That's what a Boy Scout should do."

He gave her a look of disbelief.

"Does a Boy Scout help an old woman across the street? Sure. It's in all the books. But then does he also follow her around for the rest of her life to ensure he helps anytime she might need it? No. Boy Scouts help those in need at the moment of need, then move onto something else entirely. Now Sister Renee needs you. In fact, she's why I am here."

"How? Did she contact you?"

"Her death exploded across all of my psychic bandwidth and made me aware of you. I recognized you right away and knew that there was a way that I could be a Boy Scout as well, maybe help you for a moment, before moving on."

"What is it about her death that drew you?"

"The *yazata*. That's what you called it, yes? I would see it burn if I could. But you can't die. If you do, it escapes and will go in search of another, maybe even a young girl like Sister Renee, convincing her that it is a demon so that those even more powerful will come and it can inhabit them. Yes, I know her story. She told me and it's proof that the battery inside of you should never be fully charged."

"If I don't feed it, it will take me over, Faood told me. He said the only reason it doesn't have any need to own me is because it's already had so many souls to devour. The team and I talked about it. Each soul was a doorway, and by traveling through them all, it forgot who it was."

"Faood is right. If it gets too weak, it will seek you out."

"Then what? What is it I need to do?" he asked, so tired of the whole damn thing.

She reached over and touched his closed fist. "We'll work on that. We'll figure it out together. Let me help you, Boy Scout. Let me be there for you."

He stared long and hard, then eventually nodded. In doing so, he felt the stress leave his body. When she was finished with her food, he stood and bagged his own meal. Once he was outside, Boy Scout handed it out to one of the many homeless who made Hollywood Boulevard their place in the world. One small part of the game—helping another player, then moving on. That's who he was, he supposed.

An incremental helper.

A Boy Scout.

Now if only he could figure out how to help himself.

Chapter Thirty-One

Malibu, California

BOY SCOUT AND Charlene walked up Orange Avenue to the football field for Hollywood High School. Noaks's helicopter had just landed. They hopped over the fence and ran low until they were able to board the helicopter. After Boy Scout climbed in, he reached out and helped Charlene aboard, who seemed nonplussed about the new ride. They sat facing rearward. Poe and an operator Boy Scout had never seen, dressed in full combat kit, sat opposite him. The man's face was mostly covered by a ballistic mask. A monkey harness was attached to his gear to keep him from falling to his death. He held an M4 like he knew how to use it.

Boy Scout helped Charlene into her headset and then put on his own, without which they'd never be able to hear over the roar of the blades.

Poe stared hard at Charlene.

Boy Scout ignored the look and gestured to the operator. "What's going on? I thought I said no backup."

"This isn't for you. This is for me," Poe said.

The answer was so odd that Boy Scout didn't know how to reply.

Noaks lifted the chopper into the air and banked towards the Hollywood sign.

"Who's she?" Poe asked, pointing at Charlene.

"It's not polite to point," she said. Then turning to Boy Scout, she added, "I don't like him."

Boy Scout raised an eyebrow. A psychic saying she didn't like someone was as good as a dog growling at a stranger. Maybe he should pay closer attention to Poe and his endgame. After all, no government agency was really here to help people—especially a team as secretive as Special Unit 77.

"This is Charlene Johnson," he said. "Charlene, this is Lieutenant Poe."

Poe shot Boy Scout a glare.

What was going on? Everyone was still all friendly, right? Boy Scout thought about how he was going to explain her. Something like, *This is the lady I thought had come and joined us when I was taken over by the Berber, but she really wasn't there, just like the first and only other time we met her when we were actually floating in a pond covered in shit and snot and dreaming the whole thing.* Uh... no. Maybe just keep it simple.

"She's an old girlfriend of one of my men," he said.

"This is a tactical military operation," Poe said.

Boy Scout added, "She's also a psychic. I think she might help."

Poe mouthed the words *psychic* but said nothing more.

Boy Scout figured they were at about a thousand feet. He traced the 10 as it raced east and west, the 405 on down towards the curve, then the 110, which shot straight to the Port of LA Bel Air was below them as they headed toward the hills of Topanga State Park.

By now, Lore and McQueen would have prepared the home like they'd planned. He shouldn't feel worried, but the appearance of the tactical operator out of the blue had sent a thumb of worry along his spine. Not that one man would make much of a difference, but his presence was like the tip of an iceberg. And Charlene's immediate reaction upon meeting Poe accentuated that worry. He was going to have to watch Poe carefully and see what his plans were.

But in the meantime, they had their own plan to put into place.

They sat in an awkward silence until the chopper neared the Malibu coast. Wildfires had decimated the area in recent years and squares of missing homes greeted them like buck-toothed smiles. The chopper crossed above Pepperdine University, then roared over the ocean, only to descend where the sand met the water near Puerco Canyon. A single home stood without neighbors, while all the other homes abutted each other like frat boys at an initiation.

Like Faood had said, Malibu was home to the rich and famous, which was partially why they were going to conduct their business here. Along with wealth came exclusivity. Police also tended to look the other way in communities where domestic violence and recreational drug use comprised 85 percent of the crime. So instead of policing, the cops normally formed their own blue barricade, ensuring the tourists kept moving, and those who were not wanted wouldn't be willing to stay any longer than it took to get a burger and fries at The Country Kitchen off Pacific Coast Highway.

They removed their headsets and bailed out when the skids hit the sand.

Boy Scout kept his right hand over his face to keep the sand from blasting against it.

Fifteen seconds later they were standing alone on the beach, Noaks powering down the helicopter. Evidently the new plan was to leave it there.

A local resident that looked vaguely like a grown up version of a TV star Boy Scout had seen as a kid strode towards them, his face a mask of anger.

Poe glanced over, cursed under his breath and moved to meet the man.

The operator moved behind and to his right, following, his M4 pointed a few feet in front of him.

The actor began to gesticulate wildly, pointing at the helicopter and then his house.

Whatever Poe said was lost to the sound of the wind and the surf because within a minute, the actor had deflated and turned to go back to his home.

Poe and the operator waited until the man was inside, then returned.

"What did you say to him?" Boy Scout asked.

"None of that shit now," Poe said. "Come with me." Then he pointed to Charlene. "And you stay here."

Poe started to move. When he saw Boy Scout hesitate, he turned back. "I said, *now*."

The operator raised the muzzle of his rifle a bare millimeter. Probably not enough for a regular person to note, but it was like a semaphore to Boy Scout's worry.

What the fuck was going on?

Boy Scout began to follow Poe.

The operator followed behind him.

"I heard that," McQueen said in his ear. "I got the operator. Lore, you take Poe."

"Take it easy," Boy Scout said low, trying not to move his lips. "Let's see where this goes."

"If it goes south, they go in the ground," McQueen said.

In front of the beachside Malibu mansion, Boy Scout pictured them in the windows or on the roof, aiming down the barrels of their rifles. Both were crack shots, so if shit was about to go down, then it was going to go down in style.

After about thirty meters, Poe whirled. Hands on his hips, he thrust out his chin. "What's with the woman?"

"What do you mean? She's my guest."

"Your *guest*?" Poe scoffed. "Are you a hotel? You don't get to have guests."

"Take it easy, Poe," Boy Scout said, knowing as he did so those words rarely worked.

"I'll take it easy, all right." Poe stepped in close, taking up Boy Scout's personal space. "I'll take her and lock her in a cell so we can have the mission we planned."

Boy Scout couldn't help but smile. It'd been more than a decade since someone had been able to intimidate him and Poe wasn't going to change that. Boy Scout stood his ground.

"I don't understand the change, Lieutenant. Why are you suddenly so stressed? Why do you have to bring your own dog for protection?"

"This is the culmination of a mission I've planned for months. I've nailed down every facet and MDMP'd every angle. Then she comes along. We know who she is. She's in our database. We know she's not some damned girlfriend. She's the real deal, but she's also batshit as fuck. I don't need a crazy fucking psychic to bring down a mission we've expended twenty million dollars to accomplish."

The cursing was a surprise, but so was the dollar amount.

"What's the harm in having her here? If she's as good as you say, then we could use her as an early warning device. She'll know when something bad's about to happen."

Poe shook his head and stepped back. "No. No. No. No. No," he said, rapid-fire. "You're still not getting it. No psychic is perfect. There is no one hundred percent. She's going to tell you something and you're going to want to take action but you're not going to know whether or not she is right."

"Who says she's not a hundred percent?" Boy Scout asked.

"See? You're already questioning me."

"Who says you're in charge, *Lieutenant*?" Boy

Scout countered, stressing the rank. Then he added, "Or colonel, or whatever the hell you are."

"I've always been in charge, whether you knew it or not. The minute you accepted my help, you entered into a contract with the United States government. As their representative, I'm in charge. You and yours are contractors. By US code, you *can't* be in charge. Contractors cannot represent the US government."

Boy Scout glanced at the operator, staring pointedly at the rifle.

"And you need an operator with a gun to establish your authority." He swallowed back a dozen more things he wanted to say. He wasn't going to get anywhere like this. "What is it you want me to do?"

"I want her gone."

"It's too late for that. They saw her with me."

"The hell they did," Poe said.

The operator took a half step back, as if to make it easier for him to bring the weapon around.

Boy Scout was done.

He spun and grabbed the barrel of the operator's rifle with his right hand. He knew the guy wanted to raise the weapon, so Boy Scout helped him, lifting the barrel up, then slamming it into his ballistic mask. The man stumbled, and in that moment Boy Scout found the quick release sling, let it drop, and made the weapon his own.

The operator took two steps back, went down on a knee and pulled free his pistol. He shoved the weapon out in a two-handed grip aiming directly for Boy Scout.

Before the operator's arms reached full length, Boy Scout kicked the man's hands upwards.

A shot went skyward.

Boy Scout shot the operator in the thigh, then stepped in and stomped his face.

When the guy's arms went limp, Boy Scout kicked the weapon away.

He glanced at the rifle in his hand and tossed it into the surf, then spun back to Poe.

"This is what happens when you can't play nice," he said to Poe, who now held a pistol at waist level. Lucky for the lieutenant, he wasn't pointing it at Boy Scout. Had he been, Boy Scout would have broken all the man's fingers.

"I get that you want to be in charge," Boy Scout said. "I get that you're in this fucking special top secret fucking unit that no one knows about. I get that you spent twenty million dollars and have your ass puckered so tight with worry you can't think straight, much less shit straight. But don't you ever fucking ever have a man front a weapon on me. You want fratricide, I'll give you fratricide. We could have talked about this. We could have made it work. But you went too far."

Poe blinked, as if Boy Scout's words were rocks.

"I don't know what your problem is," Boy Scout said. "But it's a whole lot bigger now."

Three shots went off, impacting the sand behind him.

"And tell your man to stand down," Boy Scout said, figuring the operator probably had a knife and was about to stab him in the back. "I have both of you covered." To McQueen he said, "How about one more in the sand?"

The shot came and the sand jumped.

"Stand down," Poe said

Boy Scout heard, then saw the operator limp in his direction. The ballistic mask had been removed and the man's mouth was contorted in pain.

Boy Scout lowered his voice. "We're done here."

Poe glanced at his pistol, then shoved it into the small of his back. "Listen, I fucked up."

"You think?"

"They want the *daeva* badly. They want to test it. Figure out its powers."

"I had no doubt. But after I use it, right?"

Poe hesitated, then nodded. "Absolutely."

Charlene came up beside him. "He's lying."

Boy Scout's eye narrowed. "What's the truth, Poe?"

The lieutenant glared at Charlene as she spoke.

"I see you strapped to a table in the middle of a cell. There's no light, except for something down a stone hall. I hear screams from somewhere. It's a bad place, Boy Scout. It's a terrible place."

Boy Scout nodded. "So, not only do you want to test the supernatural being, but you also want to test me. The thing inside of me—you want to find a way to harness it. To bottle it, don't you?"

Poe shook his head. "This is bigger than you and me. This is bigger than all of us. We need to know how to defend ourselves against this *daeva*. You said there are more. What if they come looking for their missing brother?"

"Then I'd let them."

"That's never going to happen," Poe said.

McQueen and Lore appeared from outside the mansion and walked towards them. Poe had his back to them.

"You haven't seen these things in operation," Boy Scout said. "You've only heard reports. Trust me when I say that these are things you don't want to mess with."

"Concern noted."

McQueen joined Boy Scout on the right and turned to face Poe and the operator.

"I heard there was a party. Didn't want to miss it."

Preacher's Daughter joined Boy Scout on the left.

"I hate it when our invitations get lost in the mail."
She glanced at the operator. "Tom, is that you?"

The operator rolled his eyes. "Hi, Laurie."

"How's the leg?" she asked.

"Might need a few stitches," Tom the Operator
said. "Through and through. Your boss knows
how to shoot."

"Hear that, boss? Compliments all around. Tom
here was in 5th Group, or still is in 5th Group.
He wanted to date me and I told him if he could
outshoot me, then he could."

"I take it you never dated, then," McQueen said.

"No. Not even a pity date." She grinned. "Good
to see you, Tom."

Tom the Operator knew when to shut up. He
staggered in place and stared morosely at the sand.

"Now what?" Poe asked.

"We're out of here," Boy Scout said. He turned
and caught Noaks's attention, which wasn't hard
since they were the best show in town. He made
a circling motion with his arm above his head
and Noaks climbed into the cockpit and began to
power up the helicopter.

"You can't leave," Poe said.

"You asking or telling?"

"Damn it. Boy Scout. Don't force me to—"

"What? Shoot me? Lock me up?" He leaned in
so that there were only inches between him and

Poe. "I've had better than you try." He shook his head. "I would have worked with you, except for Tom here. Once you brought him into the picture it became clear where your loyalties lie, and they aren't with us."

Poe held his gaze. "I'm loyal to the United States, as you should be."

"How's that working for you?" Boy Scout stepped back. To the others, Boy Scout said, "Come on. Let's go."

He turned and strode towards the helicopter.

Charlene walked beside him.

The other two had his six.

When they were all on the helicopter and heading away, Lore asked over her headset, "What's the plan?"

Boy Scout stared at the wide, blue ocean and said, "I have no fucking idea, but whatever we're going to do, it's not going to be with Poe."

Then he called Faood and let him know what was really going on. If he was going to throw Poe to the wolves, he might as well choose which wolves to throw him to.

Chapter Thirty-Two

Our Lady of Atlas in Exile, Again

As IT TURNED out, they went back to the beginning.

De Cherge met them on the lawn of Our Lady of Atlas in Exile and welcomed them into his office. He didn't inquire about their weapons, but he definitely gave them hard looks. Once in his office, he offered everyone a seat. He wore his brown abbot robes. His right arm was in a black, molded wrist-to-shoulder cast to protect the arm that Boy Scout had damaged earlier.

To Charlene, he held out his left hand and said, "I don't believe I've had the privilege. I am Abbot Dominic de Cherge."

Charlene blushed. "I'm Charlene Johnson. Pleased to meet you," she said, on her best behavior. If she'd gotten any vibes from the abbot, she kept them to herself.

"Thank you for taking us in," Boy Scout said. "How is your arm?"

"It throbs."

"And the others?"

"Still too soon to know."

"What about Sister Renee?" Boy Scout asked in as respectful of a voice as he could. "Are there to be services?"

De Cherge frowned and stared at the surface of his broad antique wooden desk. "She took her own life, and in doing so, cannot be in God's grace."

Boy Scout's eyes narrowed. He hadn't realized they'd look at it that way. He felt the emptiness inside of him grow. "She didn't take her own life. She sacrificed herself."

"These are kind words, but we know the truth of it. I saw her body. I saw the razors. We'd hoped she would find the opportunity to heal, but for some it never comes."

Boy Scout shook his head violently. "De Cherge, you're the one who doesn't understand. She was working with me in astral projection. She gave her own life to try and help me live. She's no different than a soldier dying for his comrades in arms. She's no different than a mother shoving her child out of the way of a moving car, only to be struck and killed herself. She fought for me and to do that, she had to sever her soul from her body."

Boy Scout continued trying to explain, telling de Cherge blow-by-blow what happened.

All the while, the abbot became increasingly more agitated. By the end, he had tears in his eyes.

"I wished I'd known this before. Not that the church would understand, but I could have at least said mass by her grave."

Boy Scout's jaw dropped. "Grave? You mean she's already buried?"

"The investigation was open and shut. She's buried in a pauper's grave on the edge of the property that's normally reserved for those not in God's favor."

Boy Scout felt unusually emotional. His eyes were tight and he was almost crying. "Can we change it? Can she get a proper burial?"

De Cherge began nodding slowly, then picked up speed. "We can. Yes."

Joy surged through Boy Scout, and it was at that moment he realized the emotions weren't his. They belonged to Sister Renee. She was somehow influencing him. She was still in his head, just as Charlene had said. *Bits and pieces.* He needed to speak with her. He needed to do it now.

"If you can have someone show me to my room, Preacher's Daughter will fill you in on things."

Ten minutes later he was in a narrow room with

a single bed. One of the plaster walls was adorned with a single, roughhewn wooden crucifix. Heavy wool drapes covered the lone, high window.

He sat on the floor in an Indian position and placed his hands on his knees. He tried to slow his breathing, but it was difficult considering the events that had so recently transpired. His mind went back to Poe and the way he'd acted. Had Boy Scout made the right decision in making the man and his unit their enemy? He supposed he'd never know. But the way Poe had acted hadn't sparked any sense of loyalty. Where was the trust? Boy Scout supposed Poe had worked so long by himself that he wasn't able to trust. And if he were to believe Charlene, and he had no reason not to, Poe and Special Unit 77 had plans for Boy Scout. Not only was the *daeva* to be the test subject of supernatural investigators, but Boy Scout as well.

Boy Scout noted that his breathing was actually speeding up. He lay back and rested his legs in front of him. He closed his eyes and brought his hands to his chest. Enough of Poe and Special Unit 77. He needed to concentrate on Sister Renee. He needed to return to the astral plane and see what it was she wanted before all that was left of her was erased.

He remembered her last words as the entity chewed through her essence. She'd discovered The

White inside the entity as if it were an access point. Boy Scout knew he needed to go into it in order to have a chance at ridding himself of *yazata,* but he didn't want to enter the thing that wanted to take him over—which was why he so desperately wanted access to the *daeva*. If the *yazata* was scared of the *daeva*, then he felt safer using it as the engine to enter The White.

It seemed an eternity, but he was eventually able to unlock each of his chakras and sizzle through his third eye into the negative universe of the astral plane.

The entity crouched like a child in the corner, facing away from him.

Boy Scout approached slowly and saw a tendril of energy leaking from it like a stray string. He knew immediately what it was and reached out to touch it.

"Sister Renee."

An astral sigh. "I thought you'd never come." The words were elongated and malformed.

"I'm here now." He regarded the filament with an ache, knowing this was the last of her. "I'm told you have something you must say."

"There's not much of me left," she said.

Her words were so stretched he found them difficult to understand.

"I didn't—I didn't teach you to travel." Another sigh. "It's too hard. I can barely do this."

"No, don't go," he begged, grabbing a bigger handful of the essence.

The entity stirred slightly, but otherwise didn't move.

A word formed in his mind.

FLY.

LIKE.

WHITE.

Then another.

THINK.

FLY.

MOVE.

They repeated over and over until they were a single word.

THINKFLYMOVETHINKFLYMOVETHINK

But still he didn't get it.

And then he did. *I didn't teach you to travel.*

One immense astral face palm as he realized the universe he'd denied himself. He'd only been to the astral plane to confront his travelers, but there was so much more he could do—so much more of it— the astral plane.

Suddenly her words disappeared.

He heard her sigh.

BEFREE.

And she was gone.

He backed away from the entity and floated silently, remembering the moments in the grotto when they'd first met. He thought of her, from the young, guiltless girl traveling to Turkey with her father to rehabilitate a monastery, to the young woman who pushed an older woman in front of a train, to a nun who gave her life in an attempt to save Boy Scout from a fate similar to the one she experienced.

It was all too much.

She was too much.

He would not let her sacrifice go to nothing.

So, he turned and soared, flying through the astral plane with increasing speed.

Gravity was a construct.

Speed was an invention.

All that existed was thought, much like in The White.

He willed himself west and south and within moments found himself hovering above the Turkish Consulate. Thousands of sparks of light shone below, each one a person going about his or her business. It occurred to him that astral projection would make a great way to surveil someone. They could be followed without anyone ever knowing.

He lowered himself so that he was closer to the earth.

Streaks of light proved to be individuals in vehicles moving along gridded streets.

But, as expected, there was one light that made

them all seem dimmer. A large rectangle, something made to store something immense, move something immense, glowing from the center of the consulate. This could only be the *daeva*.

He moved through the ceiling and the upper floors, through furniture and through walls.

Everything material was construct.

He was immaterial.

When he reached the now blinding entity, he settled for a moment. He'd never been awake when he went into a fugue. All the other times it had been when the dervishes had put him to sleep. But his intuition told him it was possible. He wasn't entering the *daeva,* but using the *daeva* as an engine to enter The White.

Was it that easy?

Who was he kidding?

Still, he reached out with a single astral digit and touched—

What felt like an electric line.

Power surged through him, but he maintained the contact, thinking of nothing more than the undisturbed nothingness of The White and his desire to enter.

And just like that, he was there.

No ceiling.

No floor.

No walls.

Nothing.

Just white.

For eternity.

Boy Scout sent out thoughts, calling for Rumi to present himself. He shouted and screamed Rumi's name, but the nothing of The White absorbed everything. Twice he saw something, dark and distant, and both times he moved away from it. The last thing he needed were more travelers. He was about to give up when The White *shifted*.

He was back in Vietnam and amid the noise and stench of Saigon. But he wasn't there to see the Napalm Girl. He also wasn't there to see the Buddhist monk immolate himself. He'd been there and done that. No, this was of a different image— an image from the same Time Life Book in which he'd seen the other two images. This one was of an execution, and he was in the wrong POV. He stood with his hands cuffed behind him. South Vietnamese soldiers smoked and laughed at him. He felt as if he'd been crying. A car pulled up and the soldiers snapped to attention. A sinewy man wearing general stars on his lapels stepped out. He was hatless and he wore his uniform with the sleeves rolled up.

Boy Scout remembered the image well. It had disturbed him the moment he'd seen it. It was the first death he'd ever seen—first in a long line of dead bodies he'd seen or caused to be dead.

The Napalm Girl stood for the hopelessness of the Vietnamese—their plight—being caught in the middle of a proxy war against competing ideals, north and south backed by competing philosophical juggernauts.

The Burning Monk stood for resolve in the face of that hopelessness—a stoicism no American could compete against. A man willing to burn himself alive just so there would be pictures to remind the world about what he did and why he did it.

Even the Falling Man was about something larger. September 11th. Jesus dying for our sins. It was an image of America's youthful recklessness in the way it treated other countries, and how even a never-before-known group with few members could snap back and take a chunk out of the red, white, and blue apple.

But the Saigon execution photo had left him speechless.

In the end, it was the nonchalance that disturbed him the most.

And now he was going to witness it—or, to his horror, become the victim of it.

The general pulled a snub-nosed 38 out of his waistband. He waved it at his men as he said in Vietnamese, "Stand aside."

They shuffled out of the way but remained close

enough to watch what was about to happen to Nguyen Van Lem—to Boy Scout.

Brigadier General Nguyen Ngoc Loan, the head of South Vietnam's National Police, stared coldly at Boy Scout.

I'm not him, he wanted to shout. *Don't shoot me,* he wanted to beg. But all that came out was a whimper.

"You disgust me," the general said, puffing on a cigarette, sweat beading his brow.

He should have turned and ran. He would have been shot, but in the back was so much more bearable than in the head.

"Do you have any last words?" the general asked.

Boy Scout tried to scream but nothing came out.

"Smile for the camera," the general said.

Then the general brought his pistol to the side of the prisoner's head and fired.

Boy Scout's POV flipped. He was no longer the victim, he was the photographer.

He felt the man's nervousness and fear. Would the general let him live after the photo?

He'd just snapped the picture of a lifetime, the nonchalant general firing into the head of a bound man, the bullet already on its way out the other side of the man's head, the hair tousled, the face misshapen. The picture would go on to be plastered across the front page of every major newspaper in the western world, would win the photographer a Pulitzer Prize, and would stand to symbolize the savage horror of the entire war. It would go on to haunt the general until his dying breath.

The general lowered his pistol and turned to the camera. He smiled.

The photographer took his picture, but no one would ever care about this one.

"The Vietcong—they killed many of my men and many of your people," the general said, then walked away. He paused to light a cigarette, then got in his car, and was driven away.

Lem lay on the pavement, blood pouring from the hole in the back of his head, forming a pool that was the color of deep black tar.

It was then that Boy Scout realized the entire scene had been played out in black and white, much like the picture.

Then Lem opened his eyes and spoke.

"You have these images inside of you that are terrible, yet you choose to remember them."

"I remember them *because* they are terrible," Boy Scout said. "Those who cannot remember the past are condemned to repeat it."

"That sounds like something I would say."

"It was George Santayana. A Spanish philosopher."

"In my day, the Spanish were always at war."

"They discovered bull fighting and red wine and found peace," Boy Scout said.

"Then you make peace with the universe. Take joy in it."

From the fortune cookie comment, it had to be Rumi. "Tell me about the *yazatas*."

"Do you think I am yours to command?" the dead man asked.

"We've met before. You told me you are studying the *daeva*. You're the one who told me they were older than humanity. What were the words you said about the *daeva*? *Maybe the Big Bang wasn't an explosion, but a bullet shot out of a rifle. The question we should be asking ourselves is who fired the rifle? I can hear their echoes. I can see their writing on the sand of my dreams. I can even parse the memories of the sleeping* daeva *who remember a different place—a place with more dimensions, where they were many and moved quite differently than they do today.* Then I said, *Perhaps the explosion that created our universe destroyed theirs.*"

"I remember this, yes. But was that before or after? Time flows differently here. The dimensions available to us through the *daeva* are mirrors of their own dimensions."

"I ask again. Tell me about the *yazata*s."

"I can see now why you ask. You have one inside of you. How I missed it before, I don't know. It's as if you've come fully formed to The White. What is my aspect?"

"You are the Viet Cong soldier lying dead in a black and white universe."

Suddenly there was color, so blinding and so raw that Boy Scout couldn't help but shield his eyes. Along with the color came the noise, only now the events were going backwards. He watched as Lem rose to his feet and the bullet slammed back into the gun.

The general turned to him and grinned.

"Where were we? If we're going to speak, I might as well be the shooter rather than the victim."

Boy Scout had given up wondering how things were done in The White.

"You were going to tell me about the *yazatas*," he said.

"What do you think they are?" Rumi asked.

"Some posit they're demons. Evil spirits."

"The darkness that lurks at the edges of each civilization. Yes, we need to put a name to that which scares us. Demons. *Yazatas*. That could be so."

"Are you telling me that you don't know?"

"I think you have a better answer. I've paid for my knowledge with time. What have you paid for yours?"

Suddenly the general raised his pistol and shot Boy Scout through the head.

The universe flipped and Boy Scout found himself hovering outside of the *daeva* and back in the astral plane.

He willed himself to return home and hardly noticed that the entity was looking at him as he slammed home into his physical body.

Chapter Thirty-Three

Our Lady of Atlas in Exile

DE CHERGE HAD given them a larger room, which they used as a common area.

Boy Scout entered and sat roughly on the couch.

Charlene and Preacher's Daughter glanced at him, but were deep in conversation.

Charlene shook her head and looked at Preacher's Daughter. "You're getting it wrong, girl. Demons never appeared in the Old Testament. They're a product of the Greeks translating various versions of the Bible and the fourth century Vulgate."

"Nice try," Preacher's Daughter said. "What about Deuteronomy 32:17-17? *They made Him jealous with strange gods; With abominations they provoked Him to anger. They sacrificed to demons who were not God, To gods whom they have not known, New gods who came lately, Whom your fathers did not dread."*

"What about it? That's the line everyone goes to when they want to argue the presence of demons. But it's all translation issues. The original Hebrew text never really had a word for demon."

"Careful, Charlene," McQueen said, an amused look on his face. "Preacher's Daughter doesn't like to be wrong."

"Easy, big boy. I'm not wrong," Preacher's Daughter said.

"Oh, yes you are, dear." Charlene took out a stick of gum. She placed the gum she'd been chewing in the wrapper and folded it up, then inserted the stick of fresh gum into her mouth. Once she'd masticated it into a snapping mess, she continued. "As I said, the original text never had a term for demons. It was the Greek use of *daimoniois* that was taken and translated in the Latin, which is why we are here now. For instance, the whole purpose of the Deuteronomy passage, and the later passage in Psalms 106: 36-37, was to poke fun at those worshipping gods of foreign peoples. In the first case, it was the Israelites. In the second, it was the Canaanites. Those were spiritually territorial verses designed to inform the reader that they needed to stick with the God that brung them."

"Whapow," McQueen said smugly.

"As far as devils were concerned, every reference was used to dis Baal worshipers. Again, used merely to make sure that the readers of the Bible stuck with the God in context. In summary, there are no demons or devils in the Old Testament, only idols worshipped by other people."

Preacher's Daughter stared at Charlene for a moment, then shook her head. "Where did you come from?"

"Indiana originally, but I'm in Arizona now."

"And here I thought you were just an above average psychic hairdresser astrologist."

"We've never met, remember? That was all in one of your dreams. But I did feel it. And the other time, too."

They all turned to Boy Scout.

"You look exhausted, boss," McQueen said.

"Rumi says hi, by the way."

"You saw him? You entered The White?"

"I did. Or at least I think I did."

"What did he say?" Preacher's Daughter asked.

"I asked him about the *yazatas* and he turned into a South Vietnamese general and shot me in the head. He said I need to earn the knowledge."

"You all live such interesting lives," Charlene said.

"Says a Chinese curse always," Preacher's Daughter said.

"We were talking about demons," McQueen said.

Charlene pointed at Boy Scout. "That nasty little beast inside of you wants to come out, but it wants to do it on its own terms. It's starting to figure out what it is."

"So, you can see it?" Boy Scout asked.

"I can see it, and I can also see a woman."

Boy Scout shook his head. "She's gone. I just saw the last of her."

"No. She's still there. She's just... changed. She's now part of the *yazata*. She's younger. And she knows you. I can see her smiling."

"Sister Renee?" he asked, air leaving him. "She's alive... or whatever she is? I thought she'd died."

Charlene chewed on her thumbnail for a moment. "Nope. Not dead. Say, does anyone have any food around here?"

McQueen straightened from where he'd been leaning against the door. "That's what I was thinking, too. Maybe a pizza."

Preacher's Daughter mouthed the word *FAT* at McQueen.

"Everyone hold your horses," Boy Scout said. "Put what you mean into context for me." He glanced at Preacher's Daughter and Charlene.

Both women nodded, but it was Preacher's Daughter who spoke first. "Sister Renee called the thing inside of you the King of Demons. One has to wonder if that's an actual title, or a term derived from her Christian point of view. As Charlene has adequately discussed, there was no mention of demons in the Old Testament, which is the one derived from borrowed stories and ideas, especially Zoroastrianism."

Charlene shook her head as if it were the saddest thing and mouthed the word *adequately*.

"Biblical evidence provides several theories that try and clarify what are popular beliefs," she said out loud. "One is that demons are spirits of deceased wicked men. But Psalm 9:17, Luke 16:23, and Revelation 20:13 all indicate that these spirits would be in Hades. Another theory is that demons are spirits of a pre-Adamic race, but there's no support in scripture for that. In Corinthians 1, the Bible declares that Adam was the first man. Another theory is that demons are the results of an unnatural union between angels and women in Genesis 6. I particularly hate this one. Not only is this pure supposition, but don't even get me started with the fact that angels were injected into the Bible to make it more spiritual. Then there's the theory that the word demon is simply another name for fallen angels."

"Thanks for the Wikipedia entry," McQueen said. "But what does this have to do with anything? Or is it something we can talk about over pizza?"

"What it means, dear heart," Charlene said, "is

that if there were no demons in the Bible, then there are no demons at all unless they're something that the Europeans developed in the fourth century."

"Wait," Boy Scout said. "If there are no demons then, what was all that about Kamaris and the Ars Goetia? What was in Sister Renee that made her—" No one knew what she'd been told, so he kept it to himself. "What about Sister Renee? What about the exorcism?"

Charlene tutted. "Oh, there's something. It's just not a demon."

"Really? What's in a name?" McQueen asked.

"Then what is it?" Boy Scout demanded.

Preacher's Daughter thrust out her hip and crossed her arms. "Why don't we see what Charlene has to say?"

"I'll pick what's behind door number three," Charlene said. "They are the spiritual remnants of a pre-Adamic race."

The Children of God, Boy Scout thought.

"You believe in spirits?" McQueen asked.

"Said the fella whose friend was stuffed with them," Charlene said. "Yes, I believe in spirits. Newton's Law of the Conservation of Energy said that energy can neither be created nor destroyed. The spirit is pure energy. It has to go somewhere."

McQueen's eyes narrowed. "I'm not sure that's what Newton meant."

Charlene shrugged. "Doesn't matter what he meant. He was merely stating a universal truth."

"They were around before Adam, then," Boy Scout said.

"Lots of things were around before Adam. Animals, bugs, insects... probably even the *daevas*. None of which were mentioned in the Bible. Some weren't mentioned because they were details. Others weren't mentioned because the Biblical architects didn't want them included."

Preacher's Daughter nodded. "The *daevas* were first mentioned 5th century BCE. In the initial Zoroastrian *gathas* they weren't evil. But as the religion progressed and became more popular, they were labeled as evil and much of what you see in the Ars Goetia regarding the names of specific demons comes from the list of *daevas*. Even back in the 5th century BCE, they were talking about beliefs that existed for many centuries before then. These beliefs could have been made based on actual evidence, or on superstition. What we do know is that the *daeva* exist. We've seen them in action."

"I remember them well." Boy Scout sighed, images of them flashing through his head. "Where are you going with this?"

"In addition to the *daeva,* there are also the *yazatas*. I've been doing some research with the material provided by the Black Dragoons care of

Special Unit 77. Some have the original Persian gods as *yazatas*, but more research seems to say that they were extraordinarily tall humanoid beings who were worshipped and revered by man."

"*There were giants on the earth in those days*," Boy Scout murmured.

Charlene stuck out her tongue. "I hate that one."

Preacher's Daughter broke into a smile. "Exactly. And what if those giants were the *yazatas*? It would explain why they have access to The White, just as the *daevas* do." She raised a hand before anyone could chime in. "I also want to point out that their first appearance in comic books was in the giant-sized *Conan* published in 1974. What you might not know is that the time period in Conan that the events take place was fifteen thousand years BCE, during the Hyborian Age."

"So now we're supposed to believe Stan Lee?" McQueen asked.

"Robert E. Howard," Boy Scout corrected. "He literally invented the sword and sorcery genre." He nodded to himself and chuckled. "He also used the books of Bullfinch's Mythology as source material for his Conan stories. The same books that mention the Zoroastrian religion."

"It's in comic books now?" McQueen said, surprised.

"Everything's in comic books," Boy Scout said.

Chapter Thirty-Four

Our Lady of Atlas in Exile

"WE NEED TO come up with a solid plan," Boy Scout said later, after they'd eaten.

Sadly, the food wasn't the pizza McQueen had been hoping for. Instead, it was a hearty beef stew with homemade bread served by the monks and nuns of the monastery. While Boy Scout had appreciated the meal, McQueen had complained bitterly about his lack of access to pepperoni.

"How long do you think we have before Poe comes after us?" McQueen asked.

Boy Scout looked at Charlene.

She shook her head. "Don't go thinking I'm in charge because I have information not available to you. That's the problem with people once they find out I'm a psychic. They lose their interest in doing things. They stop thinking on their own and start depending on me. They stop being agents of action."

Boy Scout nodded, then stared into space. "Our earlier conversation about doors had me thinking. There might be a way for me to get this thing out of me. I might actually survive doing it."

"But," McQueen said. "Where's the *but*?"

"But it would involve returning to Afghanistan and luring the other *daeva* here."

Both Preacher's Daughter's and McQueen's jaws dropped.

Preacher's Daughter was the first to recover. She shook her head and laughed hollowly. "That's a place I wouldn't wish on my worst enemy. I'm so done with Afghanistan."

"Seriously?" McQueen asked. "You want us to go *back*?"

Boy Scout shook his head. "Not you. Me."

"Don't think you're going to go there without me," McQueen said, ever loyal.

Boy Scout placed a hand on McQueen's shoulder. "I appreciate it, man, but you can't go the way I am."

"Astral projection?" McQueen asked. "Can you even do that—I mean travel somewhere?"

Boy Scout told them about his last trip and how he'd spied on the *daeva* in the consulate. "If I can do that, then I can go to Afghanistan."

"But didn't Charlene tell us that every moment spent on the astral plane is one where you might get attacked?" Preacher's Daughter asked.

"She did, but it's the only way I know to get this thing out of me," Boy Scout answered. "I can't go to the consulate. It's under surveillance. The dervishes try and move anything even remotely the size of the *daeva* and the FBI will pop them. So, it's either sit here and wait for the *yazata* to realize I'm ripe for the taking, or become that agent of action," he said, nodding to Charlene.

"What are you going to do in Afghanistan?" Preacher's Daughter asked.

"I'm going to find the *daeva* and let them know where their missing brother is. I'm guessing they're going to want him back. Then I'm going to ask if they want the *yazata* inside of me and offer them a way to do it."

"How are they going to get it out of you?" Preacher's Daughter asked.

"I'm still working on that, but I have a solid idea."

"I just love it when you build the missile in flight," McQueen said. He whistled and added, "Yeah, in-flight missile repairman."

Boy Scout shrugged. "If I fail, then it's only me."

McQueen frowned at him. "What if I learn to astral project? It can't be that hard."

"It was at first, and it doesn't always work out. I think I have an affinity for it. I was deeper in The White than any of you. I think by doing what I did there, it made my ability to astral project easier."

"But you won't have us to protect you," McQueen said.

Boy Scout closed his eyes, took a breath, then opened them so he was staring alternately at McQueen and Preacher's Daughter. "You can't spend the rest of your life protecting me. You have lives of your own, you know?"

Preacher's Daughter stood and strode to the other side of the room. She whirled, fury torturing her features. "Don't you think we know that? Don't you think we understand we're putting our lives on hold because of you? We could walk out anytime. There's no one holding a gun to our heads. My contract was long over."

Boy Scout didn't say a word.

"All I ask is a little appreciation. After all, we've spent the better part of six months working to get you free from the effects of our last mission."

Boy Scout pointed behind her. "There's the door. No one's holding you here."

She glanced behind her and then back at Boy Scout. She looked at McQueen for help, but he just sat and watched with wide eyes. "Are you fucking kidding me right now? Did you really just ask me to leave? After everything I've done for you?"

He stared at the ground. "I'm just saying that if you want to go then you can go. I'm not holding you back."

"Of all the—" Her anger dissolved for a moment as she fought tears. She slapped them away. "If that's the way you want it, then fine." She looked around the room, her eyes dead, but her voice mangled with emotion. "I got nothing keeping me here."

Then she was out the door and slamming it behind her.

No one spoke for a full minute.

Boy Scout merely stared at the floor. Although he'd hated saying what he had, there was a reason behind it—no, there were three reasons buried in Afghanistan and he didn't need another one.

"Now that was something I didn't expect," McQueen said. "You going to go after her?"

"No," Boy Scout said simply.

"What do you mean, no? Boss, I'm not sure you were paying attention, but Lore just walked out the door."

"I was paying attention."

"You were? But then why—" McQueen got to his feet. "Someone's got to stop her. Aren't you going to—" He cursed under his breath as he opened the door and slammed it behind him.

All Boy Scout could do was stare at where

McQueen had departed. He said to no one in particular, "That's a damned sturdy door."

"You know she's not coming back," Charlene said.

"I know. It's what I was hoping for."

"They feel like they deserve some appreciation," she said.

"I'm sure they do, and they deserve for me to say something." He turned to look at her. "But if I do, then they're going to keep watching my back until one or both of them dies. I can't have that."

"You can't always change the future," she said.

"But I can change the way everyone plays the game. You said that. Listen, I'm a fucking death magnet and about to invite a squadron of demi-gods to descend on Los Angeles so they can free one of their kind. Bad shit will ensue. People will die."

"Then why do it? You that desperate to get the *yazata* out of you?"

He sighed. "Never *that* desperate. If it was just me, I'd walk into the desert and take care of it myself. But this is bigger than me. I don't like the idea of the dervishes having a superhuman entity at their disposal. They don't deserve it. The thing is no better than a prisoner being kept to fuel their desire to live forever." He leaned forward. "You know what Faood said? He said if I keep this thing inside of me and feed it the souls of travelers, I can live forever, too. Do you know the significance of three thousand, nine hundred and forty-two?"

She shook her head.

"Faood said that's the number of graves outside of the cistern in Afghanistan. Three thousand, nine hundred and forty-two. That's the number of people killed by the dervishes. And it doesn't include the souls of the travelers they collect and feed to the *yazatas* inside of them. One thousand more? Two thousand more? I can't reward that by inaction. You want me to be an agent of action? I'll be a fucking agent of action." He got to his feet. "I'll be a fucking agent of action," he repeated. "I'll burn the place down. LA can take it. She's had far worse done to her than a few demigods rampaging through a building or two in Westwood. And if every last damned dervish dies in the process, then this Earth will be better off for it."

He walked out of the room feeling more exhausted than he'd ever been.

He'd sleep for a year if he could, but time was ticking.

Sleep was for the innocent and he was way past being innocent.

He went to his room, closed the door, and lay on the floor.

Chapter Thirty-Five

Astral Plane

IT TOOK HIM two hours to enter the astral plane. The pain and ache on Lore's face cast a pall over his motions like a dead moon across everything he tried to do, and try as he might, he couldn't get rid of it. He thought about chasing after her several times, or even just calling her. Wondering if that small gesture might ameliorate his shame. But he couldn't bring himself to do it. Her life was more important than his own peace of mind. So he let the wound fester until the rot of it collapsed upon itself.

Once in the negative space of the astral plane, Boy Scout couldn't help but stare at the root of it all—the *yazata*. If anything, it seemed larger than it had been. Was it coming into its own? Was it realizing what it was? He feared touching it, worried that he might get sucked in and forever lose himself. But was that so bad? What would the world be like without Boy Scout? He doubted it would ever realize he was gone. He was less than a blip on its radar. If anything, the world might be a better place.

While the dervishes would no longer be targeting him, they'd still be after Preacher's Daughter and McQueen. If there was only one thing he could do, it would be to help them—ensure their continued existence on this damned planet. To that end, Boy Scout headed west. He willed himself to move faster and faster, not yet able to just move and appear in another place. He knew there was no such thing as distance on the astral plane, but he couldn't entirely wrap his head around the concept, so the best he could do was to travel at the speed of thought. He soon found himself above a vast darkness, which had to be the ocean.

Moments passed before he saw any hint of life, but when he did, he stopped and stared in awe at an immense being of light that moved languidly in the abyss below him. For a moment Boy Scout wondered if it might be a new creature, some astral being that existed only on the plane. But then he realized that it must be a whale. He saw the ghostly shape and how it tapered to nothing, the massive creature pushing through the darkness of the astral ocean.

Whales had always been a totem for him, their existence proof that there were things so much larger than what a man could be. He'd never really understood his need to see one in the wild, but it had driven him to make attempts between contracts in Afghanistan and Iraq. He'd gone to Monterey Bay twice, where he'd boarded whale watching ships. But the closest he'd come was a glimpse of a fin and the splash of a tail. Try as he might, he'd never been able to see one in all of its gigantic glory. Frustrated at his inability to connect, after extensive research, he'd gone to Frederick Sound in Alaska and joined a kayak tour. This special tour occurred only once per year because of the whales' migration, but he'd timed it perfectly. Nine immense, two-person kayaks floated in the center of the sound, and around them swam a pod of whales. Not only had he'd seen several breach the water, almost leaping completely into the air, but many came close enough for him to touch.

Boy Scout had actually wept with joy in those moments, but he had never taken stock of what had been so significant—so important. Now he knew. His interaction with the *daeva* had informed a part of him that he hadn't known needed defining. The ache to know that there is something large out there outside of the human spectrum.

He felt drawn to the beast below.

He knew he had to travel, but he wanted to touch it, feel its thoughts, its power.

He moved lower and lower, following the creature like a bird of prey. This was the closest he'd ever get to truly flying and he enjoyed soaring over the essence that was the whale.

Even lower, until he felt like he was underwater, although there was no water in the astral plane.

Soon he was close enough to touch the creature. In the material plane, the whale would weigh upwards of fifty-five thousand pounds. Adult females were larger than their male counterparts, clocking in at fifty-two feet. But here, like he was also, they were weightless, seeming to fly in the silence.

Then like an astral lamprey he reached out with his left hand and touched it.

The feeling was electric and immediate.

A great sense of longing and loneliness filled him. Searching. Missing. Wanting. A sense of looking and not finding. What was it missing? What had it lost? And then it came to him. Whales mated for life and this majestic thing was alone. It might live another fifty years and never know peace. Moving along its migratory and feeding routes over and over and over until it either died or was killed by an illegal whaler.

Boy Scout felt gut punched with the truth of it.

He imagined what it would be like for him if he was forced to walk the planet, never able to find the one he loved, the one he needed. One more reason his decision of never getting married had been a rock-solid plan. Then again, humans could remarry as well as fall in and out of love. Human love was a capricious thing that had less to do with a genetic need to bond than it did to entice men and women to procreate.

Boy Scout noted that his hand was pulsing with energy, growing brighter and brighter by the moment. The longer he stared, the faster the pulses came and the brighter it shone until he could barely regard his own hand. Was the whale giving him power? Was it reenergizing him? Or worse, was he taking power from the whale?

A flash of an eager grin on his own face filled his mind for a single, shocking second.

The *yazata* was hungry.

He tried to push away but lacked the strength. The *yazata* had pulled up to an all-you-can-eat whale essence buffet and wanted its fill. But how much was too much? Boy Scout could see the lessening as it happened in real time, the whale growing dimmer and dimmer by the moment. His outrage and desperation exploded across the astral plane with his pain, but he still could not remove his hand.

The whale dimmed, then dimmed some more, then became nothing more than a lighter outline in the darkness. Dead. Once a whale, now floating in the astral Pacific as so much dead meat.

He felt the wrongness of it.

He felt the guilt of killing such a miraculous creation.

Determined to do something, Boy Scout sought The White. He willed himself to change, to move, to become something other than he was, just so he could be somewhere else. He refused to be witness to this calamity. He didn't know whether it was his will or by greater design, but in a flip he was no longer lamprey to a dead whale, but standing in the middle of a Vietnamese highway talking to Napalm Girl—Phan Thi Kim Phuc.

The roar of fire in the background threatened to drown out everything, but it wasn't so loud he couldn't hear the words coming from her mouth.

"What are you?" she asked.

Her flesh had been burned and the smell of it made his gorge rise. Still, he struggled to answer.

"I am Boy Scout," he said.

"What is Boy Scout?"

Who was he speaking to? Could it be the *yazata*?

"I am who you are inside," he said with the most trepidation he'd ever felt.

It felt like an eternity passed, then she said, "Ah,

so it *is* you. But what are you? What is this I am being in your mind?" She held out her arms and he had to look away. She was nine and naked. Speaking with her thusly felt incredibly unseemly. He wondered absently why the *yazata* had chosen this image.

He paused before he answered, trying to honor the image while informing the entity.

"You're an infamous picture from my memory turned real. You are Phan Thi Kim Phuc, also known as Napalm Girl. Her own country burned her village with fire and she had so many burns on her back, she was forced to run down the road naked after stripping off her burning garments."

"Why would her own country burn her village?"

"Another army had entered her village and her own country's army sought to get them out. They used a bomb that made fire stay longer than it should."

Another eternity seemed to pass, as if the *yazata*'s thoughts were as somnolent as the whale's.

Napalm Girl tilted her head at an odd angle. "How did they make fire stay longer? Was this magic?"

"Of a sort. What is your name?"

"The sound of it would blind you and cause your ears to bleed. I still need you. I see in your mind much killing. I see in your thoughts much violence.

I see murder. Ironic that it was us He tried to remove, when all along it was you. This thing I am being, this girl who has been burned by your own. You are a group that kills as a way of life. You profit by it. Death merchants. Why should you be allowed to continue?"

Boy Scout felt the need to defend his species, but he knew he had to tread carefully. "What of you? Why were you removed from this Earth?" On a hunch, he continued. "Why was it that God made a great flood come to rid the Earth of your kind?"

The Napalm Girl crossed her arms and straightened. She began to grow until she was three times the size of Boy Scout, towering over him, but she was still Phan Thi Kim Phuc, naked and burned.

"Because we were superior. We were first. Then came your kind, breeding like rats, small and inconsequential. I remember, you know. You were favored and we were asked to make way for you. But who were you to supplant us? Who were you to think that us first people needed to be replaced by a trivial race called man?"

Boy Scout realized that he hadn't formed his body and did so, willing it into being so that he could better relate to the creature that was the Napalm Girl.

"This wasn't our decision to make. God made this decision."

"It wasn't your god who did this. It was our gods. They agreed to do this in order that they should live. We were the first. We lived here before your god ever came."

Boy Scout was in new territory now. He wasn't sure how to proceed. What the *yazata* was saying was unprecedented. History that no human had ever been witness to. But what was he to say? Could he just ask it to leave? It was clear what it wanted. It wanted him, and now that it knew what it was, how to access and exercise its power, what was going to stop it? Then he realized that he had nothing to lose. The *yazata* had him. He was like a fish in a net, unable to move and slowly dying from being out of its natural environment. He was like the whale, except that he'd be kept alive and it was his spirit that would be consumed.

"What did you do with Sister Renee?"

"That one. She was my last. Her energy was imperious."

A curious choice of words. *Imperious.* "Why do you say that?"

"She tried to take me over. She tried to free you from me."

An empty joy surged through him knowing this. Even in the end, she had fought.

"What did she do?"

"Even now I can feel a small part of her

lurking about, hiding behind thoughts and ideas. Mimicking memories. Attempting to elude my attempts to consume her completely."

"She's still alive?"

"Alive? What is this concept? I was alive once. Then I wasn't. Now I will be again. Your words have no meaning in the universe of me." The giant arms of the Napalm Girl snapped out and suddenly a doll-sized version of Sister Renee was there, struggling, arms beating against the fingers that held her, legs kicking. "She surfaced for a moment. That was awkward, wouldn't you say?" the Napalm Girl asked the thing in its hand. Then she lifted the doll-version of Sister Renee to its mouth and swallowed it whole. A grin spread across the face of a girl he'd formerly only seen in agony. "Finally," she said. "The last and final taste."

The Napalm Girl increased in size once more until Boy Scout barely came to its knee.

"Do you understand now? Do you see how you are so insignificant? You sought to worship us and your god became jealous." Napalm Girl shook her head. "Petty, that."

Boy Scout didn't know how to respond. It was as if his ability to be his own agent of action had been taken away. He stared at the great being in front of him, so much like a whale, but lacking the virtue of innocence. Did the whale treat the other things in the sea as this one did humans on land? Was the whale worshipped or treated as another being in the mélange of the oceanic life pool?

He couldn't be sure how much time had lapsed as he thought these things, but eventually the Napalm Girl stirred.

"Now this is different."

And then everything flashed to darkness.

Chapter Thirty-Six

The Middle of Fucking Nowhere

JUST AS SUDDENLY Boy Scout was strapped to a chair and everyone was arguing. He looked down at his wrists to discover they were tied to the arms of a chair. He tried to move his feet and discovered they, too, were affixed to the chair's legs. He tried to speak, but fabric had been stuffed in his mouth and tied around the back of his head. His chest felt heavy, as if he were wearing weights.

Preacher's Daughter was squared off with McQueen, both of them face to face and standing in front of Boy Scout.

Charlene stood back from them but seemed ready to step between the pair.

"You shouldn't have made that promise," Preacher's Daughter shouted.

"I had to. You saw what it was doing. The damned thing would have killed us all," McQueen shouted with equal velocity.

"He's back," Charlene said.

"What do you think we're going to be able to do in seventy-two hours?" Preacher's Daughter yelled.

"You prolonged the inevitable."

"At least now we have an inevitable," he yelled back.

"He's back," Charlene repeated.

Preacher's Daughter said, "What do you mean he's—" Then she turned to stare at Boy Scout.

McQueen did as well, then rushed over. "Is that you, boss? Are you really back?"

Preacher's Daughter bent down and stared into his eyes. "This better be you," she said, removing the gag. To McQueen, she muttered, "If you're going to ask him a question, you really need to make sure he can speak."

Once the gag was removed, Boy Scout worked his mouth, but there wasn't any moisture. His mouth was raw and as dry as a desert.

Charlene brought him a water bottle and tilted it so he could drink.

When the bottle was empty, he nodded and she stepped back.

"Is that really you, boss?" McQueen asked again.

"I—I think so," Boy Scout said. "What—what—my arms."

"Let me get those," McQueen said and started to untie them.

"Hold on a moment," Preacher's Daughter said. "What's the safe word?"

"You do realize that the *yazata* knows everything Boy Scout is thinking, so it would also know the safe word. You do realize that, right?" McQueen asked.

"I don't give a shit. I want him to tell me what the safe word is or else we're not going to untie him."

Boy Scout struggled to remember. His mind was a fog and felt at once too full and completely empty. "Safe word?"

"We talked about it," she pressed. "What's your safe word?"

He still couldn't remember what she was talking about. But then things finally clicked into place. He remembered killing the whale. He remembered speaking with the giant version of Napalm Girl. And he remembered what they'd joked about being his safe word.

"Rumpelstiltskin," he said.

Preacher's Daughter exhaled and nodded. "That'll do."

She untied his left wrist while McQueen untied his right.

"What happened?" he asked.

Preacher's Daughter glanced up. "You don't remember anything?"

He shook his head. "Last I remember I was in The White."

They moved to his legs.

He rubbed at his wrists and noted the deep gouges made from the rope.

"Why did you tie me down?" he asked.

"You don't remember anything?" McQueen asked.

"Nothing. Zilch. Nada. Please, someone tell me what the fuck just happened."

Preacher's Daughter and McQueen finished and stood back and stared at him.

"Nothing *just* happened," Preacher's Daughter said. "It's been happening for three days."

Boy Scout blinked. "Three days? I was gone for—What did I do?"

"You shot a ray of light out of your mouth that disintegrated the fucking wall, is what you did," Preacher's Daughter said. "Then you almost obliterated us."

A ray of light? "Please say you're joking." He looked at McQueen.

"Sorry, boss. Not even joking. One minute we were sitting around drinking, the next you came out of your room like a fucking monster with rays of light coming out of your mouth. It's one of the reasons we gagged you."

Charlene approached with her cell phone and held it out.

"Watch the video," she said.

Boy Scout watched in fascination as his image stood in the center of the screen, rays of light shooting out of his mouth, his eyes aglow.

"How did I... How did you..." He looked at Preacher's Daughter. "I thought you left."

She shrugged. "I came back. I knew you were just being a dick and trying to save me, but it's up to me what battles I decide to fight and not fight. It's not your choice. As far as how we subdued you, it was de Cherge. He had a stun gun and hit you with it three times. Then we tied you up and brought you here."

"The *yazata* might be all powerful, but it still has to deal with a human body," McQueen said. Boy Scout looked around and realized he was in a large motor home with pull outs.

"Where is *here*?"

"In the middle of the desert in Death Valley," Preacher's Daughter said. "Seemed appropriate."

"De Cherge let us use one of his RVs. He said he'd prefer it if we didn't come back. I think he was afraid you might burn everything down."

"He certainly gave us enough," Charlene said. "It's also important that we be here."

"What is it you know?" Boy Scout asked.

"I can't tell you."

McQueen harrumphed. "She's like that. She does the *I know all* followed by the *I can't tell you*."

"And she enjoys it," Preacher's Daughter said.

"Do you really think knowing when everyone is going to die and when everything is going to happen is a blast?" Charlene asked.

Preacher's Daughter leveled her gaze at the other woman. "I think you've made it your own."

"Why were you two arguing?" Boy Scout asked.

McQueen held out his hands and patted the air. "Now, hear me out before you get mad, boss."

"Why am I going to get mad?" Boy Scout asked, frowning.

"Maybe because you're wearing a suicide vest rigged with explosives," Preacher's Daughter said.

McQueen spun to her. "Lore!"

Boy Scout looked down and for the first time saw what was weighing him down. It looked like a fishing vest that had pipes sewn into it, all with wires leading to a central point in the back. The weight he'd felt earlier had been the bombs attached to him. He flashed to the boy and his mother's orange-scented fingers. Then he got pissed.

"Get this off of me!"

"I can't," McQueen said miserably. "I won't."

"What do you mean *you won't*?"

McQueen held out a remote control that could only be the detonator. "The vest is stitched closed so that you can't take it off. The wires all go to a receiver in the small of your back, which you can't reach. This is the detonator."

"I fucking figured that out, McQueen. Now I'm going to ask you one more time. Get. This. Off. Of. Me."

McQueen shook his head and seemed about to cry.

Preacher's Daughter stepped forward. "He really can't, boss." She held out her hands. "Now, hear me out. The *yazata* wasn't fucking around. He had complete control of you and was ready to level all of us. You don't have the power to do anything anymore. The only reason you're back is because of the deal we made with it."

"What deal?"

"It's a gamble that McQueen made. I didn't like it at first, but we didn't have a choice."

"What's the fucking deal that has me in a suicide vest?" Boy Scout asked, almost shouting.

"The *yazata* gives us three days to see if we can get rid of it. The vest was our bargaining point."

Charlene fidgeted with her phone for a moment, then held it up.

"I have a video of that too."

Boy Scout watched the small screen as McQueen

leveled the threat.

"The vest is rigged with twenty pounds of explosives. Pipe bombs filled with screws all linked to a central receiver. I'm going to blow you up. It will kill my best friend, I know that, but it will also knock you back into The White. You've probably been waiting an eternity to get your hooks into one of us. Do you want to wait another eternity? Or do you want to have a chance at possessing my friend?"

The view shifted to Boy Scout, tied to the chair and gagged. His eyes glowed supernaturally.

"I think you need to give it a yes or no question," Preacher's Daughter said from off camera.

"Blink once if you understand me."

Boy Scout blinked once on the video.

"Give us one month to figure this out and if at the end we can't, then you can possess Boy Scout."

Boy Scout blinked twice.

"Fine, then two weeks."

Boy Scout blinked twice again.

"Fuck. Then how many days?"

Boy Scout blinked three times.

"Three days? Three fucking days?"

Boy Scout blinked once.

Charlene pulled her phone away.

Boy Scout stared at his deadly new attire. "So, I have three days," Boy Scout said. "What are we going to do in three days?"

McQueen looked even more miserable. "I don't know. I just knew we needed time."

"There really wasn't any choice," Preacher's Daughter said, laying a hand on McQueen's beefy shoulder.

"So the three of you made a deal with the devil and gave me three days to live."

"Don't count me as a part of this," Charlene said. "I already know how this turns out."

"And you'll keep it to yourself." Boy Scout said.

"Mostly," Charlene said. "But I'm not just along for the ride. I do have a vested interest."

"But you won't tell us." Boy Scout shook his head and pushed himself shakily to his feet. He felt dizzy and had to grasp the chair for balance. "Ain't this great? We got a psychic who won't tell anyone anything, and three operators who don't know what they're doing, but they made damned sure that one of their own was wearing a suicide vest so they could blow everyone the fuck up. Now, that's what I call a plan."

Chapter Thirty-Seven

Still in the Middle of Fucking Nowhere

THEY FED BOY Scout three cans of pork and beans. He hadn't known how hungry he was until he smelled it heating up. He figured that later the legumes would do a number on his digestive system, but he didn't really care at this point. He had roughly seventy hours to figure out how not to die and little information to go on.

He'd failed miserably in the astral plane. He'd intended to get to the *daeva* and try and communicate with it about their missing *brother*. Instead, he'd been distracted by the ghostly image of an astral whale. The more he thought about that, the more he wondered if it hadn't been the *yazata* manipulating his emotions in order to draw power from it. Then he remembered that they had encountered another whale, and another after that. He couldn't be entirely sure, but he felt as though he'd touched many more than just the one.

Had he drawn power from many whales?

How many were they?

Had he killed them all?

Maybe that's how the *yazata* had gotten so powerful. If it had been able to siphon off the life force of so many of the creatures, it might be unstoppable now. They'd gotten lucky with de Cherge and his stun gun. As much as Boy Scout hated to admit it, using the suicide vest was mad genius. The *yazata* needed Boy Scout to be alive and the threat of death would ruin all its plans.

When he finished eating, McQueen came back inside and sat heavily on the couch.

Boy Scout didn't know what model RV this was, but it had two couches, an easy chair, granite counters in the kitchen area, a table that could seat four people comfortably, and a bathroom off a back bedroom.

"You put the bombs together?" Boy Scout asked.

"With a little help from Radio Shack and Home Depot."

"Where'd you get the gunpowder?"

"This is California. They barely even sell guns, so gunpowder was out of the question. I used ammonium nitrate from fertilizer, and sodium azide from vehicle airbags. Took about a day to construct them."

"And they're not going to go off anytime soon?"

"If they do then we're all in trouble. Frankly, I'd keep my eye on Charlene." McQueen smiled grimly. "If she starts edging away from you, then you know shit's about to blow up."

"Literally." Boy Scout glanced at his watch. "What gets me is that this thing is listening to us right now. It could take me over any second. What's to stop it from coming out and just killing you?"

"Because of the dead man's switch. All three of us have transmitters. Any one of us can activate it in a moment and none of us care if we die."

"What about during the night?" he asked, absolutely horrified.

"We sleep in shifts."

"Like you've never fallen asleep during guard duty," Boy Scout said. "This entire situation is *not* making me happy."

Preacher's Daughter came in from the back. "Nor should it." She stood in front of Boy Scout, crossed her arms, and waited. "Well?"

"Well what?" he asked. Then he realized what she wanted. He shook his head and stared at the floor. "I was trying to save you," he said.

"I get that." Her foot began to tap. "And?"

"I didn't want to see you die."

"And?" Her foot tapped faster.

"And I'm sorry."

The tapping stopped and she took a seat beside McQueen.

"There. That wasn't so hard now, was it?"

Boy Scout felt an almost overwhelming feeling of friendship, of the bond that had formed between the three of them. Where he'd been close with all of his team members, these two were at the core and had always seemed to be there. McQueen especially. A scene from the movie *Heathers* flashed through his mind and he couldn't help but smile.

"What's so funny?" McQueen asked.

The moment in the movie he'd remembered was when the father of one of the two jocks killed by Veronica and JD, played by Winona Rider and Christian Slater, stands up at the funeral of his son and proclaims that the two dead boys were gay, based on the evidence that JD and Veronica had planted at the scene of the murders. They hadn't been, so what the pair had done was doubly horrible because they changed the way the dead boy would be remembered by his father. Although the movie was about high school and mean kids and cliques, it could have been about the military, which was why so many military folks loved the deadpan, gallows humor that the screenwriter had infused into the script.

"I'm thinking of *Heathers*," Boy Scout said.

McQueen groaned. "Talk about clichés."

Preacher's Daughter's grin grew wide. Then in a melodramatic voice, she turned to McQueen and said, "*I love my dead gay son!*"

"I'm going to punch you," McQueen said flatly.

She put her hand over her heart. "*My son is a homosexual and I love him. I love my dead gay son.*"

"I'm really going to punch you."

She grinned madly. "Do you know there's even a Broadway musical called *Heathers*? They have an entire song about that." She pulled out her phone. "Let me see if I can pull it up. We can sing it together."

"Boss, can you please tell her to stop?"

"I wouldn't dare."

She held the phone up and began to read. "Oh my God. This is fabulous. Listen to this, McQueen. *They were not dirty! They were not fruits! They were just two stray laces in the Lord's big boots.* Oh my God," she said again. "I need to memorize this!"

McQueen got up and left the RV, the door slamming behind him.

Preacher's Daughter was busy reading the lyrics of her new favorite song.

Boy Scout got up and followed McQueen outside.

The heat slammed him in the face. It was late afternoon and the temperature was still over a hundred. The Mojave Desert was a flat canvas as far as the eye could see. The RV was parked along a dirt road. No other vehicles were present.

He found McQueen on the other side of the RV in the shade, where the temperature was remarkably cooler.

McQueen stared into the distance.

"She was just joking," Boy Scout said.

McQueen wiped at the corner of one eye. "Oh, I know. It didn't bother me. She fucks around like that all the time. It just reminded me of something."

Boy Scout turned and gave McQueen his full attention.

"Do you remember what I told you about? How when I first came in I pretended to be a homophobe like everyone else?"

Boy Scout nodded.

"I'd laugh at their jokes. I'd laugh at their comments. I didn't want anyone to know. And then I did the most terrible thing one could do to another human being."

"I remember. Billy Picket was his name."

McQueen turned to look at Boy Scout.

"You *do* remember."

Boy Scout reached up and cupped the other man's cheek. "Of course I do. And you've spent your entire life trying to make up for that crime."

"Just like you do, for killing that pedophile," McQueen said. "God will treat you better than me."

Boy Scout lowered his hand. "What's the connection to *Heathers*?"

"We'd just got done watching it when Billy said something that was so outrageous, I gave myself away. That's when he began to make fun of me, when he began to call me names."

"I'm sorry to even bring it up," Boy Scout said. "I was thinking about how much I love the two of you and that scene popped into my mind. Of all the scenes in all the movies, I don't know why that one."

"You couldn't have known."

Boy Scout glanced around and saw nothing but desert and scrub. "Where exactly are we?"

"Ten miles north of Jimgrey," McQueen said.

"Where the hell is that?"

"Tiny town off Highway 58. We're southwest of Fort Irwin and roughly west of Barstow. Death Valley."

"Why out here?"

"In case you blew up. We didn't want anyone else getting killed." Then McQueen asked, "How does it work?" He waggled his fingers around his head. "Astral projection, I mean."

"You just have to clear your head and imagine your whole being leaving your body through your crown chakra, or third eye."

"If it's so easy, why doesn't everyone else do it?"

"It's not so easy. I don't know."

"Did you see anyone else up there?"

"Not really. I saw the other travelers, but no astral travelers like me."

"I wonder why that is? There's seven and a half billion people on the planet. Odds are you would have seen someone. I wonder if they can they hide from you."

"If they can, then they know where we are," Boy Scout said.

He spied a plume of dust in the distance.

"We're going to have company," Boy Scout said.

McQueen nodded. "That's fine. We have plans for that." He banged on the side of the RV. "Lore. Char. Prepare for Operation Boom Boom."

"What the fuck is Operation Boom Boom?" Boy Scout asked.

McQueen grinned. "Just you wait.

Chapter Thirty-Eight

Astral Plane

"TIME FOR YOU to get inside, boss."

McQueen grabbed his shoulder, but Boy Scout resisted.

"I'm not going to let you two handle this alone."

McQueen pointed to the vest. "A stray round might do more damage than we want right now. Just go inside. We have a plan."

Boy Scout considered arguing, but there wasn't any reason to do so. McQueen was correct. Right now he was a liability. He glanced once more at the approaching dust cloud, then hurried inside.

Preacher's Daughter escorted him into the back of the RV. Sheet metal had been placed around the inside of the walls.

"Not going to keep out anything large caliber,"

she said, "But it should stop anything smaller. Just avoid the windows."

"How am I going to see what's going on?"

"You'll have to trust us," she said. She flashed him a grin, then closed the door to the back.

Full on frustration set in. His troops were about to battle without him. He'd never been good sitting on the sidelines. Boy Scout briefly considered finding a way to get out of the suicide vest, but dismissed it. As soon as the threat was gone there would be no reason for the *yazata* not to take him over. Although if the *yazata* did take him over, it might fire light rays from his mouth again and help take out the encroaching enemy in a bid of self service. He filed that away as a future possibility, but dismissed it in the here and now. He figured they had about ten minutes before the dust cloud arrived. He would never know who or what was coming unless he was able to get out of the RV.

Then an idea came to him.

His only trepidation was possibly confronting the *yazata*. He'd just have to ignore it and hope the thing would leave him alone. But then he remembered that this same *yazata* had consumed Sister Renee, and anger supplanted any concern he might have had.

He lay back on the bed. At first, he was hyperaware that he was in an RV in the middle of nowhere and wearing a suicide vest. But he pushed all of that aside and concentrated on his breathing—the same slow in and out that allowed him to hit a five-hundred-meter target.

In and out.

In and out.

In and out.

He began to unlock his chakras.

From bottom to top, each one snapped open, releasing more and more of him, until he opened his crown chakra and he sizzled out of his third eye.

It was like waking up from a dream.

Gone was the RV.

Gone was the constant tick of the air conditioner.

Gone was the weight of the vest.

Gone was everything.

The only thing there was the pulsing darkness of the dark sun and the bright evil of the *yazata*.

Which was looking right at him with maniacal glee.

A light in the darkness that might as well be an oncoming train.

It took an effort of will to turn his back on it.

But he had to.

He spun away and searched the ground beneath him. He spied four figures. One was a good distance away from the RV, of which he could just make out an outline. One was in the back of the RV, so that could be only him. One was in the front of the RV, and the final one stood beside the RV.

Boy Scout conducted an astral search of the perimeter, but other than three vehicles, there was nothing else within miles.

He surged towards the oncoming vehicles and was able to distinguish twelve figures, four in each vehicle.

He decided to try something. He moved lower towards the first vehicle and matched his speed with theirs. Then he reached out and touched the light of the figure who was in the driver's seat. He felt a white heat at the site and a flash of memories that went too fast for him to latch on to. The man's hands came off the wheel and went to his head. What was interesting was that the car slowed, its speed decreasing until there was nothing.

Was it his touch?

Could he affect regular people?

The man had grabbed his head. Had Boy Scout given him an immediate headache—a migraine, perhaps?

Could he take their life force like he'd done the whale?

Boy Scout was amazed at his newfound ability and held on until he felt immense pain from behind him. He pulled his hands free. He tried to spin, but was unable. Instead, he reached around and felt an astral arm working at the back of his head. He grabbed the arm and managed to pull it away. Now he did turn, and saw another astral person hovering near him.

"Boy Scout."

And it knew his name.

"You've fed the beast."

Boy Scout glanced to where the *yazata* sat, marking the location of his physical body, then back to the figure floating close by.

"I had no choice. It took control."

"I told you to feed it the souls of travelers. I told you to make sure it had sustenance so this very thing wouldn't happen."

Faood. And he was astral traveling.

"How did you—"

"Do you think you're the only one capable of astral projecting? What you did reverberated across the entire astral continuum."

"You mean the whale. I didn't do that. The *yazata* did."

"You think it was only one? You sucked the life force out of forty-six whales."

"Forty-six? That... can't be." Had it really happened? Had he really participated in the murder of so many whales? A great sadness threatened to overwhelm him.

"One whale would not have caused the quake that forty-six did. I saw their bodies floating in the Pacific, darker than the water, what had been bright life snuffed out by your excessiveness. The scene was a veritable astral tourist attraction for a while. All sorts of travelers followed the ripples to the source and saw what you did."

Boy Scout could picture it all—cetacean after cetacean, meant to live for half a century or more, now floating dead and rotting, life extinguished because of his inability to control the hunger of the beast within him. He glared at the *yazata* and could not wait to be rid of it.

"What you did is a stain upon your soul, Boy Scout."

He couldn't help but say, "But it wasn't me."

"You still don't get it. The *yazata* is you. You are the *yazata*."

Boy Scout fumed at the idea. He was no hunter. The idea of killing something or someone who didn't pose a threat was anathema to his world view. Never would he even consider it, so to be accused of such a thing, to be an accomplice to such an event, made him physically and spiritually ill. But he didn't have time to mourn. He had a more immediate threat to deal with. "Call your men off," he said.

"No can do. They want their pound of flesh."

"And you want me."

Faood paused, then said, "Not until you did what you did. Now that it's self-realized, it can't be used for what we need. But we can study it. We can use it to further our means. Without your spirit attached to your body it makes what we want to do far easier."

"You intend to kill me for that?" Boy Scout said, pointing at the *yazata*.

"Kill is the wrong word. Release you from your physical body would be a more appropriate descriptor."

"And then you're going to tame the *yazata*," Boy Scout said.

"There's no taming it once it knows what it is. It's made you into a monster. Why it hasn't consumed you already is a mystery." Faood moved closer. "If you let me remove the silver cord then I will call my men off. You can float into the dark sun and see what's on the other side."

"Or burn up."

"Do you think so? I believe it's a gateway to somewhere else."

"Then feel free to investigate. I'm not going anywhere."

"But your team—how many are left who haven't been killed because of you?" Faood stared at the surface of the material plain. "Preacher's Daughter?

McQueen? And I see another—do you think three against twelve are good odds? Come now. Let me free you from your problems and your men will go unharmed."

"I thought yours wanted their pound of flesh and you can't stop them."

"Maybe I haven't tried hard enough."

The proposition was fair. One life for three. Boy Scout had had enough of death. He'd seen too many of those who had entrusted their lives to him die. And for what? So some VIP could make a meeting? So a convoy could make it down a road? So an HVT could sit in a cell and be badgered with questions from an FBI Special Agent? As capricious as the offer sounded, maybe that was his alternative. Maybe this way he could guarantee the lives of the few who remained.

But it wasn't a hundred percent. Even Faood didn't seem to be convinced he could talk the dervishes out of attacking. And if it wasn't a hundred percent, then he'd be sacrificing himself for nothing.

"I considered your offer, Faood. I really did. But I think I'll pass."

"I was afraid you'd say that."

Faood surged towards Boy Scout at impossible speed, grabbing him and propelling him across the astral plane so fast that the life forces in the cities blurred beneath him. Faood had completely taken him by surprise. Boy Scout struggled to remove the man's astral hands from around him, but as soon as he'd move one, Faood would grasp with another. Remembering the battle with the Berber, Boy Scout invented more arms to push Faood away but Faood was faster at growing more and more arms as well. Soon each of them had a dozen appendages fighting with one other, but Faood always uncannily maintained the upper hand.

"Clever. How did you learn to do this so fast?" Faood asked.

"I had advanced training," Boy Scout said, thinking of Sister Renee and the days she'd been locked out of her body, her only freedom to explore and understand the astral plane.

"I thought this would be easier. Still, I've been doing this for over a hundred years," Faood said. "Fighting you is like fighting a child."

Worry crept into Boy Scout's desperate attempts to be free. "Where are you taking me?"

"Kilauea volcano in Hawaii. One of the only things that can destroy an astral body is fire from the earth. Not manmade fire, but god-made fire. The fire of creation."

They were over complete darkness now which could only mean the Pacific Ocean.

Boy Scout's efforts increased as he fought to be free from Faood. To die in a volcano while in astral form wasn't in the cards. He had to find a way to get free of the mad dervish, but Faood was so strong, so fast. Boy Scout brought his legs up and wrapped them around Faood's astral hips, then pressed, using a jujitsu move he'd learned long ago. Sure enough, Faood lost his grip.

But only for a moment.

Before Boy Scout could do anything, Faood grabbed his feet and continued propelling him towards astral Hawaii.

Boy Scout pulled himself into a ball and kicked hard.

Again, Faood lost his grip.

Boy Scout took that moment to scramble away and head for what he thought was east, back to the mainland.

But Faood was impossibly faster. This time he grabbed Boy Scout by the front of his legs and changed directions, sending them back to their original trajectory. But he'd made a mistake. Faood's head was literally near Boy Scout's crotch, and Boy Scout reached down to the back of the dervish's head and grasped the silver cord that protruded. He pulled and Faood screamed. But it wasn't coming loose. He pulled harder and Faood tried to slap his hands away.

Boy Scout saw a brightening from behind his head and instinctively knew what it was. They'd traveled so fast so soon. Such was Faood's power. How could he ever hope to win this fight?

Boy Scout wrenched at the cord and Faood screamed louder.

They stopped suddenly.

Faood let go of Boy Scout's legs.

"I'm a hundred years stronger than you. You might cause me temporary pain, but you cannot possibly win the day."

Then, like an adult to a misbehaving child, Faood grabbed Boy Scout's wrists and easily pulled them off the silver cord. Then he latched onto Boy Scout's feet, swung him around three times, and released him.

Boy Scout hurtled towards the volcano, the visage of an impossibly white pit of light tumbling as he somersaulted in the astral plane. He thought of McQueen and Preacher's Daughter. He thought about Charlene. He thought of the *yazata* that had such immense power. To die like this would be... Then he remembered something Faood had said. *You still don't get it. The* yazata *is you. You are the* yazata.

And he stopped on a dime mere meters from the pool of light—the fire of creation.

He surged across the empty space to Faood and grabbed him.

"I am ten *thousand* years stronger than you."

He willed himself back to his material body and moved instantaneously there. One moment he was hovering over a Hawaiian volcano the next he was hovering over an RV in Death Valley, and he had pulled Faood with him.

"How can you—?"

This close, Boy Scout could make out Faood's features.

Faood's worry.

Faood's fear.

"You told me. I am the *yazata*. I consumed the life forces of forty-six whales. I have their power. You are *nothing* to me."

And then he hurled Faood into the *yazata*, feeding the beast the enmity of his species.

Chapter Thirty-Nine

Operation Boom Boom

BOY SCOUT DIDN'T waste a moment on his astral victory. Instead, with his newfound power he blipped to the battle, which was just beginning. Like a god, he stared down at the scene, making sense of it in mere seconds. Where he'd thought his own astral battle had taken time, the events beneath him in the material plane were still unfolding. It was as though he was using a night vision device that rendered everything alive in stark, blurry white.

The three vehicles were near the RV now, moving slowly, side by side. Half their occupants were dispersed on the ground, running beside the vehicles.

Two people were still in the RV. He imagined the one in the front was Charlene. At least she'd know when to duck, if necessary.

The figure in the shadowy lee of the RV was either McQueen or Preacher's Daughter. Whichever it was, the other was offset by forty-five degrees from the front of the RV and about a hundred meters. Although there was no way Boy Scout could be sure of the reason for that position, if it'd been him, he'd have used it as a sniper's roost.

Remembering what he'd done earlier, Boy Scout decided to see what he could do to help the others. He chose the vehicle in the middle and blipped to it. He shoved his hand into the face of the driver. The vehicle twisted to the right, colliding with the other vehicle. Electric energy shot up his arm as images buzzed through his consciousness. He started to contemplate the morality of his actions and whether or not he should be using his astral abilities like this, but dismissed the thought immediately. The enemy was presenting an overwhelming force and he needed to use any means necessary to save his team.

He blipped to the driver in the left vehicle, who was still trying to go in a straight line, and shoved his hand into his face with the same reaction.

Boy Scout felt a sort of shaking, as if the universe were going to tear itself apart.

Then again.

He felt pieces of himself flaking away, as if

something was happening to his essence.

Then Charlene was leaning over him and screaming into his face, "WAKE UP!"

Groggy from the instantaneous transformation back to the material plane, he blinked and brought a hand to his head. He quickly closed his chakras.

Then he heard it outside. Explosion after explosion.

"What's happening?" Each word took effort.

She stood up straight and crossed her arms. "There. I did what I came to do."

He managed to sit up. "What are you talking about?"

She stood in the doorway to the room, arms crossed, leaning against the frame. "Explosions are like volcanoes. The stuff of creation. Even in astral form you can't survive."

Boy Scout climbed shakily to his feet and stumbled to the window, where he spied all three vehicles smoking and on fire. The left-most vehicle was all but obliterated—the place he'd been moments before.

"I would have been killed," he said, both as a statement and a question.

She nodded. "Yes, you would have ceased to exist."

He spun back to her even as gunfire opened up from both sides.

His eyes narrowed as he spoke. "Why did you help me? I thought you wanted us to be agents of action. I thought you weren't going to help any of us. All the *we can't change the future* crap you spouted."

She made a face like there was a foul smell. "Faood would have changed the future. I can't have that."

"What? How?" The battle was distracting, but he wanted—no, *needed* to hear what she had to say. A single shot sounded louder than the others and came in metronomic intervals of three seconds. That had to be McQueen with the sniper rifle. "Explain."

"It'll take too long. Go help your friends. Go help McQueen."

He started to move, then his eyes widened. *McQueen.* She'd given him a warning.

Rounds raked the side of the RV, several piercing the metal and zipping through. He held an arm over his face and hit the door running, grabbing the Walther off the couch as he went.

The door slammed open.

The light was fading and the temperature was dropping. Twilight had arrived rather quickly.

Preacher's Daughter knelt beside the steps leading into the RV, holding an HK 416, sighting down the barrel and firing in three round bursts. "We were flanked," she snarled.

Two dervishes who had been running towards them went down.

She stood and shot each of them in the back twice for good measure.

"I thought you were supposed to be inside so you didn't get blown up," she said.

Gunfire came from the other side of the RV, but now none of it was pointed towards them.

Boy Scout ignored her and snatched the rifle away from her. He ran to the back of the RV, brought the rifle up, and cornered the back with the barrel. He saw the three smoking vehicles, which looked like they'd been razors. Several dark figures lay dead or dying on the ground beside them. He also saw five more low crawling towards McQueen's position, which was slightly higher than theirs by about five feet.

What made the other man's roost the best place to fire from also made it vulnerable for what the dervishes were doing. They were already within ten meters of the position, and in order for McQueen to get an effective shot, he'd have to show his head. He tried several times, but each time, the dervishes laid down fire. Working in concert as they were, McQueen would soon fall.

Boy Scout brought his rifle up and began to fire single shots into the enemies.

He caught one, then another, but missed twice

more. Then the bolt locked to the rear.

"Magazine," he yelled.

"Can't—we're out," she yelled back. "Hold on."

"I can't hold on," he whispered.

He dropped the rifle, pulled out his pistol and ran for the nearest dead body. He fired his pistol as he ran, but knew he had zero chance of hitting the dervishes. He just wanted their attention.

Ten meters out from the nearest dead dervish, he saw one of the dervishes who was advancing on McQueen turn and fire in his direction. Boy Scout felt the passage of the bullet as it zinged by his ear. He dove, hoping that the impact wouldn't set off his suicide vest. It didn't, so he crawled furiously for the weapon he'd seen peeking from beneath the body.

A fucking Uzi.

Almost completely worthless, yet, using the body as a base, he laid the barrel over the dead man's back and pressed the trigger. The weapon buzzed to life, sending thumb-sized 9mm rounds in a straight line, the shots eating up the sand. He used the line as an aiming device and drew it right to his target who pitched backwards when the miraculous final round smacked him in the face.

Boy Scout tossed the Uzi aside, surged to his feet and ran to the next dead dervish.

This one had an Uzi as well, but when he tried to replicate his trick, he discovered the weapon was empty.

He dropped it aside and ran to the next body. This one also had an Uzi. It was like they'd gotten their TTPs from binge watching *Miami Vice*. He would have grabbed the weapon, but Boy Scout could see it was empty, bolt locked back to the rear.

He heard screaming from the other side of the RV as Preacher's Daughter sprinted towards McQueen's position. She had picked up two AR15s from dead dervishes and she fired one on the run.

The last two dervishes on the ground turned toward her and fired, but she kept coming.

Now that she had the attention of all the dervishes, McQueen took the moment to stand in his roost and pulled his pistol.

He was about to fire when two things happened.

Preacher's Daughter took two rounds in the chest and she fell, her momentum causing her to pull the trigger and send a round into the slim space between the lower part of McQueen's body armor and his belt. He fell backwards without a sound.

Both Preacher's Daughter and Boy Scout yelled, "No!"

She climbed to her feet. The rounds had caught her high on her body armor. She'd have a bruise, but live.

One dervish was still alive. For some reason he also stood, looking at his three targets. And fuck it all if he didn't try to dance.

Preacher's Daughter butt-stroked him for his efforts and he went down, eyes rolling into the back of his head. She fell to her knees beside McQueen about three seconds before Boy Scout arrived and did the same.

McQueen had sprawled in his hasty fighting position, legs akimbo, one arm above his head and holding the pistol, the other covering the wound. Blood was already soaking through the spaces between his fingers.

"I feel like John Wayne in *The Cowboys*," he gasped.

Boy Scout crouched over him. "Wrong movie, my friend. He was shot in the back in that movie."

"Then it was *Rio Bravo* or *El Dorado*," McQueen managed.

"Same movie, different actors, except for Wayne," Boy Scout said.

"Will you two stop your fucking Hollywood repartee?" Preacher's Daughter cried. Tears covered her cheeks. "I am so sorry, McQueen. I am so damn sorry."

"Don't worry about it, kid. You were right." He smiled weakly. "I'm getting fat. Body armor rode up a bit."

"How bad is it?" Boy Scout asked.

McQueen winced, lifted his hand to peek at the wound, then returned it. "Does the pope fart in the woods when a tree falls?"

"Lore, help me get him back to the RV."

They each took an arm, but McQueen leaned heaviest on Boy Scout. They limp-carried him to the RV. They struggled for a moment getting him up the steps, but finally managed to push him onto the couch. Boy Scout removed McQueen's body armor and checked for an exit wound. He found it two inches to the right of the spine.

"Someone get this started and on the road," Boy Scout ordered, searching the cabinets for medical supplies.

"No can do. Two of the tires are blown," Preacher's Daughter said.

Boy Scout glanced at the window at the three burning hulks. "Fuck."

Then Charlene was there, holding a first aid kit in her hands.

"You knew," Boy Scout said, taking it. "You fucking knew and you let him get shot."

Charlene remained silent as he dug into the first aid kit. The small plastic box of Band-Aids was meant to fix a hangnail, not treat a gunshot. Still, he took the ACE Bandage and tore it in two. He put one section in back and stuffed the hole, then used the remainder for the front. He'd seen duct tape somewhere earlier and ordered someone to bring it to him. Meanwhile, he wanted to keep

McQueen awake.

"Why Operation Boom Boom?" he asked.

"We had three UAVs on the roofs with pipe bombs attached to them." He grimaced as Boy Scout hoisted him up to wrap the duct tape around the ACE Bandages, holding them in place. He laid McQueen back down. "When the vehicles came, I operated the UAVs from my position and kamikazied each of them into a vehicle. Blew them up good."

"Shouldn't it have been called Operation Boom Boom Boom, then?" Boy Scout asked, trying to smile.

McQueen stared at him for a moment, then shook his head. "You were always smarter than me, boss."

"That's why I'm the boss."

"We have to do something," Preacher's Daughter cut in.

McQueen shifted and made a face like he'd impaled himself on a spear. Then his expression softened and he began to breath shallowly, probably to minimize the pain.

"What is there to do?" Boy Scout said, sitting back heavily. "If we try and carry him, we'll never make it." To McQueen he said, "What do you want me to do?"

"You said they were the same movie," McQueen murmured. "Tell me about them."

Boy Scout had been there before. He remembered holding SSG Pavarnik's head in his lap as he bled out from too many wounds to patch back in Iraq. "Tell me a story, Starling," he'd said. All he'd wanted was to hear another voice—something to connect him to humanity for the last time. So Boy Scout did as he was told and gave McQueen words to anchor himself to the living.

"There were actually three movies, all done by director Howard Hawks. *Rio Bravo*, then *El Dorado*, then *Rio Lobo*. They were all essentially the same, about a sheriff trying to protect his town from bad guys. Dean Martin played the drunken sheriff in *Rio Bravo* and Robert Mitchum played the drunken sheriff in *El Dorado*. They both had a sidekick. In *Rio Bravo* it was the singer Ricky Nelson playing Colorado. In *El Dorado* it's James Caan playing Mississippi."

"Was that James Caan from the *Godfather*?"

"Sure was. Sonny Corleone. A funny thing about *Rio Bravo* is that Robert Mitchum was supposed to have a limp and he kept forgetting which leg to limp on. If you watch the movie you can see him limping on the left sometimes and on the right."

McQueen stared into space long so long that Boy Scout thought he might have died.

Every second Boy Scout's chest felt more and more hollow.

But finally, McQueen took a deep breath and said, "Sort of reminds me of when we were in the fugue. We kept replaying the same thing, trying to get it right. Maybe if we'd had Howard Hawks, we could have finished sooner. Tell me about the last one—what was it?"

"*Rio Lobo*."

"Yes. *Rio Lobo*. Is that the same as the others?"

"It starts out different, but in the end everyone is barricaded in the sheriff's office just like the others."

"Why'd the director repeat it?"

"Trying to get it right, I guess. Maybe the director, Howard Hawks, was in his own fugue."

A moment passed where McQueen had closed his eyes. "What was there to get right?"

"I suppose he had a vision and kept trying to make real life fit into it."

McQueen laughed, then coughed, then laughed again. "Funny how you call the movies real life."

"Can I get you some water?" Preacher's Daughter asked. "Can I get you anything?"

"Sure," McQueen said. "I feel so dry."

Boy Scout and Preacher's Daughter met each other's gaze and shared their desperation.

She got up and grabbed a bottle of water, opened it, and dribbled some of the contents into McQueen's mouth.

McQueen coughed once and his eyes fluttered.

"Don't blame yourself, Lore. I can see... see it in your eyes. It was a firefight. Crazy shit happens in a firefight."

Boy Scout could blame himself as well. Maybe if he'd taken Faood up on his offer, McQueen wouldn't be lying here.

"But it was my bullet fired, from *my* gun that got you," she said, and cried.

"Technically you were using one of the dervish's rifles," Boy Scout said in barely a whisper.

She looked down into what was probably a bottomless pit of regret and wiped her face with her sleeve. "Still, I was the one who fired it."

"I love you, Lore," McQueen said.

"I love you, too, my big fat gay hipster."

McQueen tried to laugh, shuddering with the effort. His eyes closed for a long moment, then opened again. He turned his face to Boy Scout. "Remember our conversation about *Buffy the Vampire Slayer*?"

"First John Wayne and now *Buffy*? What is this?" Preacher's Daughter grabbed McQueen by the sleeve.

"Hush now," Boy Scout said. "Yes, I do. You said that I was Buffy. You even said I should change my call sign."

McQueen smiled weakly. "We agreed that Lore was Anya, the vengeance demon."

"I remember that."

McQueen's eyes squeezed shut as though he was about to cry. Then he opened them again. "What about me? I don't want to be left out. Who am I, Boy Scout? What character am I, Bryan? Am I even in the show?"

Boy Scout's face softened as he cupped McQueen's cheek. "You're Xander."

McQueen frowned. "Why him? He has no power. He's just a regular dude. He... he's pretty much comic relief."

"You don't get it," Boy Scout said. "You're the expert of the show and you don't even see it. Sure, he has no power. Sure, he's sometimes comic relief. But so are you."

Preacher's Daughter broke in. "Xander's arc was about trying to get others to respect him. Don't you see it, my fat gay hipster? You spent your entire career trying to show people that it's cool to be gay and fat and hipster."

McQueen coughed, then smiled thinly. "I'm not fat," he said. Then added, "Well, maybe a little."

"See, Xander is the heart of the show," Boy Scout said. "Without him, the show would be lost, which was why he was in every episode but one. He grounds the others. He makes them more human. Among all the monsters and demons and slayers and vampires, Xander is the most human of them all. That's what you do for us, McQueen. You make us more human."

McQueen stared at Boy Scout for a long moment. Then, "Fuck me, boss. You're going to make me cry."

"Which was something that Xander would definitely have said."

Then they all cried, even Charlene—right up until the sound of a helicopter roaring past, making them all stare hopefully at the roof.

Chapter Forty

Why It's Called Death Valley

PREACHER'S DAUGHTER LEAPT up and ran to the window. She stared out a moment, then said excitedly, "It looks like Noaks." She grabbed a rifle and headed to the door. "Going to check."

When she was gone, Boy Scout asked Charlene to get him a wet rag. She brought it to him and he wiped McQueen's face clean. He was pallid and sweaty. He desperately needed medical attention. The helicopter could be a life saver.

A minute later, Preacher's Daughter came back to the RV.

Poe was right behind her.

Boy Scout reached for his pistol.

"Easy, Boy Scout. I'm just here to help."

Boy Scout's eyes narrowed. "How'd you know

we were here?"

"I saw everything from satellite. When the dervishes made their move, I made mine and tried to get here in time." He nodded to McQueen. "I saw him go down. How is he?" McQueen's eyes were closed, but he was still breathing.

"We need a Level One Trauma Center."

"Nearest one is Las Vegas. Fort Irwin is closer. They could at least stabilize him." Poe, who had been edging close to McQueen to see how he was doing, suddenly backed to the door. "Wait a minute. What are you wearing?"

"A suicide vest."

"What the fuck, Starling?"

"If I don't wear it the *yazata* takes over," he said in monotone. Damned if he wasn't tired. "Long story."

"Are you serious?" He glanced at Preacher's Daughter. "Is he serious?"

She nodded.

"Those things going to go off?"

Boy Scout looked at Poe. He wished he didn't have to answer dumb questions, but if they wanted a ride, he'd need to at least cooperate. "I hope not. Instead of worrying about me, can we get McQueen some help?"

Poe hesitated, then nodded. "Let's get him to his feet."

Together they carried McQueen to the waiting helicopter.

Noaks was in the front seat and appeared concerned. He acknowledged Boy Scout with a friendly albeit worried nod.

They laid McQueen across the floor rather than trying to strap him into a seat.

Tom the Operator sat near the closed far door. Across from him sat a dervish, his hands and feet shackled to the floor.

"I found one alive," Tom said. "He was hiding behind one of the vehicles. The rest are dead."

Boy Scout glanced at the operator and growled.

Poe said, "Nothing funny is going on here, I swear."

"Let's just get McQueen to the hospital," Boy Scout said.

"We could use our first aid kit in the helicopter, but I'm afraid we might do more harm than good. Looks like you staunched the bleeding."

"He's bleeding internally," Boy Scout said. "Nothing we can do about that here."

"Then let's get him to help."

Everyone climbed aboard. When Charlene was about to get in the helicopter, Poe said, "Where is she going?"

"With us," Boy Scout said.

"I don't think so."

"Listen," Preacher's Daughter said. "I don't know what hard-on you have for her, but she's coming with us." She gestured to the desert. "There's nothing out here and nowhere to go. We can't leave her. We won't leave her."

Poe looked as if he wanted to argue the point.

"What if the dervishes come to collect their dead and find her?" she asked.

Boy Scout could tell the man liked Preacher's Daughter.

Charlene remained silent through it all. Of course she did—she knew what the response was going to be before anyone did. "Okay, you're right." Poe held out a hand and helped Charlene board.

Boy Scout situated himself on the floor with his legs spread and McQueen laying between them, his head on Boy Scout's lap. He held his old friend with both hands.

Once in the air with their headsets on, Noaks said, "Twenty-two minutes' flying time to Fort Irwin."

After a few moments, Poe said, "The Turkish Consulate is gone."

"What do you mean, gone?" Boy Scout asked.

"The creature it held—the *daeva*—others came for it."

"How did they—" The whales. The same way Faood had known. "That must have caused quite the disturbance."

"It would have, but they were invisible to the naked eye." Poe pulled out a tablet and pressed a few buttons, then held it out. "This showed up on thermal."

And there it was. Eleven giant thermal images with impossibly long arms pulling apart the building as they worked their way to free one of their own. Chunks of walls and floors and ceilings were hurled into the street, landing on cars and trucks. Bystanders must have been mystified as to why the building suddenly just came apart. Boy Scout watched, entranced, for several moments, then saw them board their thrones and roar away.

"What's the official story?" Boy Scout asked.

Poe raised an eyebrow. "They're going with highly localized tornado."

"Who's going to buy that?" Preacher's Daughter scoffed.

Poe shrugged. "It's LA. They'll buy anything. Give it a day and they'll stop asking questions. Give them a week and they'll forget it ever happened."

Boy Scout remembered when he'd first seen them in that valley so high in the Hindu Kush where the JSOC Colonel was making a drug deal. They had been invisible at first.

"Where did they go?" Boy Scout asked.

Poe looked at him. "I think they were headed this way."

"You think they were..." Boy Scout sighed. "Why didn't you tell me first?"

"Getting McQueen help was more important. We can fly faster than they can, anyway."

"How can you be so sure?" Boy Scout asked, remembering his increasingly dexterous ability to move on the astral plane.

"Hey, we could have not come," Poe said, exasperation clear in his voice. "We've put ourselves in harm's way just by being here."

Boy Scout nodded. "I get it. Do you think they're coming after me?"

"Or what's inside of you. It's another reason we're here. Even with our differences, I couldn't leave you behind."

"About our differences," Boy Scout began. "I—"

Poe cut him off. "I'm sorry I even tried to do what I was going to do," he began. "I spoke again with the House Subcommittee and we agreed to call everything off. There were too many procedural violations and laws we would have to break to imprison you, not to mention the federal ban on human experimentation."

Boy Scout shook his head. "Human experimentation? I don't even want to know what you had planned."

"It wasn't me," Poe insisted. "I was just the delivery man."

"I was just following orders," Boy Scout said sarcastically.

Poe could only frown.

"I'm just happy cooler heads prevailed," Boy Scout said.

"Now you can walk down the street and not be in fear of getting picked up," Poe said.

Boy Scout stared out the window on the helicopter's side door and nodded. "Sure." Then he turned and made eye contact with Charlene. He scowled as he said, "I know you knew he was going to get shot."

She nodded.

"You could have warned me sooner," he said through gritted teeth.

She shook her head, eyes imploring for him to understand. Finally, she said, "But I did warn you."

"Too late. You warned me too damned late. I don't get it." He lowered his gaze back to McQueen. "Why'd you help me and not him?" he asked, patting McQueen's chest ever so gently.

"Faood did something he shouldn't have. He needed to be taken off the board."

Boy Scout tried to make sense out of her words. "Taken off the board?"

She cocked her head and paused, staring into space. Then she seemed to come to a decision and returned her gaze to him. "Faood wasn't who you thought he was," she said carefully. "Faood was Rumi. Rumi discovered how to take over a *yazata* and forced it to merge with Faood, creating a single entity. He lives within you now. You have both the original *yazata* and Rumi inside of you."

"That's impossible! I saw the *yazata* consume the essence of Faood."

"The *yazata* did try, but it was unable to succeed. Even as strong as it was, Rumi's self-awareness saved him."

Boy Scout's mind was spinning. He had so many questions he wanted to ask. He settled for, "What was Faood... going to do?"

Charlene inhaled before she spoke. "Bring on the end times. Rumi knows the truth of it all."

"Bring on the—how would he do that? Why?"

"He believes that the greed and murder and hatred of the world is because of overpopulation. He'd see it changed even if it meant the deaths of billions of people," Charlene said.

"Are we talking about the end of the world as in the Rapture? Or the end of the world because of something that man did?"

"He wants to release all the *yazata*. He's been gathering them in a single place. He wants to release them in the world and let them be free."

Boy Scout remembered the video of the rays of light shooting out of his mouth. He remembered the power of the being inside him when he confronted it. Having the world populated with hundreds, if not thousands, of these creatures would certainly mean the end times. Did Rumi really want the world to end like that? It also explained why Rumi had been so easy to find. He was always there, because he knew where Boy Scout was. The reason Faood no longer searched for Rumi was because he'd already found him and had been taken over.

Charlene placed a gentle hand on his shoulder. "You'll gain understanding when this is over, Boy Scout. You're part of the greater picture. You always have been. It's why men and women are drawn to you. There are those of us who are major players in the ultimate game. You are one of them."

"What are we playing for?" he asked hollowly, still trying to come to terms with the idea that the world might end if he wasn't able to find a way to get the *yazata* out of his head.

"What is it you always play for, Boy Scout?" Charlene asked, her voice soft. "You want the world to be a better place. You want children not to be abused. You want their mothers not to be killed. You want those who would do people harm to be removed from the game board. All of these things are good and necessary. More importantly, you want the world to *continue*."

He stroked the side of McQueen's head.

"He was playing for those same things," he said, his voice pleading for understanding. "McQueen was playing for them too. He always was."

"No," she said tenderly. "He was playing for you. He would have done anything you'd asked, trusting that you knew what was going on."

"She's right, boss," McQueen said with barely a whisper. "I would have."

Hearing McQueen speak brought a surge of hope to Boy Scout. He looked down at his friend's face. "Hey, you're back. How are you, my friend?"

His breathing hitched twice. He grimaced. "Just a quick visit, I think."

"Do you want me to tell you a story?" Boy Scout asked, trying to keep McQueen awake. Awake, he had a better chance to live.

"I'm all storied out, I think." McQueen drew in a shaky breath and locked eyes with Boy Scout. "Pocket. Get it out."

Boy Scout felt first one of McQueen's pants pockets, then the other. He felt a lump and pulled it out. It was an old Crown Royal bag, deep blue felt with gold writing. Boy Scout looked inside and saw three sets of dog tags, jumbled and twisted together.

"I kept them for you," McQueen said.

Boy Scout saw one of the names and a lump formed in his throat. He didn't need to see the others to know what they were. Narco. Bully. Criminal.

"Do me a favor," McQueen began, then exhaled a final time, his life rattling slowly out.

"What kind of favor?" Boy Scout shook McQueen lightly. "What kind of favor?" Then he shifted to his knees and brought McQueen around so he could gaze into the man's face—slack-jawed, eyes open and staring forever. "What kind of favor?" His voice rose. "McQueen, don't you die on me. Don't you die!"

But there was nothing there. McQueen's eyes were blank and empty.

Boy Scout sagged to the floor and held his best friend. He fought back tears, seeking anger instead. Anger at the dervishes. Anger at the *daeva* and the *yazata*. Anger at Billy Picket for laughing. Anger at every man or woman who'd ever made fun of McQueen. Anger at the universe. Anger at God. Anger at himself for leading his friend to his ultimate demise. Anger at Rumi for wanting to end the world.

Preacher's Daughter quickly unbuckled herself and threw herself down next to him. She put her arms around both of them. Her shoulders shook with her sobs. She held on until Noaks spoke through his headset.

"We have company," he said.

She climbed back into her seat. "What is it?"

"Twelve things in the sky west of us. Burning. Coming straight for us."

"Can we outrun them?" Poe asked.

"I'm trying, but I don't think so," Noaks said, his voice tight.

"What should we do?" Poe asked Boy Scout.

Boy Scout didn't answer.

Poe shook his shoulder. "Come on, what should we do?"

Boy Scout shrugged off Poe's hand and glared at everyone in the cabin. "Let them kill us all."

Chapter Forty-One

Death Valley

NOAKS BROUGHT THE helicopter down in a scream of engine noise and airframe groans. Everyone grabbed onto their seats or the straps near the doors. Boy Scout locked his legs around the bench seat across from him and held onto McQueen. Someone else's hands held the straps of his vest. Just when everyone thought they were going to crash, Noaks flared and bled the momentum away so that after a hundred meters, they were able to touch the skids to the ground without killing everyone inside. Still, the slam was enough for Boy Scout to see stars.

He was the first to be able to move. He scrambled to a standing position and threw open the door nearest him. "Everyone out. Get away from the helicopter."

He slung McQueen's body over his shoulder and began running into the dark desert.

Preacher's Daughter and Charlene were soon on either side of him.

After about a hundred tough meters, he stumbled to a stop and tripped to his knees. Out of breath and gulping air, he eased his dead friend's body to the ground.

Poe and Tom the Operator came next, dragging the dervish behind them.

Noaks was just now unhooking himself from the helicopter.

Boy Scout looked to the sky and saw a dozen burning objects, like asteroids flying in a V formation, the air around them rippling and on fire, heading directly for the helicopter. They moved with purpose and began to decelerate.

"Noaks, hurry!" Preacher's Daughter yelled.

He grinned and waved, then went back inside the helicopter for something.

Two of the *daeva* separated themselves from the formation and zoomed in low.

Twin beams of light shot from them into the helicopter, exploding the machine. A ball of fire erupted from where it had been, and soon pieces of the chopper were raining down. The force of the explosion knocked Poe, Tom the Operator, and the dervish face first to the ground. They pulled themselves up and limped the rest of the way until they joined Boy Scout.

"What the fuck," Tom the Operator said to no one at all.

"Welcome to our world, Tom," Preacher's Daughter replied.

Boy Scout stared at the sky and watched the formation change. Soon it was above them. Within moments they were all surrounded, one *daeva* for each hour of the clock, burning like a ring of biblical fire.

"What now?" Poe whispered.

The sound of the *daeva* was a pulsating thrum, coming every three seconds.

"You think I know?" Boy Scout responded. "Everyone, get behind me. If they want me, then let them take me."

"No," Preacher's Daughter said. "I won't lose another one of you."

"We might not have a choice. I tried to help. Maybe we'll not die." He noticed Tom the Operator had raised his rifle and was aiming it at one of the *daeva*. "If you don't put that down they will kill you."

Tom the Operator glanced at him, visibly shaken, but lowered the weapon.

Boy Scout knelt beside McQueen. He cupped his dad friend's cheek for a moment, then grabbed the man's dog tags. He broke them off and dropped them into the bag, then stuffed the bag in his pocket. Standing, he glanced at Preacher's Daughter, then stepped forward a dozen paces. It was now or never. "Here I am. Come and take what belongs to you. I don't want it inside of me anymore."

"What are you doing?" Poe asked, still whispering.

"Inviting them to the party," Boy Scout said, his voice holding a slight tremor. In the face of all this supernatural power, who wouldn't feel fear? "Let's hope we survive it."

As one, the *daeva* lowered themselves to the ground, like a ring of fire drifting to the earth. Any one of them could take all of them out. Boy Scout's group of humans lacked the firepower to do even any one of the demi-gods harm. Now, with twelve of them, they could take out an army. They'd all seen what the rays of light could do to the helicopter and Boy Scout remembered how it had evaporated Criminal. Their survival was totally at the *daevas'* whim.

Once earthbound, each of them stepped out of their burning, shield-shaped thrones to stand in front of it. Backlit by fire, their figures could be made out. They were tall, each one ten or twelve feet high. Humanoid in shape, their arms ended in five finger talons that reached to their knees. Their oval heads were devoid of hair. Their eyes glowed, as did their chests, although one was far dimmer less than the others, likely the one held prisoner by the dervishes. They began to close the circle, stepping in unison towards the group of humans.

The *daeva* could be aliens, based on what they looked like. What was it, the grays? But these immense creatures weren't small and probably didn't abduct people or experiment on cattle. At least, Boy Scout didn't think so, but he could see where someone might think they were aliens. And to think that they were as old as time itself.

The *daeva* no longer thrummed. Now they approached in eerie silence.

Boy Scout couldn't help but back up, his body traitor to his barely gripped courage.

When they'd closed the circle, they reached out and grasped one another's hands, the glowing in their chests now flowing through all of them, until they burned brighter and brighter.

Boy Scout felt someone press against his back and looked. It was Poe, eyes wide.

Preacher's Daughter and Charlene hugged each other.

The dervish prisoner shook uncontrollably.

As did Tom the Operator. Boy Scout was convinced that the man from 5th Special Forces

Group was probably in the one percent of the bravest people on the planet, but he'd never been in the presence of a demi-god—much less twelve of them.

Boy Scout knew it was now or never. He felt the *yazatas* inside of him. He felt their fear. He felt their anger. He needed to do something before it did instead of him. So without thinking about it, he walked over to the nearest *daeva* in the circle, reached with a hand, and rested it where two of the *daevas'* hands met.

He'd anticipated an electric pulse of power, but it was subtler than that. It was more like putting his hand down on the hood of a powerful car, the engine causing a deeply harmonic vibration. Boy Scout felt their power and watched as the glow from their union joined him, the light moving up his arm and to his shoulder. The things inside of him screamed for him to stop, to let it go, but he refused. Instead, he squeezed harder. It wasn't long before he was completely infused with their power. It felt neither good, nor bad... but he felt the power nonetheless. He felt as if he could lift buildings or shatter walls. But he also felt a sense of loss—deep, impenetrable loss—and sadness. An eternity of sadness.

Then he was transported, back to that street in Saigon where a monk had just set himself on fire. The smell of burning flesh mixed with car exhaust was enough to make him gag. Bicycles passed them as if the sight of a burning monk was normal, ringing their bells for the temerity of holding up traffic. The fire sparked, whipped, and roared in a voice of its own. A car honked. A merchant shouted for people to sample his wares. The monk burned before him, stoic and unmoving, staring at Boy Scout with all the volition of an angry god, which it was.

"We feel the presence of our own. Our children. What is it you do with them?"

"They have attached themselves to me and will not let go," Boy Scout answered. He willed himself to form, then watched as his hands, arms, and legs materialized. He felt his body and it felt real.

"It killed the great beasts of the water," said the Burning Monk. "It took their power. We felt it all the way around the world."

"I was coming to tell you about what the dervishes had done to one of your own. I was going to help you rescue it, but I see you've already been there."

The fire crackled and burned, the skin melting off the monk, but he refused to move. Time passed, then it spoke again. "We followed the residue of power to you and found it being held. We took apart the place it was buried within." The monk paused. A woman's scream filled the air. "Why is it that you would help us?"

"This thing inside of me wants to take away my freedom. It wants to be me. I can't let that happen."

"These are our children—our sons. We hid them away until we could bring them out again."

"The dervishes found them. They took them from where you hid them in The White and have been using them to live forever."

The sound of a dozen voices merging into one. "They took them out?"

"They use them and take their power."

The Burning Monk stood and strode over so quickly that Boy Scout backed away. He could feel the heat, see the monk's eyes scorching in anger. "We will kill them all," it said, the voice now merging with a non-harmonious many.

How was Boy Scout going to get it to understand the nature of the dervishs' theft? "Do you remember the cisterns and where they kept one of yours?" He thought hard of the time there, remembering the smell of the sludgy water in which they were kept. Images of Bully and Narco and Criminal being killed juxtaposed with that of a *daeva* held with chains. The old dervish, Sufi Sam, sitting and guarding them. It was a place he'd been forced to be for more than six months—not forced, *tricked*. Faood had told him and his team that if they couldn't find a way to undo what they'd done, the world might end. And like the naïve Boy Scout he'd been, he'd believed them. The irony that it had been Rumi all along did not escape him.

Gone were the streets of Saigon. Now he was in the cistern, or at least his memory of the cistern, recreated by the *daevas*. The ancient, hollowed-out walls were the same. The pool with the underwater pedestals where they had sat were the same. Even the chains that had held the original *daeva* the dervishes had used as a power source, hanging empty from the ceiling, were the same.

The Burning Monk materialized in front of him.

"We know of this place. Your people killed us here," it said, once more a single voice.

"We were fighting for our lives. We have no enmity to you, but you couldn't distinguish between us, the victims, and the dervishes, the perpetrators. They had imprisoned one of you here and were using it to get into The White and take your sons. The dervishes brought us here against our will, to help them and lure your sons to us. Your sons came as moths to a flame when we were in The White. Your children are lonely and confused. They've been in The White for so long, they no longer know why they were put there. They no longer know who they are."

"What good are they to you?"

"Not to me, to the dervishes. They used the power of your sons to help themselves live forever.

They take your sons, what we call *yazata*, from where you've hidden and merge your sons with their own souls, then feed the *yazata* the souls of others so that the dervishes might live longer."

Suddenly Boy Scout was in a different land altogether. Gone was the cistern, replaced by a land of meadows and trees. The verdant earth was covered in grasses that swayed in the wind. Far in the distance, the surf boomed. Cattle with impossibly long horns were being led by giants, while smaller humans followed. A city stood in the distance, its walls a burnished bronze that glowed dully beneath an impossibly blue sky. The smell of clean air contrasted the stench of the cistern and the streets of Saigon. He'd never smelled air so pure.

Boy Scout became aware that he was beside someone new. He turned and beheld a *daeva* in royal regalia. It wore a purple robe. A necklace of gold and diamonds hung about its neck and on its feet were jeweled sandals. As it turned to him, Boy Scout was struck by the awe he felt for the being. He wanted to kneel and fought to remain standing, such was the sense of its stature. Not because it was almost twice as tall as he was, but because of the reverence it inspired. It was easy to see how these beings could be worshipped.

It gestured with long arms. "This was our land. Everything was at peace until God created you. At first, we were able to live together, but you began to displace us." The *daeva* sighed. "We were his sons first."

So, Preacher's Daughter had been correct in her supposition.

"Did He tell you to move your sons?"

"He tried to drown them, so we hid them," the *daeva* said simply.

"Did God try and drown you as well?"

"We had agreed to banish ourselves to the sky and leave the events of man to Him."

Boy Scout watched as the men and giants worked together in the scene before him. "Why did He do this? Why did He come and supplant you?"

The *daeva* looked upon Boy Scout. "Why does any child want another child's toy? Why does any man want another man's wife? And if you are as powerful as He was then, who is to stop you?"

Boy Scout repeated the words in his mind. Were they really talking about God—*the* Biblical God, as if He were real? Boy Scout believed, but only in that slight *it might be true* way that most Americans believed. To have this entity speak to him in such an offhand way about God was almost too much. It was like the entirety of the Bible had suddenly become fact. His thoughts were jumbled with the possibility. But then he realized the words the *daeva* had used.

"You said *as powerful as He* was *then*. Is he gone? Is our God gone?"

Boy Scout held his breath.

The *daeva* took a moment to respond. When he did, it was like a wistful pronouncement. "Not yet, but soon. His time is waning. When He leaves, when He moves on, we shall return, as will our sons. We will bestow onto our sons all the lands that have been taken away from them and give back to them that which was stolen."

"What will happen to mankind?" Boy Scout asked, waiting for what he hoped would be an encouraging response.

It was anything but.

In a voice louder than any other time, the *daeva* said, "If He does not take them with Him, they will be damned."

Boy Scout was stunned. What the *daeva* was speaking of sounded a lot like Revelations and the end of the world. The information had always been there, but instead of the end being caused by the devil or demons from Hell coming to Earth, it was the *daeva* and their offspring, their sons, who would reclaim their inheritance—this planet Earth.

The Rapture was real.

Chapter Forty-Two

The White

Now, KNOWING WHAT the *daeva* knew, the end of the world could come tomorrow, next year, or next century. Understanding their sense of time was impossible. The twenty-four-hour clock was a human construct based on the realities of the rotation of the Earth. Dimensional topology indicated that time and space weren't the same everywhere. As insane as it sounded, Boy Scout couldn't worry about the end of the world now. He had more personal issues to deal with. It was now or never. The *daeva* had shown Boy Scout how the world used to be before God decided the *daevas'* sons needed to be replaced with man. The *daeva* had also shared what was going to happen when God moved on, basically leaving man to once again worship the children of the *daeva* or the alternative—to cease to exist entirely. "I desire to give back two of your sons."

"We could just take them from you," the *daeva* noted in an almost academic way.

"Could you do that? Could you just take them? Would I survive it?"

"Through our connection we see them in you. Each is now attached to your soul. To take them would be to take all or part of it. The architecture of man has never been familiar to us, nor has the nature of your soul. You are as different from us as we were different from those who came before."

Boy Scout wondered what it would be like to have half a soul. Could he even survive without it? What was a soul but his life force? And if he survived, would he be different? Was the soul the place his character resided? His self? Was it the locus of who he was, and without it would he be nothing but an empty shell? Each question was more horrifying than the first. He didn't want to know the answers.

"I'd rather keep my soul intact, thank you."

"But there is no other way."

"There is a way if you are willing to render a little assistance."

"What would you have us do?"

"Allow me to use you to enter The White. Each

one of you will afford me the possibility of getting these two to release my soul."

"You say possibility. What if it doesn't happen?"

"Then you can take them as you wish. It would be nothing for you to let me try. It would be everything for me."

"We will give you a moment," it said. Then he disappeared, as did the old Earth, only to be replaced by nothing. The universe was now nothing more than a completely white landscape. There was no up or down, left or right, or front or back. There was only *white*.

Now what? Boy Scout wondered. His grand idea had come to him based on Preacher's Daughter's conversation about doors. Each of the twelve *daeva* would represent a new doorway. The problem with the *yazatas* inside of him was they knew what they were. Boy Scout postulated that if he could make them forget, they might just loosen their hold on his soul. But if he believed Charlene, one was Rumi. Rumi wasn't merely a *yazata*, he was something else entirely—whatever you could call a human soul that was able to overcome the son of a *daeva*.

A black figure appeared on the horizon.

Boy Scout willed himself to be still.

When it was close enough for Boy Scout to make out its features, Boy Scout gasped.

"Your memory of him is strong," Rumi said from McQueen's mouth. He was dressed in jeans and McQueen's hot pink *Come Yank At Hanks* shirt.

"We were close," Boy Scout said, remembering to form himself. "Why did you choose this form?"

"Because I need you to trust me. I detected that this is the most trustworthy image in your memory. You'd trust this man more than anything or anyone."

Boy Scout felt the pull, the need to trust, but ignored it. "It's just an image. The real McQueen is dead. There's no reason I should trust you regardless of what you look like. You've been deceitful."

McQueen reached up and cupped Boy Scout's cheek. "Not telling you something is not the same as lying. I never lied to you."

Boy Scout jerked his face away. "Do not touch me like that."

"But isn't it the way you two were together?"

"How we were together has nothing to do with you. You want to destroy the world."

McQueen tilted his head and frowned sadly. "Not destroy it. Remake it."

"You would free the *yazatas?* I have seen what a single one can do. How many are there? Thousands?"

"Tens of thousands. I have tracked most of them

down and placed them together. They talk and begin to remember. When they finally do, they will need to be released."

"Or what?"

"You heard the *daeva*. God will soon leave us. Would you rather the end of the world come as a surprise, or would you like to fashion it, shape it, control it?"

"I'd rather the world didn't end, period," Boy Scout said.

"Stop acting so small. You are the universe in ecstatic motion," Rumi said through McQueen.

Boy Scout shook his head. "For the love of Christ, enough of the fortune cookie nonsense."

"It's not nonsense," Rumi said. For the first time Boy Scout could detect the entity's frustration. "I'm trying to make you understand. You have the ability to think large instead of small. You think about yourself. I think about the world. Change is inevitable."

"Your ego is fathomless, Rumi. That you think you can change the way the world ends is an explosion of arrogance like the world has never seen."

"You heard. You saw," McQueen shouted. "The *daeva* want back what was theirs. They want a return of their rule before the advent of man. I have been working to fashion the way their children see the world. When they are released, they will not act as before, but will allow us, mankind, to guide them."

Boy Scout opened his mouth as the full realization of what Rumi's plan was. "You've brainwashed the *yazatas*? You're going to be in control. You will be their god. They will all follow *you*!"

"They were a blank canvas," McQueen said softly. "I recreated them in our image."

"And what of their fathers? What of the *daeva*?"

"They will be viewed differently. Their memories of the time before has been changed. The *yazatas* will see them as enemies of man—which they are."

Boy Scout was astounded at the planning that must have gone into this effort. Rumi's understanding of the dimensional topology and how to navigate it was beyond anyone's comprehension. To think he'd been on a celestial scavenger hunt for hundreds of years, just so he could elevate himself to the divine, was amazing. "All this time, all this effort—it wasn't just to live forever. You had a much greater purpose. When our God leaves, you want to take his *place*."

"The world is a dirty thing. With the help of the *yazata*, I will make it clean again, just as it was before man came and spoiled it."

Boy Scout was so furious, he spat, but nothing came out because he was in The White. Not only did he feel used, he felt humiliated. It was one thing to try and keep the *yazata* from harming humanity, but it was another altogether to *subjugate* them—intellectually enslave the *yazata* to do their bidding. They had been on the Earth long before mankind and deserved a better destiny than being the whipping boys of a small man whose only contribution to the universe thus far was to inspire thousands of Hallmark editors and fortune cookie makers to one-up themselves. That this evil man had chosen McQueen to use as a vehicle to try and convince Boy Scout made it exponentially worse.

Still, Boy Scout tried to stay calm. He needed to control his emotions or his plan would never work. As it was, everything was merely theoretical based on the conjecture of some Notre Dame University scientists. But now it was more important than ever to succeed. Before it had been only his own soul that would be obliterated. Now Boy Scout was fighting for the souls of tens of thousands, because if Rumi's plan came to pass, each of the *yazata* would need a vessel in which to reside.

He closed his eyes and willed the world to silence.

He was almost to that point when he heard the words, "Oh no, you don't."

He snapped his eyes open and saw McQueen backing away. "I now see your plan. I should have anticipated it. I should have been paying more attention. But it is too late for you." He raised his arms and shouted, "Behold! Once the offspring of the Sons of God, they are now the Partners of Man."

The White opened up and thousands of spiders rained down upon Rumi, each the size of a Labrador with the face of McQueen, each scrambling over the other and making the mating call of a monkey. The deluge continued until they were piled impossibly high. Spider after spider, each one representing a trapped soul, but in this case, a *yazata*, for Boy Scout had no doubt that knowing his mind couldn't be co-opted, Rumi had decided to release them on his own. The pulsating mass continued to grow until it made a mountain of souls shaped like human-faced spiders. The cacophony was fantastic in its dissonant clamor, overwhelming Boy Scout's senses to the point where he could hardly think. The face of his best dead friend on each of the spiders surrounding him was terrifying in its invention.

Then the sound suddenly stopped, and the silence seemed louder than the noise.

As one, the spiders turned to look at him.

Boy Scout knew what would happen next.

He turned and ran, which meant moving as fast as he could in the opposite direction.

His plan had been for him to be calm to easily

move into the astral plane, but there was no time for that now. He had to trust his instincts.

The mating calls of the monkeys came from behind him again, rising. He had no doubt that they were behind him as the sounds rose once again to mind-deafening proportions. Rumi was trying stop him from doing the one thing that might possibly stop everything. If only he could run, move fast enough, then he could—

Hope blossomed in Boy Scout for the first time as he realized what he'd forgotten. Space was nothing more than a construct. Gravity and friction only existed because he expected them to. He didn't need to run when he could fly. He didn't need to fly, when he could just—*be*.

He willed himself into the astral plane, and like a shot he was surrounded by a black void.

Each of the *daeva* glowed blindingly bright, encircling him. The two *yazata* glowed almost as bright as they stood beside him, grinning. One tried to grab him, but Boy Scout shifted again, touching the next *daeva* in line.

Back into The White, but this was a different one...

Because each of the *daeva* represented a different *dimension*. No, each was its *own* dimension, which was why once captured, they could remain hidden from their own kind. At the moment, because they were touching, twelve dimensions were merged, each able to see into the other, but that wasn't the norm. Once they separated, so would the dimensions be separated.

A darkness broached the horizon as the horde found him.

Mating calls demanded for him.

But he was too fast.

Where they ran, Boy Scout could just *be*.

Back in the astral plane, then to the next *daeva*.

And the next.

And the next.

He moved so quickly between the white and the black of the astral plane that his reality became a flickering newsreel where a single man flipped back and forth.

Over and over.

Black.

White.

Black.

White.

Black.

White.

Touching and being, moving and shifting, becoming and devolving, until he was nothing more than a human bullet traveling through time and space and dimensions.

Black.

White.

The faster he moved, the more he understood. The more he understood, the more he forgot.

Black.

White.

Just before he lost track of everything, he touched each of the *yazatas* and brought them into The White.

Each stood before him, an avatar, faceless, barely even a human-looking form.

Boy Scout willed himself back into existence, his hands, feet, and body forming. He'd forgotten who he looked like so allowed his face to form as it must. Who he was, what he was... all just gone.

"Where are we?" one of the avatars asked.

A word formed in his mind, one he'd been hanging onto through each of the transitions, repeating it over and over until it became him. He fought to remember it. He struggled with the shape of it. Finally it came, fully formed. The word was *Rumpelstiltskin,* and with it came the smiling face of Preacher's Daughter as she said it. Then everything returned, slamming home so that Boy Scout was once and truly himself. The world was full of doorways and he needed only a single key. The safe word that had started as a joke saved him.

This was it. This was the end game. Now he'd discover whether or not the doorway effect was real, or if it was mere fantasy. He'd managed to make it through, but had the others?

"What have you done?" said the other avatar, forming into the figure of a small Persian man—Jalāl ad-Dīn Muhammad Rūmī.

"You remember?" Boy Scout asked, disappointment slamming into him.

"Barely. What you did... what you did was impossible," Rumi said. "All of them... you made them forget. How is it you could do this?"

Boy Scout felt a surge of pride at having outwitted such an old soul and saved the world while doing so. Not only had he been able to make at least one of the *yazata* attached to him forget, but the horde of *yazata* that Rumi had collected had chased him until the very end, going through doorway after doorway after doorway.

"The doorway effect. It's why you can't find your car keys most of the time. Whenever you go through a doorway, your mind takes the immediate information and stores it. The more doorways the more storage until you have a jumble of information."

"Car keys?"

"Or who you are? Your dimensional topology didn't take into account such a simple thing. The mind stores events in particular orders." Boy Scout remembered how Preacher's Daughter had compared it to RAM and ROM, but if Rumi didn't even know what car keys were then he couldn't fathom a computer. "I forced them all to move through so many doorways. They barely knew what they were to being with. All they had to do was stop and they would have remembered. But now they are as they were before your interference. They are once again lost to time and memory."

"All that effort. All that work." Rumi's face sagged so that he did look like a very old man. Where he'd always seemed so damn sure of himself, his voice barely held a breath. He stared at the avatar beside him and in a raw voice said, "You've doomed us all. You've ruined what I've been trying to fix for hundreds of years!"

"Or saved us," Boy Scout said. "We can't know. We weren't meant to know."

"The soul has been given its own ears to hear things the mind does not understand," Rumi said. "If you had paid attention, the answer would have presented itself. You have to be open for it, but you walk around being so closed, so confident that you know what's right and what's wrong."

"Then why are our answers are so different, Rumi? How can both of us be wrong?"

Rumi sighed. "Because our questions were so different."

A Burning Monk appeared.

Then another.

And another, until Rumi and the *yazatas* were surrounded by twelve Burning Monks.

"Who are you to have taken a son?" one of the monks asked.

"You have replaced him," said another.

"What made him ours is no longer," said another.

"We have seen what you have done," said another.

"We all saw the shapes of our sons and what you did to their minds," yet another said.

"And it was this one who returned them to the way they were," said yet another, pointing at Boy Scout.

"You should never have come," another said.

Rumi looked from one to the other, fear beginning to etch on his features.

Then Boy Scout knew the truth of it. The *daeva* might never have found where Rumi had been hiding their sons if Rumi hadn't released them. By dragging them through each of the *daeva*, Boy Scout had made the demi-gods aware of the truth of what Rumi had actually done.

One of the monks morphed into the form of a South Vietnamese general, his sleeves rolled up, a .38 Special in his right hand. He walked up to Rumi and raised the pistol.

"The wound is the place where the light enters you," Boy Scout said.

Then the general pulled the trigger and a beam of light fired into Rumi's head, dissolving him.

And then Boy Scout was back in his own body, sagging on his knees, gasping and retching until the contents of his stomach heaved onto the desert floor.

Hands grasped him and helped him to his feet.

He looked around.

The *daeva* were gone.

Charlene smiled grimly and nodded.

Poe, Tom the Operator, and the dervish stood several feet away.

Preacher's Daughter held him up.

"Did you do it?" she asked. "Did it work?"

"I think so," he said. "I feel different. I feel strong, but I'm so damn *tired*. Where did they go?"

"Each their separate way. One moment they were here, the next, nothing but beams of light." She used the back of her hand to wipe away something on Boy Scout's face, then wiped it on his suicide vest. She made a face. "You have vomit on you," she said.

Chapter Forty-Three

Fort Irwin

AN HOUR LATER, they found the road to Fort Irwin. Boy Scout told Poe and the others to walk on ahead. His going was slow. He refused to let go of McQueen and had carried him on alternating shoulders the entire way. He couldn't help but move slower than the others.

Preacher's Daughter stayed with him.

"Rumi came to me in The White," he said. "He wore McQueen's face. Tried to convince me to help him destroy the world."

"Why would you want to do that?" she asked.

"God is going to leave us one day," he said. "Don't ask me how I know. It's a long story. It could be tomorrow, it could be next week, it could be in a thousand years, but He will move on. Rumi wanted to be the architect of the end times. He wanted to do it before it was necessary, so he could shape it."

"The Bible talks of the Rapture," she said. "It details the end of the world when God turns his gaze away from us."

"From what the *daeva* said, everything Revelations says will happen will probably happen. They know and are prepared for it. Waiting for it. Looking forward to it even." Boy Scout stopped walking for a moment and shifted McQueen to his other shoulder.

"Won't you let me carry him a little ways?" she asked.

He shook his head. "He is my burden to bear," he told her, and started walking again. "Something else Rumi said bothered me. He said I'd doomed all of mankind. I said *Or saved us.* He argued the point, and I told him *We can't know. We weren't meant to know.*"

"Some say that there are signs for us to follow— that God lays them before us to follow or ignore. Others believe in pure fate, that there's nothing we can do and the future is already settled," she said.

He nodded. "Then Rumi said, *The soul has been given its own ears to hear things the mind does not understand. If you had paid attention, the answer would have presented itself. You have to be open*

*for it but you walk around being so closed, so
confident you know what's right and wrong."*

"I can see that. But what bothers you about it?"
she asked.

"Because then I asked why our answers were
so different. He said it's because our questions
were different. What *is* my question, Lore? What
question has been dictating my life all this time?"

Preacher's Daughter sighed. "We live our
questions, Boy Scout. The answers are as fleeting
as the questions. We may never find the answer,
but we have to continue to live, hoping one day
we will."

"Now you sound like him. Fucking fortune
cookie logic." Boy Scout gave the universe a
sideways smile. "Why don't I know? Rumi seemed
so sure. What if I was wrong? Why am I so
confident of right and wrong? What if I really did
doom everyone?"

They walked on for a time in silence, grim
sadness casting a pall over everything. Eventually,
Preacher's Daughter said, "I can't believe that after
everything you've done in the world, you would be
the one to doom it."

"How can we be sure?" he asked, voice cracking.

She shook her head and gave him an imploring
look. "We can only do our best... my boss... my
friend, my leader."

The sky above the desert was so wide that they could seen storm cells making their way across it. Boy Scout counted three cells under a sky that was beginning to brighten. Monsoon season. He'd seen a five-minute deluge fill a wadi and flip a tank with its power. The thing about the desert was that even if it wanted water, it couldn't take it. The ground couldn't absorb it, so the water moved until it found its own level.

Fort Irwin was the home of the National Training Center, a place where brigade-sized elements came to play wargames with OPFOR. It was the largest force-on-force wargame area, and Boy Scout had been there several times back when he was with the regiment. Which was why he knew exactly where they were.

The painted rocks. He saw them in the distance, and as he got closer he became surer of what he was going to do.

"This is as far as I go," he said, when they drew near.

"Here?" she asked, looking around. "What's here?"

More than a hundred boulders comprised a mound in the middle of the flat desert. Each had been painted with a unit insignia. Most he recognized, but some he didn't. Probably National Guard units. He searched for and finally found the boulder with the lightning bolt of the 75th Ranger Regiment. Above the patch was the ranger scroll. He kept searching until he found McQueen's unit, 1st Special Forces Group.

"There's yours," he said to Preacher's Daughter, pointing. "4th Mechanized Infantry Division."

"Never made it out here," she said. "Never practiced war. Only made it."

"I remember a time when we didn't have any wars," Boy Scout said. His voice was beyond tired. "All we did was practice."

"People don't get killed practicing," she said. "Not many, anyway." She gave Boy Scout a long look. "Why are we here?"

"Might as well ask the desert why it's empty," Boy Scout said. He looked at her pointedly. "What are you going to do now?" When he saw her blank look, he added, "Our unit is over. Most are dead. I'm not going to lead anyone anymore."

"I figured as much." She sighed, then her shoulders sagged. She hesitated a moment and stared at the rocks. Then slowly, as if to test the words, she said, "I was thinking about joining a new unit. Special Unit 77, I think. I hear they need a vengeance demon." She flashed a tired grin as she sought his approval. "What do you think?"

"I think they definitely need a vengeance demon," Boy Scout said. "They'll be lucky to have you."

He could see her straighten a bit with his words. "What about you?"

He gestured with his chin towards the desert. "Out there, where the desert is so lonely that it dreams of crowds."

She touched his suicide vest. "What about this? What about the vest?"

He glanced down as if he was seeing it for the first time. "I think I'll keep it for awhile."

He turned away from her. The storm cells were getting closer.

"Hey, Boy Scout," she said.

He heard a tinkling and turned.

She held out her dog tags. "Take these."

He considered for a moment, then shook his head. "You're not dead. I only take the tags of the dead."

She sighed and let her hand fall to her side, the chain dangling almost to the dirt.

"You were the best of us," she said in a low voice.

"Then why are you all dead?"

"I'm not dead," she said.

"No, you're not." He offered her a solid grin. "I hope you keep it that way."

"One more thing," she said.

"What is it?"

"What is it you think McQueen was trying to say at the end? You know, when he started with *Do me a favor*," she said.

"We'll never know," he said.

"Oh, I think we can figure it out," Preacher's Daughter said. "All he wanted was for you to be happy. He wanted you not to mourn him. He loved you, Boy Scout. He loved you so much, is what he probably would have said." A tear slipped from her eye. "You know how sappy he could be."

"Sappy," Boy Scout said, letting the word roll around. Then he laughed. "That's McQueen all day long."

Then Boy Scout turned and walked into the desert, the bombs still strapped around him, thinking of the Chai Boy in the wheelchair he'd saved and the one he didn't, the smell of oranges covering the stench of his murder. He thought of Sister Renee and the torture her soul had experienced. He continued walking and thought of McQueen and the others—Narco, Bully, Criminal. Their time was over. His time was over. They'd done all they could. He climbed the boulders and stood on the highest one, staring out across a world that would end some day when God got tired and decided to move on. The storm clouds of one of the cells seemed almost close enough to touch.

He turned back to look one last time and saw her staring at him, hands down at her waist. He remembered what she'd said that had interested him the most.

In the beginning God created the Heaven and the Earth. This seems simple but is significant. We believe that God lives in Heaven. That's why everyone looks forward to it when they die so that they can finally see God. So riddle me this, Batman: how did God create the place where He lived unless He came from somewhere else? He had to come from somewhere, and if He'd just finished creating Heaven, where was that somewhere?

Boy Scout climbed down, moving out of Preacher's Daughter's view.

Topology was the study of spatial relationships and how they twisted and bent as they interacted. Preacher's Daughter's words were about God missing a spatial relationship to where he'd come from. Or that all the believers in the world never wondered about that spatial relationship. Boy Scout already knew that there were multiple dimensions from which things sprung. The White, the astral plane, the material plane were all related to each other. But there had to be other dimensions and in those others possibilities arose. Maybe there was a place where McQueen still lived. Maybe there was a place where a young Afghan boy could have a mother whose fingers smelled of orange. Maybe there was a place where a young girl from California could stay in California and never even travel to Turkey.

Just as the Painted Rocks were a doorway soldiers used to go in and out of Fort Irwin, maybe in the very creation of the universe, God passed through his own doorway and forgot where he came from. If only Boy Scout could forget so easily.

The sun rose and its light seemed to grab the world by its edges and pull it tight. The desert ran on before him until it wavered in the distance and merged with the sky. Still, he walked. His hand brushed against the vest's actuator, as it had done so many times before. He exhaled, the weight of McQueen a constant reminder of everything that had been lost.

Somewhere came the sound of thunder.

And the wind carried what remained.

Acknowledgements

THE FIRST BOOK of the duology was *Burning Sky*. It was about man's inability to overcome nature—how the inexhaustible qualities of nature far outstrip the abilities of any man or woman, even a team of men and women, to accomplish that which they must. No one left the end of *Burning Sky* without a wound. Boy Scout had the most, carrying not only the memories of his dead team mates and everything he'd done, but also the memories of the travelers within him. *Dead Sky* is about self or loss of it. How do we define who we are? Do we define ourselves by what happens to us? Sister Renee certainly tried to escape her past and rewrite her future. Are we who we associate with? McQueen's identity was inextricably linked to Boy Scout. Boy Scout made him who he was.

Only Preacher's Daughter was herself regardless of the circumstances. The men didn't know it, but she was their rock. I hope to see her again someday, maybe even in a Special Unit 77 project.

I WOULD LIKE to thank William H. Halloran for introducing me to astral travel all the way back in 1979 with his spectacularly frightening book, *Keeper of the Children*. Not only did it inspire the events of this book, but also my first book, *Scarecrow Gods*, which won the Bram Stoker Award for First Novel. Thanks also to my first reader, editor and wife, fellow author Yvonne Navarro. Thanks to my agent, Cherry Weiner, and the good folks at Solaris, Michael Rowley, David Thomas Moore, Kate Coe, Paul Simpson, Remy Njambi, Ben Smith and the rest of the team at Rebellion. Also a shout out to acquisitions editor, Jon Oliver, who has moved on to more lucrative fortunes.

FINALLY, I WOULD like to thank all of the men and women who have spent all or part of the last eighteen years fighting in Afghanistan. It's a hell of a place, isn't it? I hope to God you never have to go back again. Or to any other combat hell hole, for that matter. You are a wretched blessed bunch.

About the Author

WESTON OCHSE IS a former intelligence officer and special operations soldier who has engaged enemy combatants, terrorists, narco smugglers, and human traffickers. His personal war stories include performing humanitarian operations over Bangladesh, being deployed to Afghanistan, and a near miss being cannibalized in Papua New Guinea.

A WRITER OF more than 26 books in multiple genres, his military supernatural series, SEAL Team 666, has been optioned to be a movie starring Dwayne Johnson. His military sci-fi series, which starts with *Grunt Life*, has been praised for its PTSD-positive depiction of soldiers at peace and at war.

WESTON OCHSE'S FICTION and non-fiction has been praised by *USA Today*, *The Atlantic*, *The New York Post*, *The Financial Times* of London, and *Publishers Weekly*.

FIND US ONLINE!

www.rebellionpublishing.com

/rebellionpub   /rebellionpublishing   /rebellionpub

SIGN UP TO OUR NEWSLETTER!

rebellionpublishing.com/sign-up

YOUR REVIEWS MATTER!

Enjoy this book? Got something to say?

Leave a review on Amazon, GoodReads or with your
favourite bookseller and let the world know!

'Weston Ochse is the new voice of action science fiction'
New York Times bestselling author Jonathan Maberry

WESTON OCHSE
GRUNT LIFE
A TASK FORCE OMBRA NOVEL

Benjamin Carter Mason died last night. Maybe he threw himself off a bridge into Los Angeles Harbor, or maybe he burned to death in a house fire in San Pedro; it doesn't really matter. Today, Mason's starting a new life. He's back in boot camp, training for the only war left that matters a damn.

For years, their spies have been coming to Earth, learning our weaknesses. Our governments knew, but they did nothing—the prospect was too awful, the costs too high—and now, the horrifying and utterly inhuman Cray are laying waste to our cities. The human race is a heartbeat away from extinction.

That is, unless Mason, and the other men and women of Task Force OMBRA, can do anything about it.

This is a time for heroes. For killers. For Grunts.